A smile that made him feel like a hero spread over her lips.

The sun had pinkened her skin and her hair shone in the light. Between victory and spending the day in close proximity to Eloise, Dante wanted to kiss her.

The thought shocked him to his core. *Kiss her?* He'd been dealing with this new attraction, but to take it a step further? Too much, too soon.

He fisted his hands together to keep from hauling her against his chest.

"I knew you could do it," she said. "You were made for this case."

"Saying I'm sneaky?"

"In the best way." Her grin grew bigger. "I made inroads today, as well."

He threw his arm over her shoulder and tugged her close, one part undercover, the other part pure selfishness. It was like they fit together.

Should he be worried?

Dear Reader,

I'm so excited to introduce the Matthews brothers to you. You'll be seeing more of them in the books to come, but in *The Lawman's Secret Vow*, we begin the journey with Dante, the youngest of the Matthews clan. The brothers are on a mission to protect their mother, and being the well-meaning but suspicious sons that they are, you can imagine the lengths they'll go to in order to uncover the truth.

Have you ever wondered what it's like for police officers who go undercover? How it would feel to solve a case and put away a bad guy? Experience the rush of adrenaline by jumping into action that is just a bit over the line? For Eloise Archer, this goes against everything the by-the-book detective is about. For Dante, it's standard operating procedure. Put them together and wait for the fireworks to begin.

I love this couple. They're both so different in their process of discovering the truth, but eager to get the job done. In life, people don't achieve goals by going after them in exactly the same way. Where's the fun in that? As this couple begins to trust, something deeper develops. But do they have the courage to confront those feelings?

The books in this series will also feature Deke and Derrick Matthews, as well as a surprise heroine with her own story. Sit back and enjoy the ride, because the Matthews brothers go full tilt on life and will have you falling in love along the way.

Happy reading!

Tara

HEARTWARMING

The Lawman's Secret Vow

USA TODAY Bestselling Author

Tara Randel

H HARLEQUIN® HEARTWARMING™

Recycling programs
for this product may
not exist in your area.

ISBN-13: 978-1-335-63375-0

The Lawman's Secret Vow

Copyright © 2018 by Tara Spicer

Printed in U.S.A.

Tara Randel is an award-winning, *USA TODAY* bestselling author of fifteen novels. Family values, a bit of mystery and, of course, love and romance are her favorite themes, because she believes love is the greatest gift of all. Tara lives on the west coast of Florida, where gorgeous sunsets and beautiful weather inspire the creation of heartwarming stories. This is her seventh book for Harlequin Heartwarming. Visit Tara at tararandel.com and like her on Facebook at Tara Randel Books.

Books by Tara Randel

Harlequin Heartwarming

The Business of Weddings

His One and Only Bride
The Wedding March
The Bridal Bouquet
Honeysuckle Bride
Magnolia Bride
Orange Blossom Brides

Visit the Author Profile page at Harlequin.com for more titles.

To my police officer friends who bravely serve and protect their communities, and take time out of their busy schedules to answer my endless questions.

CHAPTER ONE

A STRONG HAND clasped Eloise Archer's upper arm, yanking her toward a deserted hallway in the Palm Cove, Florida, police department. She glanced at the hand and then looked up at the serious dark blue eyes of fellow detective Dante Matthews.

"Chambers is on the warpath. Pretend we're having a work-related conversation."

She clutched the file folders in her arms tighter to her chest, ignoring the shimmers of attraction that came with Dante's touch. It was bad enough she worked with the handsome man, was it too much to ask that she not… notice him so much? They had a professional relationship, end of story. But Dante, with lush dark hair, recently cut short after his last undercover operation, stood tall and lean, filling out his button-down shirt and jeans—very much a dream man.

Or hers, anyway.

She spied over her shoulder to see Lieutenant Chambers standing in the doorway of his office across the wide, busy squad room, arms crossed over his barrel chest. Dante was right on the mark with his assessment. Their superior officer did not look happy.

"What did you do now?" she asked, returning her gaze to his. She knew the answer. Wanted his version.

"Nothing serious."

"Really? I heard your last case had a bit of a hiccup," she returned, showing him she wasn't clueless. In fact, she probably knew more about the results of his undercover operation than he thought she did.

His eyes crinkled in the corners when he smiled at her. "Hiccup is an understatement."

"Jumped in to make the arrest too soon?"

"Not by design. Six months of undercover work down the drain, but at least I got one arrest in the end."

"Tell me what went wrong."

"It's not important." His fingers repeatedly squeezed and released her bicep in a rhythm she doubted he was aware of. That was Dante, always moving. "What is important is that I need your help."

One eyebrow rose. She knew what was coming.

"I've been relegated to desk duty until Chambers decides to give me a break. I'm behind on paperwork. Any chance I can talk you into a late-night catch-up session?"

"Reviewing reports? Why would I do that when I have my own to manage?" She held up the folders to prove her point, immediately missing the warmth of his grasp on her blouse-clad arm when he dropped his hand.

"We can go out for drinks afterward."

"I don't think—"

"That's right. You don't drink. How about grabbing some food?"

"I haven't even agreed."

A slow smile spread over his lips. "Come on, Ellie. Help a coworker out here."

Eloise's face burned. He was the only person in her life to have ever given her a nickname. "Eloise will do."

"But you look like an Ellie."

Did she? Her name happened to be a bit old-fashioned, probably the reason why her parents had given it to her when she was born. Literary professors, they loved classics from centuries past. But Ellie? The woman who dressed in a white blouse and navy or black skirt every day? Pulled her hair back in a no-nonsense bun to keep it out of her face? She was an Ellie?

Eloise tried to ignore his cologne, a musky aroma mixed with spice, tickling her nose.

"C'mon, Ellie. What do you say?"

"If I do help you, and I'm not saying I will, you'd owe me."

It was only fair she ask for something in return. She might be dedicated to the job, but she wasn't going to let him use that knowledge to push his work off on her.

His eyes lit up. "Sounds intriguing. What did you have in mind?"

Definitely not what his expression suggested, which probably included wild fun. She couldn't imagine Dante living life any other way. And why was she reading anything into it? He was so far out of her league. Besides, her one experience with an almost work romance had crashed and burned. She didn't care to replay that mistake ever again.

"My request would be that when we work together on a case, you listen to me."

He tilted his head. Sized her up. "I don't listen to you?"

"It's not so much me as other officers you've worked with. You have a bit of a rep."

Brows beetled over his eyes. "A rep?"

Like he didn't know it. "You aren't exactly a team player."

"I get the job done."

The edge in his voice told her she'd touched

a nerve. "Let's face it, you do rush into situations."

"When it's called for."

Great, the chummy coworker was gone. He had his cop face on now.

A loud cough from behind drew their attention from the conversation and back to the lieutenant.

"How about we table this discussion and revisit it later?" she suggested.

He nodded, then strode away.

"Every time," she muttered under her breath. Whenever she'd mentioned his…flaw, he withdrew. Because she called him on it? Or was he well aware and embarrassed? After all, he had cost the department an important case.

Hitching her shoulders back, she headed for her desk, ready to get some work done before any calls came in. The Palm Cove PD wasn't huge. A two-story structure, the bottom floor was the command center of the building. Desks for officers were located on one side of a waist-high wall, the detective's area on the other. Half of the desks were occupied, with low voices from fellow officers making follow-up calls or the slow tap, tap, tap of others writing up reports on a computer, and the remaining surfaces were littered with files and paperwork or messages.

A front desk situated behind glass in the lobby spanned one side of the building with a wall separating it from the officers' desks; a holding cell took up the complete other side. Burned coffee emanated from a small kitchenette down the hallway in which they'd just stood.

Upstairs held administrative offices, including the chief's domain. As the town grew, thankfully so did the budget. There were fifteen officers employed right now.

She'd just dropped the files on her desk when a chirpy voice waylaid her.

"Girl, we need to talk."

Eloise turned to find Brandy Cummings resting a curvy hip on the side of the desk. In her midtwenties, she'd been hired fresh out of college, taking over the crime scene investigation position Eloise had vacated when she'd become a detective. Brandy was eager, smart and knew every detail of what went on in the department, official and personal. Eloise admired that. Physically, Brandy was the exact opposite of Eloise's willowy shape and studious demeanor. And yet despite their different approaches to the job—hers methodical and well thought out, Brandy's spontaneous but effective—Eloise wasn't surprised when they'd become good friends.

"I overheard Lieutenant Chambers on the phone talking to someone about the sergeant position."

Eloise glanced around them. "You know you shouldn't do that."

"Do what?"

"Listen in on private conversations."

Brandy swiped a nonchalant hand through the air. "You need to know. He mentioned your name."

Her heart accelerated.

"And Dante Matthews."

And then came to a screeching halt.

"Dante? I'm surprised. The lieutenant doesn't like Dante."

"That's for sure." Brandy chuckled. tossing her thick, black hair over her shoulder. "Chambers calls him a danger and a disgrace. I swear I've seen his eye twitch when Dante's name is mentioned."

"That's harsh." Even if the danger part rang true.

Brandy shrugged. "Which means you'll get the promotion."

"I don't know," Eloise hedged. Even though she wanted the job. More than anything.

The rumors of the promotion had been circling the department for weeks, especially since they had yet to fill the sergeant position left open by a recent transfer. She'd passed the civil exam without a problem, made sure Chambers was informed of her grade and made her desire to be considered for the position known, then secretly kept her fingers crossed that she'd be offered the chance to move up in rank. She'd been on the Palm Cove police force for four out of her six years as a police officer, a detective for two, and hoped her experience weighed into the decision making.

"Chambers respects you."

Eloise straightened the files and other office supplies positioned on her compulsively neat desktop. "That's because I do my job and get my reports in on time."

"And you work well with everyone. You're good at supervising and making decisions."

"So is Dante." She remembered his earlier request. "Well, everything but desk duty, that is."

"Yes, but you are the complete opposite of reckless."

She stilled. "You say that like it's a bad thing."

"No. I mean, I've learned a ton from you. But sometimes you have to think outside the box. Dante has that ability in spades."

Eloise frowned. "I could be reckless."

Brandy burst out in a merry laugh. "Oh, honey."

"Really, I could," Eloise fumed. "Watch me."

Brandy merely patted her on the arm and strolled away to start a conversation with a patrol officer who'd just walked in.

Who was she kidding? She plopped down into her chair.

Reckless was not a word she'd use to describe herself. She always had to push herself out of her comfort zone, especially since becoming a cop, and she was extremely proud of herself.

Now she had a chance to move up the ranks. Make a name for herself. Show her parents she'd made the right decision by forgoing a career in academics, like they'd wanted, and pursuing a degree in criminal investigation. A job she loved, with a possible promotion in her future.

The phone on her desk rang. She picked it up on the third ring, infusing an authoritative tone into her voice. "Detective Archer."

"Eloise, it's Tom Bailey over in Palm Beach. Got a minute?"

"Sure."

She'd run into Tom, also a detective, at different police functions, since Palm Cove, located on the east coast of Florida along the Atlantic, was twenty miles north of Palm Beach. Actually, she'd applied to the Palm Beach PD when she'd sent out résumés, but Palm Cove had offered her a position first. Maybe one day she'd consider moving, but she liked it here and had the promotion to consider.

"We picked up a teen the other night. Lives in your area. Pulled him over while joyriding in a stolen car."

Teen car thefts were a growing problem. Auto theft was bad enough, but the underage drivers usually crashed while the police were in pursuit. It seemed they got at least half a dozen calls a month from folks who'd discovered their cars were stolen.

"So what do you need from us?"

"It's not really what I need, more of a heads-up. We're cracking down on the problem here and hope we can share information in the future."

"You know I'm happy to work together. This isn't a problem that's going away anytime soon."

"I figured you did the research."

How could she not? She'd had multiple cases on the offense, but what made it frustrating was that the underage kids were sent to juvenile detention, then released within hours or a few short days, only to become repeat offenders. Bragging rights could be found all over social media, which the department monitored, with kids posting pictures with key fobs around their necks like trophies or snaps of the speedometer when these kids drove in excess of one hundred miles per hour down the road. Worst-case scenario was if one of the kids found a weapon in a car they'd stolen, an added prize that propelled the legend they'd spread online.

"Have you noticed an increase in activity?" she asked, wondering about a possible connection. In Palm Cove, stolen cars tended to be more midpriced than high-end, but still, people weren't happy when their mode of transportation disappeared. Worse, when the vehicle was found after a wreck, the owner had impound and insurance hassles ahead of them.

"There's a small uptick."

"Okay, well, I'll keep you informed if I learn anything helpful."

"Great. So, ah, are you attending the Maniacal Mudder charity run this weekend at Soldier Park?"

"I don't think so." She tried to attend police benefits in the surrounding cities, but didn't always make every one, especially those that included running. Or mud. Who got enjoyment out of scaling obstacles while trying to keep their balance sprinting through a world of wet dirt? Her colleagues loved the challenge, but it made her shudder. The idea of landing face-first in a puddle of goop, losing her glasses and trying to blindly make it to the finish line gave her nightmares. She'd considered it once, when Dante taunted her about tagging along, but wisely chose to stay on the sidelines in the end. She was a much better cheerleader than participant.

"If you change your mind, maybe we can form a team. It's not too late to sign up."

Team up? Did he know her? She was anything but athletic.

"Sorry, Tom. I'm going to pass."

"But you are going?"

"Um... I'll try."

"Then we can hang out. There's a barbecue after the run."

"I'll see what I can do." She noticed a movement from the corner of her eye. The lieutenant ushered Dante into his office while Dante briskly knotted his tie before entering the room.

"Listen, I need to run. We'll talk another time."

"Sure. Ah, have a good day."

"I will."

She hung up, her attention already focused on the drama sure to play out on the other side of the office door. Brandy rolled over in a chair from a nearby desk.

"It's gonna hit the fan now." She practically squealed in delight. "I'd love to be a fly on the wall."

So would Eloise, not that she'd admit it out loud.

Having previously seen Dante's face when the lieutenant spoke to him, reading his body language had become second nature to her. Not only because of the annoying attraction, ugh, but because she always thought Dante made a good cop. If he could temper his restlessness, that is. He was smart, but he couldn't stand still to save his life. Was it a lifelong problem? Was he one of those guys who craved an adrenaline rush? Questions like that popped into her head from time to time, especially when he got himself into hot water with the commanding officers. And he and Chambers were definitely oil and water.

"Do you think he'll suspend Dante?"

Eloise hoped not. He was too valuable on the job, when he wasn't making rash decisions. "I have no idea."

"Desk duty?"

"He's already on that."

"Then what?"

"I'm not going to guess." She met Brandy's gaze. "And you shouldn't, either. It's none of our business."

Brandy pouted. "Can't help it. Office politics have always intrigued me."

"Don't you have a crime scene to investigate?"

"As a matter of fact, I do. I was hoping to hold off a few more minutes to see the outcome."

Eloise held back an eye roll. "If you don't leave now, someone will report you."

"Not Sam," Brandy said, referring to the patrolman currently working the same case as Brandy. "He likes me."

"Not if his job is on the line."

"True." Brandy stood and rolled the chair back. "Let me know what happens."

As if she'd be privy to the details. Dante could be very closemouthed when need be.

She watched Brandy hurry away, reminded that she had plenty of calls of her own to make. If she wanted to get the promotion, she needed to worry about herself, not the meeting going on in the lieutenant's office.

"YOU NEARLY COST us on your last assignment, Matthews."

"I went over it with you. It was unexpected. Stone caught on when he saw the police cruiser stopped outside the house. It was either reveal the op early or lose it all."

"You know the only saving grace is the fact that the sheriff's department has an ongoing investigation with related drug dealers."

"Trust me, I get it."

The lieutenant sent him a steely glance. "Do you?"

Not again. Every time something went off script, Chambers came down on him like a hammer to a nail. The undercover investigation had been right on target, until the rookie had forced Dante to make a snap decision. It was like Chambers got enjoyment out of making him squirm.

"I know the other team on this case. They'll tie the entire ring together. With the information I acquired, these guys will go away for a long time."

Chambers merely grunted in agreement.

Dante's knee started jumping. He forced pressure on it with his hand to keep the lieutenant from noticing.

"That's not why I called you in here."

But you couldn't resist mentioning it yet again, Dante thought.

"With the possibility of a future undercover case coming your way, I need to know I can rely on you to keep your cool and get the job done."

"You know I always follow protocol, sir."

"And your idea of protocol is improvising?"

Why did this conversation not seem different from the one they'd started out with?

"I'll be honest, I'm worried about you, Matthews. How many undercover operations have you been part of in the last year?"

"Three."

"And while two have been successful, I wonder if it's too much."

Okay, taking down high-risk criminals was intense work. Pretending to be someone other than himself for extended periods of time took a toll. He'd learned to conceal the fear or anxiety in a dicey situation, while reveling in the adrenaline rush during a bust. He had no problem arresting the bad people under surveillance when the time came. It was the innocent bystanders who were pulled into a criminal lifestyle by association or relationships that did a number on his head. Undercover jobs weren't for everyone, but it worked for Dante.

"I think you should sit out the next assignment. Handle more routine calls coming into the department."

Dante controlled his annoyance by staring at the family picture of Chambers, his wife and kids displayed on a credenza behind the desk. Family. It's what got him into law enforcement in the first place, a love-hate relationship he dealt with daily.

"Is this coming from you or higher up?" he finally asked.

"A mutual decision."

He nodded. At least he wasn't suspended, or worse. He'd made a mistake. Would take his lumps, even if it meant the dreaded desk duty.

"Is that all?"

"One last question."

Dante swallowed a sigh.

"Do you wish to move up in your career?"

Unexpected. Chambers had never discussed Dante's career path before. "Move up, sir?"

"You do know we need to fill the sergeant position."

"Everyone knows."

"You passed the exam. It's been brought to my attention that a supervisory position might be a good move for you."

The sergeant job? Yeah, it sounded appealing, but with his rep, he doubted he'd be in the running. And he doubly doubted Chambers wanted him in the position.

"Think about it," the lieutenant said, rising, which Dante took as his cue to end the meeting.

"I will. Thank you."

"Don't thank me yet."

As Dante closed the door behind him, he yanked at his tie. The conversation with Chambers set his mind in motion and the idea of being weighed down in paperwork didn't thrill him. Would there be reams more if he made sergeant? A definite check in the con list.

He'd just settled in his chair when Eloise caught his eye. She was busy writing something on a yellow legal pad. No doubt jotting down notes on a case or for a trial. She was organized that way. Making sure to cross all her *t*'s and dot all her *i*'s. Had mad computer skills he lacked. But there was an air of uncertainty about her that he understood. It made him want to coax a smile out of her. She took everything in life so seriously, not even recognizing his teasing until they were well into a conversation. Calling her Ellie was just icing on the cake. He knew it rattled her and thought it might secretly please her.

Beneath her starched, professional persona,

she possessed a determination that impressed him. He'd noticed it a few months back when they'd disagreed on a certain department policy. Most colleagues gave him wide berth. Not Ellie. She stated her reasoning, concise and to the point, and he took notice, real notice, of her for the first time.

And why that mattered, he couldn't say. Just knew he liked her. Admired her dedication to the job. Along with her knowledge. She had a way of catching his eye and kept him looking. What else was hidden in those still waters?

She closed a file and tapped it on her desk to even the edges. A satisfied smile curved her lips until she glanced across the room and their gazes collided. Behind her glasses, coffee-brown eyes widened. Her cheeks turned pink. He found himself wondering if she dated and, if so, what kind of guy she went for. When she turned away, he knew his procrastinating had come to an end. With Chambers breathing down his neck, he needed to get some work done.

Her phone rang, and after a short conversation, she grabbed her bag and left.

The afternoon dragged on during his stint working the front desk. Hating every minute of being confined, it irked him that he answered the phone but couldn't go on any calls.

He took a break to pour himself some coffee, hoping caffeine would give him a much-needed jolt. Maybe he'd see which guys were participating in the mud run or engage in some office gossip to perk himself up. When he went back to the squad room, he noticed Ellie had returned.

Mug in hand, he sauntered to her desk. Leaned against the side.

"Heard you're going to the mud run."

Her head jerked up. "What? Who told you that?"

"Mason. Said he heard it from some guy over at the Palm Beach PD."

"Well, he heard wrong. I have no intention of running in mud."

"Chicken?"

Her eyes narrowed at his challenge. "Sane."

"It could be fun."

"Says who?"

Her horrified look had him chuckling. "I'll take that as a definite no."

"Because my first answer was unclear?"

"Touchy."

She blinked at him. "Bleary-eyed."

"Guess my wrangling you into reviewing my reports is moot."

"I can't provide information I have no knowledge of."

"That's right, we've never worked on a case together." He took a sip of the bitter coffee and grimaced. "Although that might change. I'll be around more often."

"No new exciting cases?"

He shrugged. "Not for me. For a while, anyway."

"So you hone your detective skills in the meantime."

"Saying I'm rusty?"

"I don't know. I've never worked with you."

She'd used his words against him. He held up his mug and grinned.

"Not that I've asked not to be paired with you."

"I never thought you did."

She relaxed.

Add *nice person* to the mental list he'd been making about her earlier.

"How come you never go out with your fellow officers after work?" he asked, genuinely curious.

"I don't know. I'm not a terribly social person."

"Why is that?"

She shoved her glasses up her nose. A nervous tick he'd noticed.

"Not good company, I guess."

"Then why is a Palm Beach detective interested in you?"

Her mouth gaped open. "Why would you think that?"

"Because he told Mason."

"Good grief," she muttered under her breath, then met his gaze again. "I think work relationships are better left at work."

Interesting. History there?

"Fair enough."

The conversation lagged for a few moments. Ellie glanced at a clock on the wall. "I need to head out."

"You never answered me about dinner tonight. Two colleagues discussing work over a burger and fries?"

"I don't think it's a good idea, but thank you."

She stood, gathered her purse and slid the chair up to the everything-in-its-place desk. He wanted to mess it up and see her reaction. Instead, he moved aside as she passed, her light floral perfume following in her wake. "See you tomorrow."

"'Bye."

He returned to his desk, a little disappointed. He would have loved to wrangle the truth of why she avoided work relationships out of her, but not tonight. He settled back in and, to his surprise, finished the last of his tasks in no time.

An hour later he ran along the broad sidewalk in Soldier Park that was situated parallel to the ocean, loud, headbanging music keeping pace with his stride. After a day of being mostly cooped up, he needed to get rid of the excess energy. Running had always been a way to do just that.

Or cars. Tinkering with an engine always grounded him. He never understood why, just accepted the gift. Working on cars had not only given him focus, but he'd spent the best times of his life working alongside his dad. It was the one thing they'd had in common. And growing up with three older brothers, it was also the one thing he didn't have to fight and scratch for to get his father's attention. His bothers preferred other activities.

Coming to the end of his run, he slowed down. The sun was setting. The early-spring temperatures were still cool for Florida, but in the next months the thermometer would begin to inch up to the ninety-degree days of summer. Dante would have to get up at dawn to handle the heat while he ran, but it beat going to the gym. Just wasn't the same as getting out in the fresh air, charging past couples out walking their dogs or parents playing with their kids at the playground.

He stopped the iPod and yanked out his earbuds. Instead of raging guitars, the water crashing onto the shore greeted his ears. He gazed out over the undulating water, taking a deep breath. Salty with a mix of suntan lotion. Sunset, his favorite time of the day. He found peace watching the sun disappear from the sky, dragging streaks of pinks and oranges fading to purple with it, until the sky went black.

He loved it here in Palm Cove. His brothers, Derrick and Deke, worked in different states, and Dylan, on the opposite coast of Florida. When Dylan found himself falling in love during a case, their mother had decided to move to be closer to the only woman who, she was certain, would ever be a possible daughter-in-law. Jasmine Matthews knew how to lay on a guilt trip just as her boys knew how to sidestep her tactics. It was a game they played, more so since their father had died. Mom needed a hobby and acting like her world would end if she didn't have daughters and grandbabies worked for her.

A smile crossed his lips. He pulled out his phone and speed-dialed her number.

"Dante. It's been nearly a month," his mother accused in way of greeting.

"I was undercover. I told you and Dylan."

"Dylan's been busy chasing after criminals. You boys need to give me better details."

"We can't always do that."

"Please." She tsked. "Your father always did."

Dante knew that wasn't the case. Daryl Matthews had been on the force for thirty-five years. There was no way he told his wife everything.

"I was just thinking about Dad."

Her voice softened. "A good memory?"

"Cars."

She laughed. "You two did have fun. How's the Cobra?"

The '65 Mustang he was currently retooling. "You remembered."

"I remember everything my boys tell me."

Which was eerily true.

"Still tinkering, but I decided to paint it red."

"Racy choice. Your father would have approved."

Would he? In Dante's choice of car color or career choice?

"Something troubling you?" she asked with her weird mom ESP vibe.

"Not really. I had a conversation at work today about my career. Not sure how I feel about it."

"Since when have you not been able to make a decision? All my sons are very professional when it comes to law enforcement. I'm proud of each and every one of you, but out of the bunch, I worry about you most."

He hesitated. Asked the question he'd never wanted to broach with his mom, but now seemed like a good time. "You don't like me going undercover?"

"I'd be lying if I said I didn't have a few sleepless nights when I know you're on a case." The hesitancy in her voice made his chest clutch. "I may not know the particulars, but I know the situations you're investigating can't be good. Or safe."

"I wonder sometimes if I could handle a job that required me to sit behind a desk more. It doesn't seem natural."

Jasmine laughed. "You never were one to be happy indoors."

"Is moving up the ladder part of growing up? Dylan's arrest rate at the DEA is impressive. Derrick has made a name for himself at the FBI and Deke is a well-respected forensic investigator. They've made great strides in their careers." He tamped down the envy that threatened to bring him to his knees when he considered his brothers' successes. He loved them; he just had a hard time following in their footsteps. "I guess I just never put a lot of emphasis on moving ahead in my career until now."

"Then the question you need to ask yourself is, can you do the job?"

He thought about the sergeant's test he'd passed. Studying had been excruciating, but he'd needed to prove to himself that he could do better than being the pesky kid brother who had to find inventive ways to keep up with his siblings.

He rolled his shoulders as he considered the question. Settled with, "I'm sure I could."

"Okay, then ask yourself this. Do you *want* the job?"

He thought about his brothers again. Would he take a promotion just to be like them? To carry on the Matthews tradition to serve and protect? Or would he take a promotion, if it was offered, because *he* wanted the job?

"Guess I need to sleep on it."

"Dante, whatever you decide to do in life, know that I'm proud of you."

"Thanks, Mom."

"Your father would be, too."

He swallowed hard. His father had supported

him, but had also tried to temper Dante's reckless streak when he was growing up. Tried to find activities Dante would find interest in to keep him out of trouble. And told his son it might cost him something he desperately wanted one day if he didn't learn to control himself. Could a promotion be what he wanted? It certainly would have made his late father proud. Could he do it? The idea was planted in his brain now and he'd puzzle over it until he came up with an answer.

His mother broke into his thoughts. "When am I going to see you?"

"Maybe I can get over in the next week or two."

"Don't be a stranger. There's this cute waitress who works at the local outdoor restaurant I've fallen in love with. She'd be perfect for you. I think—"

"Mom, I gotta run. Work might be calling me."

"Might be? Dante Matthews—"

"Love you. Talk to you soon."

Dante ended the call before his mother had him talked into calling this woman and asking her out on a date, sight unseen. He hoped Dylan got engaged soon, just to take the pressure off.

As he jogged back to his truck, he thought

about work decisions, which then triggered visions of Ellie. Her lovely smile when she let her guard down. The deep brown of her eyes. She intrigued him, that's for sure, which was odd, since she wasn't his type. He went for women who were more put together in the looks department. Not that Eloise wasn't pretty; she just hid behind the glasses, tightly pulled back hair and severe clothing choices. But his mother would love her.

Reason enough not to pursue the interest he'd discovered in her. He could already hear his mom humming the wedding march.

CHAPTER TWO

"HEY, ELLIE. WAIT UP."

Eloise ignored the jolt to her heart and turned to find Dante racing through the parking lot the next morning. The sun was shining, the temperature hovered in the midseventies and Dante was calling her name. Did life get any better? She took a breath and kept her voice level. "What's up?"

The bright morning light lifted the multiple shades of brown in his unruly hair. Dark sunglasses shaded his eyes, but not the cocky curve of his lips.

"I just found out we're short a person for the mud run on Saturday."

"That's too bad." Adjusting her purse strap on her shoulder, she was disappointed by his statement, though why, she couldn't explain. She headed for the building.

"It won't be if you'd join us."

"I already told you, not interested."

"See, here's the thing. We haven't lost a

challenge to another PD in two years and we can't lose now. We need you."

She stopped. Faced him. Tamped down her annoyance.

"I can't help you."

"Sure you can. All you do is say yes, throw on clothes you don't care about getting dirty and show up at the obstacle course at eight on Saturday morning." He paused. "It's for charity."

Even though she stayed physically fit to keep up with the demands of the job and policy of the department, she wasn't very fast. Or accurate. "Dante, trust me, no one wants me on their team."

"I do."

She wished she could read his eyes. Was he serious? Merely taunting her?

"I'm sorry, Dante. The answer is still no."

She'd turned and had taken two steps along the blacktop when she heard, "Bawk, bawk, bawk."

She whirled around. "Did you just make chicken noises at me?"

He shrugged. "If the chicken feet fit…"

"I don't have chicken feet. And I'm not scared."

"What, then?"

Oh, now he was taunting her. Her temper rose and she blurted, "Uncoordinated."

Dante calmly walked to her. "Hey, it's not my intention to upset you, but we really need you. We can't find anyone else."

"Be still my heart. Picked for a team last again."

He ran a hand through his hair. "I didn't mean it that way. I just… It's a team effort. You're part of our team. Palm Cove PD, that is. We'd be honored to have you."

Now he was laying it on thick. "There's absolutely no one else available?"

"We need one more woman to even out the team. And even though you've expressed your displeasure at being part of the team, I'm hoping you'll reconsider." As backpedaling went, it wasn't much, but the chagrined expression on his face granted him points. Even more points for actually listening to her. He wanted her to join despite her refusal.

"I've never done anything like a mud race before."

"You come and do the best you can."

She did want to feel accepted, be part of something bigger than herself. She'd forever been the odd person out. Vowed one day she'd change that status. Could it start with something as dirty as a mud run?

She pushed up her glasses. "You're 100 percent certain you need me?"

He flashed her one of his charming grins. "Absolutely."

Not sure if it was the team angle or Dante's interest, but she nodded.

"Great. See you Saturday," he said, then took off as if afraid she might back out if he hung around.

Which made her want to kick herself. She had three days to get ready. Well, today was already busy with follow-up interviews in ongoing cases, which essentially left her with two days. What was wrong with her?

Marching inside the building, she stopped short when Brandy ran up to her. "Something major's going on."

Holding up her hand to ebb the flow of information, she stalled by storing her purse in her desk drawer and pouring a much-needed mug of coffee. Brandy, nearly dancing with impatience to fill her ear with the latest news, was clearly ready to burst.

After a bracing sip of the supremely awful coffee, Eloise faced her friend. "This is a police department. Something is always going on. What makes today different?"

"There's a rippling in the atmosphere. Plus, Chambers has been upstairs for over an hour."

"He goes up a couple of times a week to meet with the chief."

"I heard from the chief's secretary that the sergeant position is a priority. Like the decision has to be made pronto."

Eloise set the mug on her desk. Smoothed her black dress pants and straightened the collar on her white blouse while trying to contain her excitement. Would the chief of police seriously consider her?

"I don't suppose you heard who the likely candidates are?"

"No. That information is being monitored, even more closely guarded than the gold at Fort Knox."

Eloise blinked. Following Brandy's thought process was like participating in a Ping-Pong match. If she wasn't careful, she might get mental whiplash. Thankfully her friend was more focused when on the job.

"I can't imagine there are that many choices. As far as I know, Dante and I are the only ones who have recently taken the test."

Brandy's lips curved. "Exactly."

"You think…both of us?"

"Who else?"

Eloise sank down into her chair, her chest suddenly tight.

She knew it was a possibility they'd both be

in the running. Although, when she'd learned Dante had taken the civil test, she'd been surprised. He'd never expressed a desire to be in a more supervisory role. Not that they'd had any lengthy conversations about their desired career paths or, let's face it, lengthy conversations about anything much at all. She was lucky they got through their daily hellos. The man didn't share his personal life with anyone that she knew of; why would he announce his professional career path to the entire department? Maybe it was because of the undercover life he'd adopted to so well. Keeping secrets, and his intentions, close to the vest.

Great. Did she have to worry about competition for the job? They were both qualified, and not to toot her own horn, but she was better suited for the position. But it didn't matter what she thought. That decision came from those with a higher pay grade.

"Let's not jump the gun here," she reasoned. "Who even says they'll promote someone from this station?"

"Why bring a new person from the outside when we have qualified candidates in this very building? Besides, anyone who knows you can't argue about how awesome you'd be."

The pressure in Eloise's chest eased. "Thanks for the boost of confidence."

"You have to get the job. For the sisterhood."

Eloise laughed. "The sisterhood, huh?"

"Seriously. We have to stick together. It's bad enough we work in a male-dominated field. We have the added pressure of proving ourselves every day."

As Brandy sauntered away, Eloise considered her words. Her friend spoke the truth. The women working here did prove themselves daily, but for Eloise, this was nothing new. She'd been proving herself her entire life. First, to parents who hadn't been thrilled when she came along, leaving her pretty much to her own devices while growing up. Their academic careers came first and, as much as it hurt, had been a sterling example of the work ethic she'd adopted from the start of her career.

She'd tried to fit in, at college and on the job, but there was always something keeping her from fully joining in. Letting herself go. Something protecting that little girl who'd longed for the love of her parents and acceptance of others.

Shaking off the direction of her thoughts, she looked up when she sensed someone at her desk. Dante, holding out a slip of paper.

"Patrol called in trouble at Parson's Auto Mall."

"What kind of trouble?"

"Stolen vehicles. Damage."

She stood and reached for her badge and a small wallet holding her ID and driver's license. "Are you coming?"

"No. Still on house arre—I mean, desk duty."

She would have smiled if his disgruntled expression wasn't so fierce. Sitting on the sidelines had to be killing him.

"I wrote down the address for you."

"Thanks," she said as she took the paper, not really needing the address. Palm Cove was small enough that finding the major dealership wasn't a problem. When Dante didn't move, she asked, "Everything okay?"

"Yeah. Just a little distracted today."

Did she dare ask if he'd heard about Chambers's meeting up in the chief's office? No, she wouldn't go there. Instead she said, "Sorry you're stuck here all day."

"Hopefully Chambers gets tired of seeing me around all the time and puts me back in the field."

"You could bring him coffee. Ask him if he wants to talk about his day, what's up with his family and then, if things are going especially well, ask if he wants to talk about his feelings."

Dante shuddered. "As much as you meant

that as a joke, if the guy doesn't lighten up soon, I might resort to your suggestion."

"Oh, let me know if you do. I want to stand by the door and listen to every word."

"I'll blame you."

"Go for it," she said as she walked away. "But he won't believe that you and I ever had this conversation."

His chuckle came from behind her, making her smile. Neither of them was very chatty with Chambers, but at least she'd lifted his spirits.

"Heading out to the auto mall?" Brandy asked as Eloise passed her desk.

"Yes. You, too?"

"I am," she said, gathering her equipment.

"Want to ride together?"

"Sounds good."

Fifteen minutes later they pulled into the dealership. A patrolman stood by the front door of the glass-enclosed showroom, speaking to an agitated middle-aged man.

"Mr. Parson?" Brandy guessed as they walked his way.

"Looks like him." The dealership had two major billboards on the highway just outside town, prominently featuring the owner.

The patrolman noticed them and excused himself.

"Hi, Officer Stevens," Eloise greeted him.

"Archer. Cummings." He nodded in their direction. "Got the call when Mr. Parson arrived this morning. Two cars in the lot were stolen." He pointed to his left. "The perps used bolt cutters to breach the perimeter fence and gain access to the property. Focused on taking two newly delivered cars."

"I'll go talk to the owner," Eloise said, then to Brandy, "You can get started."

"Follow me to the location," the officer said.

Concentrating on the task at hand, Eloise went inside the bright, shiny showroom. Noticed the pervading scent of rubber and oil mixed with air freshener. Four cars were featured: two sporty models she couldn't name, an SUV and a four-door sedan. New models. All high-end.

"Mr. Parson," she said when the owner approached her. "I'm Detective Archer."

"These car thefts are getting out of hand. This is the second time in six months."

"I understand your frustration. Believe me, we're concerned about the problem."

He ran a hand over the sparse hair on his nearly bald head. "The cars were just delivered yesterday. I didn't even have time to get them on the showroom floor. It's like someone knew where the new arrivals were parked."

"Do you have security camera footage covering the entire lot?"

"Yes. Over here."

Parson muttered under his breath while leading her to an office on the back side of the showroom. A young woman, twentysomething, Eloise surmised, rushed to his side. "Mr. Parson, I have the insurance company on the line."

"Give me a minute, Stacy." He glanced at Eloise. "My office manager."

She nodded. Once in the room complete with security screens covering different angles of the property, and what smelled like a greasy breakfast sandwich and coffee, Mr. Parson introduced her to Jerry, a security guard, and said, "I'll be right back."

Jerry sat back, the chair protesting under his girth. Crumpling up the food wrapper, he tossed it across the room to the trash can, missing his mark. Unconcerned, he clicked a mouse stationed beside his computer keyboard. "Got what ya need right here."

"Did you go through the footage from last night?"

"Yep."

"Can you show me where the stolen cars were located?"

"Sure, but you won't see much. Was like the

guys knew where the cameras were mounted. Made sure to face the opposite direction."

He pulled up the footage in question. Sure enough, two people—young men, she thought—appeared on screen, their faces obscured by hoodies. One held a device in his hands, most likely a wireless code grabber that intercepted signals sent by remote keyless entry devices. Recording the code prior to trespassing on the property, it was then used to unlock the car doors. Once they'd cleared that hurdle, the vehicles started, and soon they were speeding away. As they moved into darkness, the image grew grainy, but she noticed a bright white slash on the back of one of the jackets.

Jerry pointed to another screen. "The gate barring entrance to the lot after-hours was tampered with and moved."

Explained the easy getaway.

"The main question is, how did they get the key codes? From the office?" Eloise wondered out loud.

"Impossible. Mr. Parson has always been careful with the keys, but after the last theft, he's even more diligent. I personally see that the keys are stored so that no one can hack 'em."

Hmm. Obviously someone had. Here or elsewhere?

Eloise asked a few more questions and made notes. Arranged to get a copy of the video sent to the department. This motive didn't follow the thefts they'd been experiencing with joy-riding kids. It amazed her how often owners left a vehicle running to dash inside a store or business or leave an unlocked car in the drive-way with the key left in the console. Ripe picking for a kid looking to car-hop. Not the case here. This was deliberate, a well-planned get-in-get-out before the authorities arrive.

She asked a few more questions, then went back to the dealership owner, who had returned to the showroom floor, talking in urgent tones to a salesman.

"Anything else you can tell me, Mr. Parson?"

"Only that somehow these thugs knew I had a delivery scheduled."

"Are new vehicles brought in on a regular schedule?"

"No, for this exact reason."

"Any way one of your employees could have passed the delivery information along?"

"There's only a handful who know the particulars. Stacy Monroe, my wife and my general manager."

"Is the manager here?"

"No. On vacation. He'll be back next week."

Mr. Parson's phone blared. "I need to take this."

"And your wife?" Eloise asked quickly.

"At home. This is her calling now."

Pivoting on her heel, Eloise searched for the main office. She found Stacy, a pretty brunette, hanging up the phone, tears in her eyes. "This is terrible." She swiped a tissue from the box and blotted her eyes. "I've been in line for the office manager job for months and when I finally get the position this happens."

"Do you have something to be worried about?"

Stacy's eyes went wide. "No, I just mean that we all take this personally."

"Did you mention yesterday's delivery to anyone?"

"Of course not."

"How do you think the thieves knew to go right to the new cars?"

Her chin went up. "I wouldn't know."

Upset and defensive. Did Stacy know more than she let on? Or had she messed up somehow and was worried about keeping her job?

"And all the keys are accounted for?"

"Yes." She grabbed a fancy, square key ring featuring an imprint of some kind of animal on it, passed Eloise in a haze of strong perfume that made her sneeze and unlocked a large wall safe. Inside, key fobs hung from individual hooks, along with corresponding numbers she assumed went with the car the key belonged to. "They were locked up last night."

And no one had broken into the office or safe. Didn't matter since the cars were gone, but Eloise had to follow her line of questioning.

"Look." Stacy sniffled. "I need this job. I wouldn't risk it by getting involved with stolen cars."

Until Eloise did a background check on the woman, she'd have to accept her word, but something was off here. Taking a card from the holder on Stacy's desk, Eloise said, "If I have any more questions I'll contact you."

Stacy nodded, then hustled back to the desk when the phone rang. Eloise asked other employees more questions, finally heading to her car once she was satisfied she'd spoken to each person who could supply viable information.

Brandy stood by the sedan. "Finished?"

"For now. Ready to return to the department?"

As Eloise drove, her mind went over the statements she'd taken. No one knew anything. Couldn't account for the thieves discovering the delivery date. Right now she had lots of questions that would take days to answer.

She and Brandy had just entered the squad room when Lieutenant Chambers caught her attention and motioned for her to come to his office. Thinking he wanted an update, she grabbed her notes and hurried over, stopping short when she saw Dante seated in one of the two chairs before Chambers's desk.

"Have a seat, Detective."

Eloise lowered herself, glancing at Dante for a hint of explanation as to what had precipitated the meeting. His expressionless face told her nothing.

"I called you both in here for two reasons." He met her gaze. "Detective Archer, that call you took this morning. Did it look like our teen car problem?"

"No, sir. It was too deliberate. Too planned out."

He nodded. "The dealership in Palm Cove isn't the only one to be hit in recent months. Even dealers like Marcus King, with car lots in multiple cities, are being affected. Intel leads us to believe there's a ring operating locally. We need to find it and put a stop to their activity."

"What did you have in mind?" Dante asked, interest lighting his eyes.

"Matthews, I need you to go undercover again."

Dante sat straighter in the chair.

"With your interest in restoring cars, you have an in. One of our officers, already undercover on a different case, reported unusual activity at an automotive shop under surveillance. We'd like you to infiltrate. We're hoping this leads you to the ringleader."

"Does this officer have an in?"

"Yes. You'll pose as his cousin. He'll give his seal of approval to secure you a job there."

Dante nodded. "When do I start?"

"Monday. You'll be briefed today about the garage in question, as well as the owner, who's a potential suspect." He paused a beat. "You won't be going alone."

"Excuse me?"

"I don't want a hint of failure like last time. I'm sending another detective in with you."

"To keep an eye on me?"

Eloise tightly gripped her notebook as the tension in the room accelerated.

"To make sure this operation is carried out to satisfaction."

Dante's jaw worked but he didn't respond.

"In order to make this plausible, we're going to set you up as a married man. Just a guy looking to support his family. A wife in the picture makes you less suspicious."

"And who is this wife going to be?"

No, Eloise thought. *No, no, no.*

"Detective Archer."

"Oh, no," she groaned under her breath.

DANTE GLANCED TO his left. Eloise? They were partnering him with Eloise?

"Are you sure, sir? Detective Archer hasn't had any undercover experience."

"Then I'm sure you'll show her the ropes. She's a smart woman. She'll catch on quick."

"I don't think—"

"It doesn't matter what you think, Matthews. You work with her or you don't get the case."

Eloise? How on earth was he supposed to work the case and train her at the same time? Prove to the brass that he wasn't going to screw up this investigation?

"If I may," Eloise cut in.

Chambers nodded.

"I might not be experienced, but I can certainly be an asset." She sent Dante a sideways look. Annoyance glittered in her eyes.

"I agree. You're a fast learner, Archer. And you're more than competent. While Matthews works at the shop and uncovers information there, you can work the technical end. We'll have a computer station set up at the house you two will be sharing. You'll be doing background checks, monitoring security once Matthews is employed at the shop and working the rest of your magic with a computer."

Wait. The house they'd be sharing?

"You've already closed cases involving car theft, Archer. You know how serious this is. The call you took this morning proves that the problem is getting bigger. As you said, this was a professional job. This group is organized and has insider information. We need that information, as well as to find out how they are altering VINs and bills of sale successfully. Where are the stolen cars going? It's a big deal."

"I appreciate you needing the technical end, sir," Eloise was saying, "but I'd like to be more visible."

"That's why you two will blend into the neighborhood we're setting you up in. Be active. The whole point it to collect viable intel on the car ring. We need to know participants, specific delivery schedules, dealerships they plan to hit, and at the top of the list? The name of the boss behind the ring, without your neighbors knowing exactly who you are."

Dante cleared his throat. "And who are we exactly?"

"Dan and Ellie Smith."

Dante heard another quiet groan escape his new partner. A good rule of thumb when undercover was to use a variation of your real name so you wouldn't get mixed up during the op. She was going to hate this.

"From the intel we've received, whoever is running this ring is good at hiding their identity. We need a name. Then we stop him."

"Are the feds involved?" Dante asked.

"As of right now, no. Far as we can tell, the stolen cars have not crossed any state's border."

"Then we focus locally."

"Yes. I want this one, Matthews. Archer has a good head on her shoulders. Listen to her."

He glanced in her direction. She kept her chin up, facing the lieutenant. What was she thinking about all this?

"Moving on to the next item of business. Chief Perkins and I have been discussing possible candidates for the sergeant position. Both of your names have come up in consideration."

He turned his head and met Eloise's gaze. If she was surprised, she didn't show it.

"You both have strengths that would work for the position. You both passed the civil test, and even though we haven't officially interviewed you, we know both of you well enough to determine you're ready for a promotion."

Dante planted his feet on the ground to keep from jittering. As much as he'd told his mother he wasn't sure about taking the position, he discovered he wanted it. Badly. Enough to battle Eloise over it? Yep. Did that make him a bad guy?

"The two of you pairing up as partners works to our advantage. We'll watch how you handle the investigation, your decision making, how you interact with each other. Then we'll decide who moves ahead at this time."

Eloise squared her shoulders. She wanted the job. It was written all over her. She was a good detective. Probably a better administrator than he. But he knew his fellow officers. Could be a better supervisor. Office management could be learned as he went along.

"You'll both report for a briefing in an hour. Dismissed."

Eloise hightailed it out of the room. He had to jog to keep up with her.

"Ellie. Slow down."

She spun around. "Not Ellie. Not now."

He followed her to her desk. Voices carried around them from officers busy at work, but when he noticed curious eyes on them, he realized the tension around himself and Eloise alerted them that something was up. "Fine. When we start the operation."

She stared back at him, her pretty brown eyes dark. "I want the promotion," she stated.

"So do I," he countered.

"I deserve it."

"I could use the same argument."

The thundercloud in her eyes still raged. "Then this puts us at odds."

"Not during the operation, Eloise. It doesn't work that way. We put all thought about the sergeant position aside when we become Dan and Ellie Smith. Otherwise we won't fool anyone."

"Fine, but I'll be an equal partner. I won't be your babysitter."

"Harsh."

"I'm a professional and I can do the job as well as you, even if I don't have undercover experience."

"But I do have the experience, Eloise. That's the point."

"And I have the research skills."

"Exactly. We both have our strengths." He ran a hand over the back of his neck. "I've never done this kind of op, where I had to pretend to be married. It'll be a learning curve for both of us. Instead of battling each other, let's promise to work together."

Her gaze wavered. She was an intelligent woman. A savvy cop. She might not like his words, but she would accept the truth behind them.

"I can't promise I'll be a loving wife," she said, voice lowered, still infused with irritation.

"I can honestly say I'll probably make a lousy husband."

She sighed, all pretense of anger gone. "What were they thinking?"

"That we'd make a good team?"

She removed her glasses and rubbed her eyes. "Wait till everyone finds out."

It wouldn't be long before the entire squad room discovered they'd been partnered together. He could imagine the remarks he'd have to fend off because this was Eloise he'd been teamed with. Upright and uptight, but smart and savvy.

"I meant what I said this morning. You'll make a good team member," he told her, trying to defuse the tension, but also honestly meaning it. She might not like sports a whole lot, but she was willing to try. She'd give her all when undercover. That went a long way in his book.

"That's when you were talking about the mud run."

"I was talking about being part of a team in general. I think I can trust you, Eloise."

"Think?" she sputtered, her eyes hot again. "We're going to pretend to be husband and wife, live in the same house, for Pete's sake, and you *think* you can trust me?"

Jeez. This was getting out of hand. Didn't bode well for his husbandly skills. "No. I will trust you."

Her eyes blazed. "That's right you will."

"We'll put moving ahead in our careers aside for sake of the investigation?"

"Yes. And once we've concluded the case, it's game on."

A small victory, he supposed, but he'd take it.

"Want to grab lunch?"

An *are you kidding me?* expression crossed her face.

"Work related," he bit out.

"I suppose we could discuss the upcoming investigation." Her shoulders relaxed a bit. "How we'll work together to make this happen."

She couldn't help tossing the "we" in there.

"Good. It's a date."

Just when he thought he'd persuaded her—

babysitter, really?—a whistle split the relative calm of the squad room. Dante looked over to see one of the officers send him a thumbs-up. "Promo's yours, bro," he said. Dante grimaced, almost afraid to face Eloise. He wouldn't have if he wasn't a Matthews, because Matthewses didn't run from danger. So he turned toward her.

"You have got to be kidding me," Eloise fumed. "This is insulting. I've worked hard to get where I am today. In two seconds, your friends over there have turned our vying for the sergeant's job into the makings of a frat party."

"Ignore them."

She gaped at him. "And how do you suggest I manage that?"

Before he could pin down his suggestions, Brandy ran up to them, excitement streaming off her in waves. Now it was his turn to want to bolt.

"Mr. and Mrs. Smith?" she squealed. "Just like the movie."

Just shoot me now.

Eloise sent him a wry look. "Ignore it, huh?"

"Yes. We have an important job to do. These clowns will be apologizing later when we make the biggest arrest in Palm Cove history."

She raised a brow.

"Okay, a substantial bust. And we'll do it together."

She didn't seem convinced. "Come on, let's go. Lunch is calling."

"Never mind. I have things I need to tie up here if we're going to be out of the office for any length of time."

Brandy shot him a victorious smile. "And she and I need to talk." That said, she tugged Eloise's arm.

Dante stopped her before she was pulled away. "This will work out, Eloise. We'll be professional and aboveboard."

The fire in her brown eyes warned him there might be fireworks ahead. Not that he minded an explosion every now and then. One way or another, he'd win her over.

CHAPTER THREE

HE HAD TO hand it to her. She'd shown up.

Dante had had his doubts, considering the grueling couple of days prepping their undercover stories and investigation strategy. Must have been the team loyalty he'd inspired in her. Either that or she planned on sticking it to him during the race. A smart man would keep his eye on her, and Mrs. Matthews didn't raise no dummy.

Eloise stopped at the perimeter of the teams milling around prior to the race. Uncertainty wrinkled her brow. A slender finger pushed her glasses up her nose. Man, that got him every time. She tried to hide her vulnerability, but it was like he had radar. Probably because he could relate.

Growing up in the shadows of his older brothers, barreling through life, whether it was grabbing the last pancake on Sunday morning or making a sports team one of his brothers had already left his mark on, he found himself competing for their respect. Making a bigger splash to get noticed. Hating when they'd nicknamed him Pretty Boy. He couldn't help his looks. It was genetics and he was more than that, if they'd notice. Hadn't he carved out a career in law enforcement because he wanted to be like his father? Upheld the family tradition?

Someone slapped him on the back, jolting him from his jaunt down memory lane.

"Today's the day we beat you, Matthews."

"In your dreams, Johnson."

His taunt was met with a laugh. Yeah. Palm Cove would show the other teams today. The race might be called Maniacal Mudder because of the challenging obstacles, but he and his teammates would show the other police departments a thing or two.

"This is worse than I imagined," Eloise said as she joined him. "Maybe I can get a last minute doctor's note and bow out."

"People have seen you. Can't leave now."

"Just what I was afraid of."

"C'mon over to the sign-in table."

He waited until she fell into step beside him and led them through the crowd. Before long she'd stowed away her small backpack, had a cloth square with the number eighty-three pinned to the back of her T-shirt and slipped on the rubber wristband given to the runners.

"Guess this makes me official." She rolled her shoulders and glanced around. "I feel like I'm forgetting something."

He made a swirly gesture toward her hair. "You might want a bandanna so if your hair gets loose it won't get in your eyes."

She worried her lower lip. "I didn't bring one."

"Got one in the car. Follow me."

He led her to the '65 Mustang. Hid a grin when her eyes went wide.

"Wow. That's quite a car."

"Been tinkering on it for a while. Decided to bring it out for a drive today."

The two-seater looked sweet in the early-morning light. Or maybe he was jazzed to have taken it out for a spin, windows down, a fresh breeze blowing out the cobwebs after being cooped up all week.

"This is what Chambers meant when he mentioned your interest in restoring cars?"

"Yep." He opened the door and leaned in to rummage through the glove box, pulling out a checkered square of cloth. "My dad and I logged a lot of hours working on cars like this. Mostly muscle cars. We'd restore and flip them."

"A side business?"

"Not really. It was a reason to make time to be together."

Her eyes took on a wistful gleam.

"How about you? Any hobbies you share with your folks?"

"Not unless you consider lecturing your daughter a hobby?"

Okay, then. He handed her the bandanna. "This should work."

She took it, twisted it between her fingers.

"Don't worry so much. This is going to be fun." He nodded to the cloth. "Might help keep your glasses in place, too."

Her fingers flew up to the arms of the glasses as she adjusted them. "Brought an old pair. Just in case."

"You'll do fine."

Doubt and fear competed for prominence across her gentle features. Before he could stop and think about what he was doing, Dante laid a comforting hand on her shoulder. There was a spark from the connection. At her surprised glance, their eyes met and held. The deep, coffee-brown depths started his heart to hammering, which had nothing to do with the anticipation of the race and everything to do with the woman standing before him.

As if scalded, he jerked his hand back to

his side. Eloise ducked her head. Uneasiness hovered between them.

"We should join the team," he said finally.

They began to walk away when Eloise stopped.

"You forgot to lock your car."

"No need."

"Really? With all the auto thefts we investigate, you're willing to take a chance?"

A slow grin curved his lips. "Never with my car."

She waited for an explanation.

"One, I take my keys with me. Two, I disconnect the fuel cell. Even if someone tried to hot-wire my car—and with dozens of cops around that would be stupid—they wouldn't get anywhere."

She shrugged. "Your decision."

He was about to defend himself when his phone rang. Yanking it from his pocket, he read the caller ID. His brother Dylan. "I need to take this."

"I see Brandy. I'm going to talk to her."

He watched her stroll away, shoulders hunched just a bit, before he tapped the green button. "Hey, bro. What's up?"

"Got a minute?"

"Only. Getting ready to compete in a mud race."

"A mud what?"

"You need to get out more."

"Whatever. Listen, we have a problem with Mom."

Unease skittered over his neck. "Is she okay?"

"Physically, she's fine." Dylan paused. Either for effect or composure. Knowing Dylan, the ultimate protector, Dante banked on the second.

"She's dating."

Dante blinked a few times. Had he heard Dylan right? "Dating?"

"As in going out with a guy who isn't our father."

"Our mother?"

"The only one we've got."

Huh. She hadn't mentioned this when he'd last talked to her. But then again, Jasmine Matthews could be cagey when she wanted to.

"In all fairness, our father is in the forever after."

"Yes. But she's *dating*."

Dante and his brothers had talked about what they'd do if their mother ever decided to put herself out in the dating world again. Jasmine was in her late fifties. Young enough to find interest in another man. But growing up around his parents, seeing the depth of their devotion to each other, he and his brothers had been convinced she'd never take the plunge. Apparently they were mistaken.

"When did this start?"

"I just found out about it last night. Mom swore Kady to secrecy."

Their mother had moved to Cypress Pointe, where Dylan was currently residing, to work with Dylan's girlfriend, Kady, at her family's floral shop.

"How could you let this happen?" Dante accused.

"Really? Have you met our mother? She has a mind of her own."

No joke. Still… "Have you talked to her about this?"

"She told me to mind my own business," Dylan answered gruffly.

Dante snorted. "Rich, coming from a woman who has made it her life's mission to interfere in ours." He shook his head. When their father had died, the brothers had promised each other to protect their mom, no matter the cost, and not let anything hurt her again, if they could help it. If this was one of those situations, they'd find any way possible to safeguard her. "Who is this guy?"

"She won't say."

"But being the dutiful son that you are, you found out, anyway, right?"

He paused. "She didn't exactly confide in Kady, only mentioned a man in her life, and has refused to tell me his name."

"But you'll ferret it out of her, right?"

"You bet. She isn't the only Matthews with mad interrogation skills."

Dante didn't doubt his brother for one second.

"Have you told Derrick and Deke?"

"Derrick laughed for about five minutes. Deke wanted to jump on the next plane home and start a search for the guy."

"Well, I won't add to your troubles by showing up. It'll only make Mom clam up more."

"Any chance you'll be free in the coming days if we need a brotherly chat?"

Dante inhaled the smoky scent of the grill being prepared for the barbecue lunch. His stomach growled in anticipation. "Starting a new case on Monday. I'll be undercover so I can't make any promises. I can videoconference call with you guys if necessary."

"Okay. I'll let you know." Dylan went quiet for a long-drawn-out moment. "This case dangerous?"

"Shouldn't be."

"Watch your back, Pretty Boy."

Dante ground his back teeth before answering. "Got it under control."

"I'll keep you informed."

Dante signed off, struggling to keep his cool between the Pretty Boy remark and the fact that their mother was keeping secrets from them. She'd never done that before, unless it was leverage to get him or his brothers to do her bidding. It had always been in fun, the Matthews family game, until now. He didn't like it. Not one little bit. And he was sure his brothers felt the same way.

"You all right?" Eloise asked as she tentatively moved toward him.

He controlled the scowl he was sure would scare anyone away.

"Family drama."

"Okay, well, the team is gathering for a pep talk before the race starts."

He shook off his mood and strode toward her. "Lead the way."

The group huddled together, speaking in low tones. Dante pushed forward, making room for Eloise beside him. He clapped his hands. "Are we ready?"

Everyone responded with a resounding yes, except Eloise.

"We're going to follow one another in the staggered starts. Two each from our team at a time, as well as the other departments participating." He glanced at Eloise. "There's a chip in the wristband they gave you. At the end, we'll see which team has the best time."

He raised his hand, to which the team high-fived. "Good race, everyone."

Eloise moved away, scanning the course set out before them. Her cute nose wrinkled in distaste. "Smells like soggy grass out here."

"Makes the challenge more fun."

The race announcer called the teams to the starting line.

"You're running last," Dante told Eloise. "You can watch us, get a feel for the course. If you have a hard time maneuvering an obstacle, one of your fellow runners will give you a hand." He tried to read her face, but it had gone blank. "Ready?"

She looked at him. "Our team really holds the record?"

"So far."

With a deep breath, Eloise squared her shoulders. "Okay. I can do this."

Dante grinned. He couldn't wait to watch.

THE ANNOUNCER PUMPED up the challengers with a rousing pep talk before lifting up the small, black device in his hand. A loud electronic beep sounded among the excited cries of runners, and they were off. Brandy stood beside Eloise as they watched, cute in a bright pink T-shirt and black running shorts, her thick hair pulled back in a high ponytail. Eloise had grabbed an old ratty shirt and a pair of baggy shorts she'd worn years ago when she was at the police academy. Hardly a fashion statement, but then…this was mud!

"I'm pumped," Brandy gushed. "This is my second time in a mud race."

"So it's not awful?"

"Are you kidding? You're going to have a blast."

Eloise doubted it.

She'd studied the course description when she'd logged on to the race site online. Three miles, short by most mud race standards, with eight obstacles in all. They didn't seem terribly daunting. The hardest part would be keeping her feet from getting sucked into a mudhole. Watching previous race videos to get an idea of what she'd encounter, she now stood before the real thing.

"What am I doing here?"

She had better things to focus on, like the details of her very first undercover operation. She'd made lists after the briefing, took care of personal business and started packing, even though they didn't start until Monday.

She would have liked to go over the official reports of previous car thefts today, try to find a pattern or similarities in the crimes, but that wasn't happening. Even Lieutenant Chambers had been on board with her joining her fellow Palm Cove officers in the race. Being a team player would go a long way toward the promotion.

Glancing around, it seemed like everyone but Eloise was a competitor. If they'd entered a race on reading books, she bet she'd come in first every time.

The next group lined up, ready to take off. She caught sight of Dante, looking very athletic in a tight tank top and running shorts. His leg muscles, defined as he struck the starting pose, reminded Eloise that he liked to run. She shuddered. Running had never been her forte, her average times gumming her up at the academy, but she'd pushed herself because the goal of graduating was more important than the misery of running. Could she pull this off?

The beep sounded again and Dante, a mischievous grin on his face, took off. He cleared the first hurdle, hay bales lined up end to end along the width of the course, with very little effort, then sprinted. He reached up to grab the monkey bars at the next obstacle, swiftly moving hand over hand until he jumped off. After that, she lost sight of him.

Brandy turned to Eloise. "My group is up next."

She ran off to join the others, leaving Eloise behind. Her heart quaked in her chest and she thought she might throw up. She should have stood her ground. Never let Dante taunt her into coming. But as much as she dreaded today, a part of her that had only dreamed of the opportunity was thrilled to be part of the group. After all the rejections in gym class growing up, years of hiding her embarrassment, being on this team meant the world to her. She had to do well, or they'd never ask her again.

Before she was mentally ready—would she ever be?—it was her group's turn. She took her place, swallowed hard and, when the beep sounded, took off.

The hay bale wasn't bad, a bit slippery since they'd been soaked with water prior to the race. Her team member reached the monkey bars before her. With an oomph, she jumped up and grabbed hold, dangling over the murky water below, wishing she had better upper body strength. She pulled herself, grunted— grunted!—and slowly made it across. *So far so good*, she thought.

She ran a distance before coming upon a large, shallow mud patch. Here, she would have to slither through the sludge on her knees and elbows, ducking under swinging plastic barrels overhead. Good Lord. Who came up with this torture?

She lowered herself, cringing when the cold mud slithered against her skin. She bonked her head, three times, but eventually made it through. Rising, she tried pulling the damp T-shirt from her skin, then decided to forget it. She had to keep moving.

"Hey, Eloise. Good job."

She nearly tripped looking over her shoulder to see who'd called her name. Before she could find a familiar face, she ran right up to the next obstacle, walking over a single plank of wood that rather resembled a balance beam, above water.

"Center yourself," she coached herself, stepping up, arms out to her sides for balance. She stopped once when she began to totter, throwing her shoulders back. Then she was off again.

The obstacles continued. She carried a long pole across her shoulders as she moved through a knee-deep pond, crawled through a dank-smelling tube and dashed over a hill with randomly placed buckets keeping her on a zany path, sprinting as fast as she could without losing breath between each obstacle. By now she barely noticed the warm, earthy smells, ignored her damp skin and clothing, not to mention her feet squishing in her sneakers. Then she came upon the final obstacle and stopped dead in her tracks.

An eight-foot wall, with cutout holes in the wood for the runners to scale up and over, loomed in her spotty image. She wiped the lenses on her glasses and gaped. No way.

"Get moving," people from behind her yelled as they passed her. "You can do it."

The chatter and hoots of laughter dimmed as she concentrated on the wall before her. Heart pounding, she ran to the wall, placing her feet in the lowest holes. Her soles were slippery and she promptly slid out. Grinding her teeth, she pressed down hard to keep purchase and lifted her arms to the cutouts above her. Slowly, she lugged herself to the top, wondering what her time could be. As she swung one leg over the peaked top, she could see the finish line in the distance. Along with the Palm Cove PD, standing on the sidelines to cheer on their team.

Dante stood out, waving his arms in encouragement. She gulped. Swung over the other leg. Looked down. Froze.

Was she supposed to jump?

Another participant handed her a rope. "Use this to get down."

Breaking out of her scared stupor, she grabbed the muddy rope like a lifeline. Pushed herself off and tried to rappel down. Only her hands slipped—ouch, rope burn—and her feet slid down the wet wood. Next thing she knew she was sitting butt down in the mud, recovering from the jolt to her tailbone as people dashed around her.

"C'mon, Eloise, you can finish."

She looked over to see Dante. He'd moved up the line to get a clear view of her sitting there. She'd done pretty good through the other obstacles. Why did he have to witness her ungainly fall now?

"Get up. You're almost finished."

She'd show Mr. Hotshot Matthews. With a sudden burst of energy, she rose, stumbled, then took off as fast as her shaky legs would carry her. Loud cries and applause greeted her at the end of the line.

She bent over once she knew she'd crossed, hands on her knees, heaving in great big gulps of air. Her heart beat overtime, her head hurt and her knees were red and skinned.

And what, exactly, did people find invigorating about this race?

A hand slapped her on her back. She rose, meeting Dante's amused gaze.

"You survived."

The heck with survived. "Did we hold on to the record?"

His grin dimmed a fraction. "Off a couple seconds. No big deal."

Her stomach sank. She'd cost them the victory? "I'm sorry. I...I could have—"

Dante cut her off. "Stop."

She blinked back the stinging tears blurring her eyes.

"You did great for your first time. The Sandy Beach PD signed up a ringer, so we were outmanned, anyway."

She ran a dirty finger under her nose, then grimaced.

"Are you sure?"

"Positive."

She'd blown it. For the team. Could she feel any worse?

Brandy and the rest of her fellow officers circled her, giving her praise and joking with each other. All Eloise could muster up was disappointment in herself.

"Hey," Dante said with a low voice as he leaned in close. Gripped her elbow. "You okay?"

No.

"Sure," she said, pulling her arm from his grasp. She didn't need his sympathy.

Brandy hooked her arm through Eloise's. "Let's get our complimentary T-shirt, clean up and have lunch. That barbecue smells good and I'm starving."

She limped along with her friend. In the public restroom, she took one look in the mirror and nearly burst out in tears.

"Oh. My. Gosh."

Brandy giggled. "Yeah. This race takes a toll."

Eloise's gaze slipped to her friend, as Brandy patted only a bit of mud from her fresh face, and she nearly growled.

Reluctantly returning to the mirror, she cringed. Her hair stuck out, mostly frizz pulled from the ponytail. Her glasses hung haphazardly, caked with gunk. Her shirt was stained and her legs were spotted with mud.

"Please tell me you have a brush," Eloise nearly whimpered.

"Not on me." Brandy laughed. "Don't worry. You're in the same condition as the other runners."

"If that was meant to make me feel better, it didn't work."

Brandy handed her the clean shirt. "Put this on. It'll help your disposition."

Really? At this point, nothing could make her feel…anything.

They finished up, but after stepping outside, Eloise told her friend, "I'm going to my car. I'll be back."

Brandy narrowed her eyes. "You aren't running off, are you?"

"No. I need to fix my hair before I join the team."

"Okay, but if you aren't back in ten minutes I'm going to send a search party for you."

Dragging in a long sigh, she retrieved her pack and keys and marched to her car. She tossed her ruined shirt on the back floor, quickly grabbed a brush she'd placed in the console and went to work on the tangles catching in her shoulder-blade-length hair. Then she grabbed a towel she'd thrown in the back seat and wiped off her legs and arms. Changed sneakers. Feeling marginally human again, she turned to see Dante walking her way, a water bottle in each hand. Great. Add messy insult to injury.

He handed her a bottle covered in condensation when he reached her. "I noticed you didn't stop at any of the water stations along the course. Figured you'd be thirsty."

She didn't realize how much until the cold, clear water slid down her parched throat. She chugged half the bottle before asking, "How long were you watching?"

"Just after you cleared the hay bales."

Great. Only the entire course. She forced herself to meet his blue-eyed gaze. "Sorry I cost you the best time."

He waved off her concern. "Don't worry. It's more for bragging rights. Trash talk, really."

She shook her head. "I just don't get it."

"Get what? Having fun?"

"No. This whole team mentality. I mean, I understand from a work perspective. We need to work together to put bad guys away. But sports…"

"I take it you weren't on any sports teams in school?"

"Do I look like I'm athletic?"

He took a long, leisurely sweep from her head to her toes and back. She shuddered under his perusal.

"Right now? I guess not. How about other teams? Intellectual pursuits?" He grinned. "I could see you on the debate team."

She wished. If she'd had the nerve to join back then, she would have loved to debate. Fear had taken precedence.

"I wasn't really involved in many team endeavors. Mostly stayed to myself."

"Why?"

She took another sip to stall. Why indeed? Lacked confidence, she supposed. Without parents or anyone to encourage her, it was hard to work up the nerve to join in.

"I didn't really have a lot of support. My parents are college professors. Really busy."

He tilted his head, but thankfully didn't say a word.

"I suppose now that I've run the course, next time I'll know what to expect."

"Next time?"

She cringed. Had she overstepped? "That is, if the team will have me?"

"Are you kidding? We'll take any soul willing to run through muck and then hoist back a beer." He frowned. "You will have a celebratory beer, won't you?"

Would she? She didn't drink. Never saw the appeal. "I suppose."

"That's the spirit. Let's go get some food." Dante turned and started toward the smoking grills and clusters of chatting people.

Her stomach growled, and for the first time since her clumsy descent of the climbing wall, she felt better.

"Dante. Wait."

He turned. Walked back to her.

"Thank you. For pushing me to come today.

Even though I might have cost you bragging rights, I had fun."

He threw an arm over her shoulders, leaned in and spoke into her ear. "Then it was a good day."

She turned a fraction. His face was so close to hers. She held her breath. Waiting, for what, she wasn't sure. This close, the dark blue of his eyes mesmerized her. She couldn't have moved if she wanted to.

She felt him go still. His warm breath brushed her cheek, yet he continued to stare down at her. Seeing what? she wondered. Then, just as quickly as the moment began, it ended when he moved away.

He smiled. Hitched his shoulder and she fell into step beside him.

Before long she was enjoying a tasty barbecue beef sandwich, the bold spices exploding with flavor in her mouth. She sipped a cold beer like her teammates—again, not her thing—and switched to bottled water. Found herself involved in conversation not involving the job and realized, *I'm part of a team.*

The reality shook her. Made her wonder why she'd shied away, especially once she was on her own and away from her parents' negativity. Old habits? Fear she'd mess up and hear her parents' voices in her head saying, *I told you so*? Suddenly she looked at her coworkers in a new light. She had friends, she realized. Strange, but wondrous at the same time.

"I thought I saw you on the course," a male voice said over her shoulder. She turned. Tom Bailey was there, surprise etched on his face.

"Tom. Hi." She waved. "It was a last-minute thing."

"How'd you do?"

She held her arms out at her sides. "I'm in one piece."

He chuckled. His warm eyes met hers. "Want another drink?"

She checked her water bottle. "I'm good."

"Have you eaten?"

She nodded.

"How about getting away from this crowd?"

She blinked.

"It's hard to talk over all the conversations."

"Okay." She joined him as he headed a few feet away and found a quiet bench far enough from the noise but still in sight of her teammates.

"I was hoping you would have run with me," he said.

"For another PD? I don't think that's how it's done."

Tom chuckled, a pleasant sound. "No, I suppose not. Guess I was being selfish."

"How's that?"

They glanced over the scene before them: police officers enjoying the spring day, the mild temperatures and a time of relaxation away from the demands of the job.

"I was hoping you'd like to go out with me sometime."

Her mind went blank. He was asking her on a date?

"Tom. I don't know what to say."

"How about yes?"

It had been a while since she'd been out with a guy. Work kept her busy and now she was focused on the promotion. Then there was Dante's blue eyes...

"Tom, I have to turn you down."

She glimpsed embarrassment in his eyes and, hating that she put it there, quickly laid her hand on his. "Not because I don't like you. I'm getting ready to go undercover and I don't know when I'll be free."

His face brightened. "But you'd think about it? After?"

Would she? She looked back at the crowd. Dante stood talking to a tall, leggy blonde, probably his type of woman, and decided, *Why not?*

"Sure. If you don't mind waiting?"

"No. I mean, it'll give me time to plan something fantastic."

She chuckled. "Dinner and a movie is fine."

"Not for you."

She smiled at him. He was handsome, with round cheeks, nice green eyes, sandy-blond hair. All in all pleasant, but nothing to get her heart racing like when she was with Dante. The few occasions she'd spent with Tom, they'd had a decent conversation. No witty banter, but still…nice. So why wasn't her tummy doing somersaults at the thought of dating him? Her heart not pounding out an excited rhythm?

"Listen," she said, troubled by the direction of her thoughts. She'd said yes about going out with Tom and had meant it. "I should get back."

"Sure. Okay." They rejoined the crowd. "Call me when your assignment is over."

"I will," she said, watching as he walked backward, waving goodbye.

"What was that all about?" Dante asked as he sauntered over to her side.

"Tom asked me out on a date."

Dante glanced in the direction of Tom's path and back to her. "Told you he was an admirer."

"I suppose."

"Tell him we have an op coming up?"

"Yes. He was cool about it."

Dante raised a brow.

"What?"

"I don't know. He doesn't seem like your type."

"I have a type?"

"Everyone has a type."

Hers seemed to be Dante, she realized. A depressing thought because she was no competition for the leggy blonde.

"Look, who I go out with shouldn't be of any interest to you," she said with a little starch in her tone.

"Are you kidding? Monday you become my wife."

Her heart shivered. "For the op. Not real life."

"Still…"

"Leave it alone, Dante. Let's enjoy the day."

"Sure." He glanced over at the blonde he'd been chatting up. "I'm going out for drinks later, anyway."

"Great. Have fun."

He scowled at her. "I will."

She stood her ground. Waited for him to leave.

He stared back, then finally shook off his mood. "Go home and get some shut-eye," he suggested before walking off. "We're setting up house bright and early Monday morning."

CHAPTER FOUR

RISING AT DAWN to get his five-mile run in for the morning, Dante had taken a quick shower afterward. Now, with a mug of aromatic, freshly brewed coffee at his elbow, he scanned the computer screen after signing into the videoconference call with his brothers.

Since his siblings were scattered along the eastern seaboard—Derrick in DC, Deke in Atlanta and Dylan on the other coast of Florida—this was the most efficient way to meet at an agreed upon time and carry on a conversation. All accounted for, they could discuss their mother before he left the house to pick up Eloise and start their undercover married life.

His pulse kicked up, but he ignored it.

"Hey, guys. I'm starting my undercover assignment today. I'm on the clock," he said in lieu of hello.

"Dangerous, Pretty Boy?"

Derrick always managed to annoy him. You'd think he would be used to it by now.

"Shouldn't be. Auto theft ring."

"Are you on it alone?" Deke asked.

"No. New partner." Whom he didn't want to discuss with his older brothers. "But we're together to talk about Mom."

Dante took this time to look over each brothers' face before they got into the family discussion. They all sported dark hair and varying shadows of blue eyes, carrying the olive-skinned coloring of their mother. Derrick resembled their father more than the others, with his blue eyes a lighter shade just like the man they'd all loved. Daryl Matthews had doled out wisdom, laughed liked there was no tomorrow and touched each son in a deep and lasting way. For Dante, he and his father had shared a love of cars and motors. It led to building a sense of trust with his dad that he'd never shared with anyone else. They'd spent hours hunched under the hood of one make or another, taking apart engines and reassembling them, only to make the cars faster, much to their mother's chagrin. But if his father could be remembered for one trait equally and above measure with all his sons, it was the listening and abiding love of a father.

"Let's get to it," Dylan said, taking the lead since he was the one with the limited intel on their mother and her new beau.

"Who is this man?" Deke asked, wasting no time in getting right to the heart of business. Studious and more logical than the other Matthews boys, his reserved nature served him well in forensics.

"That's the problem. I don't know."

"You don't know, or you don't *want* to know," Derrick, always outspoken, threw into the mix.

Dylan frowned. He'd been protective of the entire Matthews clan for as long as Dante could remember. "I want to know, but she's giving me the runaround."

"Which you should be used to," Derrick said, then slurped from a mug.

Dante tried a different angle. "Has Kady learned anything?"

"She overheard Mom on the phone making a lunch date for tomorrow. Once she learns the location, I'll stop by to pick up an order."

"If the place has takeout," Deke pointed out.

"Yeah. If it doesn't, I'll take Kady there for an impromptu lunch. One way or another, I plan on meeting her date."

"Whatever you do," Derrick warned in his oldest-brother tone, "don't scare him off."

"Why would I do that?"

"Dude, you get all serious and scary on people. This guy isn't a perp, so tread lightly."

"I think I know how to handle an interrogation."

"See," Derrick said after a chuckle. "You view this as work. It's life. Go easy."

"Life?" Dante snorted. "When did you become so Zen?"

"The minute I learned my mother was interested in a man who isn't our father."

"May he rest in peace," Deke said in a low voice.

They all went silent for a beat.

Dante swallowed, his throat tight as he thought of the larger-than-life man who had affected all their lives.

Derrick, the troublemaker of the tribe, held up a silver coin in the small square of video space. "Let's flip to see who leads this mission."

Dante groaned. "Really? The coin toss?"

"It's tradition," Derrick countered, a slick smile on his lips.

"And not necessary," Deke chimed in. "Dylan is right there. Let him take the lead."

"That's not how we do things."

Since they were kids, the boys had always used a coin toss to determine which brother would be responsible for a task. Clean the pool. Coin toss. Cover for the brother who slipped out of the house late at night? Coin toss. The latest had been the last time they were all together at a family wedding when their mother had requested that one of her sons accompany her to a florist convention. Dylan, needing an excuse to tag along to solve a case, lost the toss, but ended up winning the girl.

Derrick deftly rolled the coin between his fingers. "C'mon, guys."

"I know how this ends." Dylan shook his head, his bluish-gray eyes glittering.

It was frequently suggested that Derrick cheated, but Dante had yet to uncover the truth. Mostly out of self-preservation. His oldest brother could make his life miserable, since he had lots of dirt from when Dante was growing up and was not the least bit shy about using it.

"Let's forgo the toss this time," Dylan said. "Deke's right. I'm here, so I'll take the lead. As soon as I get an identification on this guy, I'll have a local PI I've worked with do a background check."

"You'll fill us in right away?" Deke asked.

"Yes."

On the screen, Dante watched Derrick rubbing his palms together in glee. "I see an intervention in our future."

"Not so fast," Dante warned. "This is Mom we're talking about."

The brothers all paused, identical expressions of exasperation on their faces. Jasmine Matthews would not be happy her boys were spying on her, even with altruistic motives.

Deke glanced at his watch. "Guys, I have to run. Text or call when you get a lead."

They said their goodbyes and Deke signed off.

"What's up with him?" Dante asked. He hadn't spoken to Deke in a while, but it was clear he was preoccupied.

"Court case," Derrick simply said, the one brother who kept tabs on everyone, whether they liked it or not.

"I need to get going, as well," Dylan said. "Talk to you soon."

After a moment, Dante and Derrick were the only brothers left.

"Tell me, who's your partner?" Derrick's tell-me-everything, I'm-your-buddy tone didn't fool Dante.

Shoot. Dante was hoping none of his brothers would pick up on the fact that he'd quickly changed the subject when asked about his assignment. "Another detective in the department."

"Who has a name?"

"Of course."

Seconds ticked away.

"I can do this all day," Derrick finally said, then took another sip from his mug. If anything, working for the FBI had taught his brother patience.

Dante let out a tight breath. "Eloise Archer."

Derrick swallowed. Considered. "Eloise. Hmm. That's a decidedly female name."

"Because she's a female."

"And her role is?"

"Undercover wife."

"Huh." Derrick paused, his eyes twinkling with mirth. "This is new for you."

Dante reined in his impatience. "And your point?"

Suddenly the humor was gone and Derrick was all business. "You're going to be in a very intimate situation. Living under the same roof. Pretending to be in love. It can be easy to cross the line."

"I think I can handle a fake temporary marriage."

"But you've always gone undercover alone."

"And your point is?"

Derrick's expression didn't waver. "Look, bro, you tend to live for the assignment. Throw yourself in 100 percent, all of the time."

"That's not crossing the line."

"No, but it can happen."

Was he saying…? "You crossed the line on an op?"

Derrick went uncharacteristically quiet for a taut moment. "I didn't cross the line," he said, "but the temptation was there. I ruined a good working relationship. A friendship. There's no coming back if one or both of your emotions get tangled up."

His brother thought he'd endanger the op by falling for Eloise? The old anger flared. "Eloise and I are coworkers. End of story. There is nothing to worry about."

Derrick pinned him with a steely look, the same look his father had sent him on more than one occasion, which made Dante squirm. "Make sure it stays that way." Just as quickly, Derrick's facial muscles relaxed. "What's she like?"

"Smart. Methodical. Focused."

"Right, right." Derrick gulped his drink and then asked almost offhandedly, "Pretty?"

"Asks the serial dater."

"Hey, I'm not ready to settle down."

As long as Derrick's first love was out there, somewhere, Dante doubted he ever would.

"So…"

Eloise was attractive. Not in the conventional sense, Dante had to admit, but who cared about convention? Pretty, even when she was buttoned up in her work wardrobe. Which got Dante to wondering, what would she dress like when it was just the two of them, a newly married couple moving into a new neighborhood?

Derrick coughed.

"Yeah," Dante answered. "In an understated kind of way."

"Interesting." He paused a beat. "Single?"

Finally, he'd had it up to his eyebrows with all the questions. "What does that matter?"

"Going back to my original warning. Don't be reckless and cross the line."

Dante ran a hand over the back of his neck. He loved his brothers, but he'd show Derrick, and the others, that he could carry out this op without any emotional collateral. "Anything else?"

"You seem a bit put out there, Pretty Boy."

"Don't call me that."

Derrick shot him a know-it-all grin, then he was gone.

"Yeah, what do you know?" Dante asked the empty screen. He closed the lid of his laptop and rose, returning to his last-minute packing.

Crossing the line indeed.

As per the op details he and Eloise had laid out, he was to pick her up at her apartment at eleven. They'd place the boxes with their clothes and personal items in the bed of the truck they'd use during the investigation and arrive at the rental house together. Just a pair of newlyweds ready to start life. With any luck, some of the neighbors would be around, although it was a workday. Still, there were always a few nosy types who managed to spread the word of any activity through the grapevine. By dinnertime, he and Eloise should be the talk of Orchard Street.

He pulled comfortable jeans and tees from his dresser drawer and threw them in the box, along with running clothes and a few dressy shirts and slacks, just in case. He wasn't up on the latest styles, but he wanted to do right by Eloise. Correction. For the op.

"What is wrong with you?" he muttered under his breath. Like Eloise really cared about his fashion sense. Cared about him personally. This was her first undercover gig. That's what was important to her. Knowing her, she had it all plotted out, from the meaning behind every article of clothing she packed, to her personal effects. You could only plan so far ahead, he'd told her. That was the nature of the op. Spontaneous, life-altering decisions had to be made, depending on what happened in any given situation. Thinking off the cuff was the name of the game. He hoped she understood that early on. And realized this was a job only.

No emotions getting tangled up.

By ten thirty he was packed and ready to roll. Fake ID. Department-issued and personal cell phones. Service weapon. Badge.

He tapped Eloise's contact number in his phone.

"Hello," came her breathy answer.

Her voice caught him off guard. "Eloise?"

"Yes."

"Right. This is Dante. Just checking to see if you're ready."

"Yes, um—" she sounded distracted "—just about."

"I'll be there in fifteen."

"Fifteen?" Was that panic? And was there another voice in the background? "Are you busy?"

"No, I… Brandy is here. I had some last-minute things to tie up."

"Okay. Can you finish up by the time I get there?"

"Yes." Her voice was back on firmer ground. "See you soon."

He ended the call, staring at the cell. Had this mission thrown her for a loop? They hadn't even started yet. Still, she was handling it, which he had to admire. She'd added smart suggestions to the plan, like coming up with a code word to use in front of others in case they needed to talk or trouble occurred. They'd settled on *news*, which was generic enough but served its purpose. All in all, he decided they might just make a good team.

He took one last sweep of the house. This was why he didn't have pets or plants. He was free to come and go without responsibilities strangling his life. See, he wasn't interested in a relationship. Not with Eloise or anyone else. Derrick and his needless cautions…

Shaking his head, Dante grabbed his keys, decided everything was in order for the duration of the assignment, then locked the door. Lowering his shades over his eyes, he walked to the truck. The sun was shining, the breeze was blowing, and his mind shifted into undercover mode.

Like it or not, today was the first day of marriage for Mr. and Mrs. Smith.

As he jumped in the sweltering vehicle, a dark cloud obscured the sunlight. He glanced out the window, a sense of trepidation washing over him. This op was make or break for his career. He needed to keep a wary eye on the prize so his partner didn't swoop in and steal the spoils of their hard work.

"HE'LL BE HERE SOON."

Panic coursed through Eloise. Not because Dante was on his way, she assured herself. More because this was her first undercover op and she was keenly aware of the pressure.

"Calm down. You'll do fine." Brandy fluffed Eloise's hair, releasing the scent of a flowery shampoo and hair product, then stepped back. Cocked her head to admire her handiwork.

"Well done, if I do say so myself."

Nerves gripped her. "Can I look now?"

"Knock yourself out."

Biting her lower lip, Eloise rose and turned slowly, afraid to face the mirror. Which was foolish, of course, since she'd caved at Brandy's suggestion of a makeover. Her reasons were valid: a new persona to match her fake life, a chance to really see if she could pull off a stylish new look and, mostly, a confidence booster. This assignment was important, not only for her career, but for her self-esteem. She knew she was a good cop. She wanted to prove she could handle more responsibility.

"Are you going to look or not?"

Eloise blinked against the contact lenses she'd been putting off wearing on a regular basis. After much practice, she'd been able to apply them successfully, but she wasn't sure they were for her. Maybe they'd become second nature, much like this assignment? She could only hope.

Shaking off her thoughts, she made a one-eighty and stared at the stranger in the mirror. Blinked, this time out of shock, not the itchy eyewear.

"Well?" Brandy prodded.

"I… Wow." Eloise reached up to lightly touch her new hairstyle. "I barely recognize myself."

Her friend preened. "I'm good."

"No one is going to argue that point."

Eloise moved her head from side to side. Her hair, usually pulled back into a tight bun, flowed over her shoulders in layers. Highlights brightened the normally dull brown into myriad shades she'd never noticed before. With her glasses gone, her coffee-colored eyes glowed. Her makeup, understated yet effective, made her cheekbones stand out. She'd consider herself pretty, if the idea wasn't outlandish.

Don't mess with makeup, her mother had admonished. *You just aren't the sort to carry it off.*

If only Mama could see her now.

"Brandy, I'm at a loss for words."

An atypical frown tilted Brandy's brows. "Oh, no. Is that bad?"

A full smile bloomed over Eloise's face.

Suddenly, she looked and felt like Ellie Smith. "On the contrary. I love it."

With a whoop, she hugged her friend, thankful Brandy had suggested the makeover. She resembled the type of woman handsome and confident Dante Matthews would fall for and marry. Or rather, Dan Smith.

Brandy giggled and held her friend at arm's length. "And you even took my fashion advice."

"Can I share a secret?" Eloise asked in a hushed voice.

Brandy bounced up and down on tiptoes. "Now we're talking."

"Most of the clothes draped over my bed? The ones you okayed? I didn't need to go out and buy them. I already had them stored away."

Confusion crossed Brandy's pert features. "Why on earth would you buy cute clothes and not wear them?"

Eloise shrugged, old insecurities clogging her chest. "It's a long, boring story. But the point is, I know how to shop for trendy clothes." A bubble of laughter escaped her as she thought of all the times she'd bought something pretty on impulse only to imagine her parents' criticism and stuff the item in the back of the closet. "Me. The woman who always wears suits."

Brandy grinned. "Explains our shopping trip. You went straight to the style of clothes perfect for you. To be honest, I thought it was a fluke."

Eloise laughed.

"I'm sorry," Brandy rushed to say, her cheeks revealing a touch of pink. "You just needed a reason to come alive, kind of like a butterfly when it finally sheds its cocoon."

"Thank you, Brandy. I needed this shove."

"My pleasure." Brandy took Eloise by the shoulders and turned her toward the bed. "Your hubby will be here soon. Let's get these outfits packed."

Her coworker was right. Dante would be here any minute and she was far from ready.

The thought stopped her. This was unlike her. Yet a sense of—was it freedom?—filled her to overflowing. She should have gone undercover a long time ago.

"Where did you two meet?"

Eloise folded a blouse and placed it in the box. "You know, at the police department."

Brandy rolled her eyes. "No. Where did Dan and Ellie meet?"

Her hands stilled. Good grief, had she really just blown her cover? Thank goodness this was Brandy she was talking to, not a new neighbor. A sliver of doubt assailed her. Maybe she wasn't as ready for this op as she thought.

"At the park. Sunset."

"Nice." Brandy tossed a few more articles of clothing in the box. "You did memorize your cover story, right?"

"Of course. You just caught me off guard."

"You can't make a mistake, Eloise."

"I know." And she wouldn't. This assignment was too important. After all, it might earn her a promotion. *Focus*, she admonished herself. "I think the makeover threw me." She tucked her elbows into her sides, her hands straight on either side of her eyes, like blinders. "Straight and narrow. I'll be careful and fully in character."

"Good, because if you mess up, Dante will never let you hear the end of it. Or Lieutenant Chambers. He's counting on you to do a good job."

Right. No pressure. "Thanks for reminding me."

"Have you decided what you'll do if Dante goes off script?"

Eloise folded the top of a full box. "I have actually. I came up with alternative scenarios to those we discussed. Dante really stressed that I be ready to improvise."

"Then it sounds like you have everything under control."

They both hefted boxes and carried them to the small foyer by the door. Eloise dropped hers with a huff. "As much as I can be."

Brandy moved to the coffee table, held up the key Eloise had given her before slipping it into her purse. "I'll stop by periodically. Make sure no disasters have taken place in your apartment."

"Thanks. I'm probably overreacting but…"

"Yeah. I get it."

"You have all my emergency numbers."

"Yes."

"My folks' number."

"Yes."

"My—"

"Stop." Brandy tugged her purse strap over her shoulder. "I have everything under control here. You're going to be fine."

Eloise placed a hand over her swirling stomach. "This is it."

"You're prepared. You're smart and have good instincts. Stop worrying."

"Right. Being a cop is my life. I've trained for just such a scenario." She squared her shoulders. "I can do this."

"You go, girl."

Her stomach dipped. "What if I can't do this?"

Brandy puffed out a breath of air. "Think of the promotion."

"Promotion. Right."

"And don't let Dante charm you into going against your cop instincts. Listen to your gut."

Eloise chuckled. "My gut?"

Brandy patted her slim waist. "We all have a gut. Trust it."

The doorbell rang. Eloise's eyes went wide. "He's here."

"Yep." Brandy took the few steps to cross the room, opened the door. She smiled at Dante, who'd dressed for the move in a navy T-shirt, worn jeans and running shoes. "C'mon in. Your wife has been waiting for you."

"You're loving this, aren't you?" he grumbled.

Brandy grinned. "You know, I really am."

Eloise swallowed hard. Smiled a normal greeting to her fellow detective. "I'm all set. Just load these boxes in the truck and we're ready to roll."

Dante stared at her, not saying a word. Did he hate her new look? Had she thrown him off by not giving him a heads-up? Deep down, she'd been excited to see his reaction, except, in her mind, he'd smiled and told her how great she looked. The silent treatment was making her sweat.

"Dante?"

"Yeah, I, ah…" He ran a hand over the back of his neck. "You look different."

"Brandy and I thought I should create a new appearance for the assignment."

"Huh."

Brandy nudged his side with her elbow. "So?"

"Yeah. You look nice."

Nice. Nice?

"Oh."

"Sorry. I wasn't… You look good, Eloise."

"That's Ellie to you, Dan."

A slight smile touched his lips.

"I like the look, Ellie."

She tamped down her disappointment—really, what was she expecting?—and calmly morphed back into cop mode. It was better to live there, anyway. Facts, procedure and being prepared got the job done, not makeovers and expectations from male coworkers. She'd be best served to remember this.

"I have one more bag in the bedroom. I'll be right back."

Before she could leave, Brandy hugged her again. "Be safe. Be smart."

"Always."

Her friend turned to Dante. "Behave."

He nodded.

Brandy glanced back and forth between them and grinned. "Ha. You guys are going to have your work cut out for you."

CHAPTER FIVE

DANTE WAS FLUMMOXED. Plain and simple. It was the only word he could come up with to explain his current state.

He flinched when the door closed behind Brandy with a bang. Eloise stood on the other side of the room, a flicker of hesitancy in her eyes. He hated that he was the cause of her discomfort, but c'mon. She was stunning.

Again, her understated beauty captured him. He'd sensed it was there all along, just disguised under her professional work persona. Why? He had no idea. Was she trying to hide herself? Her hair was…gorgeous, and her eyes without glasses? Deep and inviting. But something was off. It took him a moment to realize she wasn't wearing a suit. Today a bright floral blouse and dark jeans with sandals were her clothing choice.

Stop. This is the same woman you work with every day. Pull it together.

"So, uh, why don't we get your things

loaded and head out," he suggested when the awkward silence stretched for too long.

"Right." Her crisp tone brought him back to reality. Her movements, efficient as she collected her purse and overnight bag, reminded him that this was Eloise of the neat desk and tidy reports at the Palm Cove Police Department. Her looks would most likely turn a few—make that plenty—of heads, but she was a detective. His partner. The woman who didn't shy away from an assignment or make waves when he tweaked procedure to catch a criminal. Well, not many, anyway.

He grabbed a box, carried it to the truck as he brought his new awareness of Eloise under control, before returning for the second. "Is this it?"

"Yes. Should I have more?"

"I don't think so. My mother always over-packs. I figured most women do."

"That's a very general assumption," she said, starch in her voice. "And not at all accurate."

Oh, good. Work Eloise was definitely back. "Yeah, if she was here, my mother would read me the riot act, as well."

"I like your mother," Eloise said as she locked the door, swinging her hair over her shoulder. Sass. He liked it. And so would his mother, heaven help him. The woman would be all over him to date her. Jasmine Matthews could never meet Eloise Archer.

Once they were settled in the truck for the twenty-minute ride to their new living arrangement, Dante tossed her a key ring, which she caught midair. "Your set to the rental house."

"Thanks. Have you seen it yet?"

"Drove by but haven't been inside. The PD was able to secure the lease last minute, so we're in the dark together."

"I'm sure it'll be fine. We're there to work, anyway."

Right. Work. The promotion.

"I do know that the computer system is up and running," he told her. "The techs went in on the sly last night and got you all hooked up."

"Great." She dropped the ring in her purse. "What do you know about the neighborhood?"

"Working class. Mixed ages, but lots of families. Rico Battles, the suspect I'm supposed to contact at the auto garage, lives a few doors down. He'll be my boss."

"Convenient."

"From what we could determine, there are some stay-at-home moms and a few retirees, but most of the other adults work."

"I'll connect with ones at home since I'll be working from the house."

"Are you okay with that?" Dante shot her a glance. "I know you want to be in the middle of the action."

"Once you get hired, talk up my computer skills so that they want to use my services. Until then, I'll keep busy one way or another."

He tapped his thumb on the steering wheel as the conversation with his brother repeated in his head. "I want you to know that I'll listen to your suggestions as we move along on this case."

She sent him a puzzled frown. "We already established we'd hear each other out as the investigation unfolds. Why bring it up?"

To make sure this remains professional. "Conversation with one of my brothers this morning." He glanced at her out of the corner of his eye. "I don't want any problems between us, Eloise."

"Stick with our initial plan and we won't."

He nodded. "Don't be afraid to remind me of that if I go rogue."

She turned her head to stare out the window. "Oh, believe me, you'll hear about it."

Swallowing a chuckle, he turned off the main road down a quiet, tree-lined street. Most of the houses were older, single-family ranch-style homes with stucco or wood finishes, in varying conditions. There was an occasional two-story and a few Craftsman-style homes. Children's toys littered front yards. A tree house peeked out from the branches of a large oak in a side yard. Some properties needed the grass mowed, while pristine landscaping beautified others.

"I did a search on the neighborhood," Eloise said as she checked out each house. "It's pretty popular. Houses don't go on the market here often. We're lucky to use the rental."

"The chief pulled a few strings."

Dante slowed about midway down the street, turning into a driveway.

"Here we are—1027 Orchard Street." He turned off the ignition. "Welcome home."

Eloise had leaned toward the windshield, her perceptive gaze taking in everything.

The well-maintained one-story house was painted a bright yellow, with white shutters. Neatly trimmed bushes lined the length of the foundation. Two smaller windows, curtains drawn, flanked the large picture window in the center of the home. A flag with bright flowers greeted them as it swayed from a holder by the front door. Best of all, in Dante's opinion, it had a two-car garage. He planned on moving a car he'd been working on here in order to keep up with their cover.

"What do you think?"

"It's lovely. To be honest, I wasn't sure what to expect. I could only pull up a picture of the outside of the house from satellite imagery."

"Think you could live here for a couple weeks?"

He swallowed hard at her luminous smile. "Depends on the interior." She opened her door, hopped out of the car and raced up the brick sidewalk to the front porch, keys in hand. Finding her excitement contagious, Dante followed, stopping her before she entered the house.

"Hey, wait a minute."

She turned before slipping her key in the lock, her brows lifted on a question.

"We're newlyweds. I need to carry you over the threshold."

She gaped at him. "You're kidding, right?"

"Not one bit." He took the key from her hand, unlocked the door, pushed it open, then proceeded to scoop her up into his arms.

"Whoa," she cried, her arms quickly winding around his neck to hold on. This close, he inhaled the exotic whiff of jasmine. Her hair fell over her shoulders, revealing her graceful neck. Her coffee-colored eyes were wide with surprise.

This close, it would be easy to lean in and kiss her. What husband wouldn't? Except he wasn't her husband and no doubt she wouldn't appreciate his advance. Her gaze met his, accessing the situation. Softening as the moment stretched out. It took every ounce of strength he had not to kiss her, anyway.

Instead, he said, "What better way to announce to the neighborhood that the newlyweds have arrived?"

She cleared her throat, her gaze darting everywhere but at him. "Do people follow this tradition these days?"

"The Smiths do." He spun her around, then stepped inside the house. "Just so everyone knows we're crazy in love."

He immediately lowered her feet to the carpet and moved away. *Too close, Matthews.*

"Wow," he heard Eloise utter as she viewed the comfortable living room filled with a sofa, armchair, coffee table and large-screen television. Worked for him.

After closing the door, he followed her to the kitchen at the back of the house. Not updated, but not ancient, it would work. Eloise stood before the sink, gazing out the window. "There's a great big patio out back."

"Guess the Smiths will be grilling."

"Do you know how?" she asked, all business. Good.

"Yeah. My dad was an ace at the grill. I learned from the best."

"We can have a party right away."

"Or we could get settled first."

She glanced over her shoulder. "Funny."

"I try."

While she puttered around the kitchen, Dante checked out the sleeping arrangements. A spacious master with a bath was located on one side of the house, two smaller bedrooms with a bathroom between them on the other. The back bedroom was already furnished with the computer system Eloise would use while they investigated the auto thefts.

He heard a phone ring—Eloise's cell, he assumed—and kept checking out the rooms. The smaller front bedroom would work for him, but he wanted to give her first choice. "Hey," he called as he cut through the living room. "Care which bedroom you bunk in?"

When she didn't answer, he detoured to the kitchen. Her back was to him, her voice lowered. "I really can't talk, Tom. I told you after we finish the case."

Silence.

"Right. I promise I'll call."

Dante backed out of the room. Tom. The cop with a crush on Eloise. Now, more than ever, his brother's words made sense. If Eloise was interested in Tom, he needed to keep his distance. They were partners, not romantically involved. Her promise to Tom was proof that while Dante found himself distracted by her, he wasn't her choice. She needed a nice, stable guy, not someone who could easily drop everything for a dangerous assignment.

But that wasn't her problem. From here on out, he'd honor the line. No questions asked.

She exited the kitchen and poked her head into the master. "Nice room."

"It's yours."

"Really? Just like that?"

"What, did you expect a coin toss?"

Her brows angled in confusion.

"Family thing," he explained. "We toss for big decisions."

"Oh, well, we can if you want."

By the look on her face, she wanted the master. "Nah. You take it. I don't care where I sleep."

Her smile was reward enough for his magnanimous gesture.

"Let's bring our belongings inside."

They ventured out to the truck. Just as Dante had hoped, the curious were headed in their direction. An elderly woman with a cane made her way from the house next door, while a younger woman with a baby on her hip crossed the street.

"Here we go." He spoke softly into Eloise's ear. Felt her stiffen. "Relax," he said just as the women arrived.

He took her hand in his. "Good afternoon, ladies. I'm Dan and this is my beautiful wife, Ellie."

WHAT WAS HE up to? Besides establishing their cover, that is?

He hadn't said much about her transformation. She didn't know whether to be relived or miffed. The whole idea was to make her appear less severe, more approachable, but she'd at least hoped Dante would approve of her makeover. After all, she'd done it for the sake of the operation, which is what they were both focused on. Why was he acting so weird?

Dante bumped her with his elbow, jerking her from her thoughts. She flashed a smile at the two women.

"Hi," she gushed, mentally telling herself to rein it in. "You're our first visitors."

The young woman, with her blond hair in a braid, grinned at them. "Hi. I'm Betsy."

She pointed over her shoulder. "My husband, Steve, and I live across the street."

"And who's this little guy?" Dante asked, chucking the baby's chin.

"Baxter."

"He's adorable," Eloise added. She hadn't really been exposed to children very much, having no siblings or married friends with kids of their own. While she liked them, in an abstract sense, she watched the baby drool all over his mother's shirt and held back a cringe.

Dante caught her expression and chuckled.

Best to turn her attention elsewhere. By now, the elderly neighbor had joined them. The woman breathed heavily, holding up her hand, gesturing that she needed a minute. Eloise wasn't sure if she should do something, but took Dante's lead and politely waited.

Finally, the woman smiled. "Well, hello. I'm Martha Jamison," she announced, sticking a shaky hand out.

Eloise took her outstretched hand. Soft and wrinkled, a great strength belied the woman's grip, taking Eloise by surprise. When she met the woman's clear blue gaze, she realized the woman might be up there in age, but she had all her faculties. A familiar scent surrounded her. Shalimar, Eloise thought, reminding her of the grandmother she missed. While her parents had been less than nurturing, Grammy Beth had made time for Eloise, always encouraging and loving. Until she died when Eloise was ten. Without realizing it, she hung on to the woman's hand longer than necessary.

"My, my, you're certainly friendly."

Eloise abruptly let go of Martha's grasp and shoved her hands into her jeans pockets. "And happy to be home."

"I was quite surprised when I learned Ted and Janice were going away and had rented out the house. Usually I keep up with these sorts of things."

"It was last minute," Dante confirmed. "Ted is a family friend and offered the house to Ellie and me while they're gone."

"Where, exactly, did they go?" Martha queried.

"Out west. For a visit."

Martha brightened. "To see the kids, I would imagine."

"You would be right," Eloise chimed in.

Martha looked Dante and Eloise over. "They're certainly lucky it all worked out. You seem like a very lovely couple."

Dante threw his arm over Eloise's shoulders. "Newlyweds actually."

Martha placed a weathered hand over her heart. "Congratulations."

"I remember those days." Betsy sighed as Baxter tugged at her shirt collar.

"Enjoy the baby," Martha advised. "They grow up much too fast."

"I agree." Betsy hugged her son close. "You guys moved in at just the right time."

Dante removed his arm and fixed his attention on Betsy. Eloise missed the connection as soon as he stepped away. "And why is that?"

"We have our monthly block party this weekend. It'll be a great time for you to meet everyone on the street."

Dante grinned at Eloise. "Hear that, honey? We're moving in just in time for a party."

"I think you planned it," she teased.

"I do like a party."

Betsy chuckled. "I should get home. Baxter needs a nap."

They said their goodbyes and Betsy hurried across the street.

"I suppose that's my cue." Martha pushed on her cane to start her walk back to the house.

"Hold up. I'll go with you," Eloise told her.

"How very nice, dear."

Dante raised a brow. "Meet you inside?"

"Of course. Where else will I go?" She blew him a kiss, a fun and flirty gesture so out of character, but decided Ellie Smith would be bold enough to fling air kisses at her husband.

She fell into step beside her neighbor. "Should I call you Mrs. Jamison?"

"Oh, no, Martha is fine."

Eloise nodded.

"I suppose you'll have lots of questions about the neighborhood," Martha said.

"Yes. It'll take us a while to settle in, but Dan and I are happy to be a part of the community."

"Newlyweds, you said?"

She tried to beam. Wasn't sure if she succeeded. "That's right."

"I bet you had a short engagement."

Her brow furrowed. "Why would you think that?"

"Just a hunch. The way you both smile at each other."

How, exactly, did she smile at Dante? She wanted to know, but couldn't ask. "You're right. The idea of marriage sort of sneaked up on us and—" she snapped her fingers "—here we are."

"Your husband is very handsome," Martha said.

"He is," Eloise agreed. That little fact she didn't have to make up.

"I'm delighted you're here." A glimmer of sadness crossed Martha's eyes, but was quickly gone. "With Janice away, it will be just me hanging around. Most of the parents around here work. Betsy is home most days, when she's not off at a mommy group."

They reached Martha's covered front porch. "Please come by for lemonade when you have a chance."

"I will," Eloise replied as she watched to make sure the older woman entered the worn-looking house safely.

There was something about Martha that spoke to Eloise. It might have been the joy of life tempered with just a bit of loneliness. Martha tried to hide it, but Eloise recognized a kindred spirit when she saw one. She knew just how suffocating loneliness could be, having always been on the periphery of things growing up, wishing she belonged.

The window curtains moved and Eloise waved at her new neighbor before loping back across the grass to her new home. She found Dante in the kitchen, his head in the refrigerator.

"Hey," he said as she walked in, slamming the door shut. "We need to go grocery shopping."

"You brought all our things in?"

"Yep."

"Then let's go shopping. We can unpack later."

With a detour to her bedroom to grab her purse off the bed, she turned to find Dante lounging in the doorway, shoulder pressed against the frame, arms crossed over his broad chest. "What was that all about?"

She frowned, confused. "Martha?"

He nodded.

"She's home all day. I figure she'll be a decent source of intel."

"Good call."

He didn't move. His sober expression didn't change.

"Did I do something wrong?"

"No. Our first interaction with the neighbors went well. You played your role nicely."

Relief washed over her, but quickly faded when Dante's expression remained the same. "Why do I get the feeling there's something you're not telling me?"

He opened his mouth, paused, then said, "Don't get attached to the neighbors."

"Excuse me?"

"I saw how you and Martha clicked. Getting too close can be...problematic."

Frustration tangled up her nerves. "You explained all that back at the department when we were prepping for the operation."

He pushed off the frame, big as life, and stepped a little farther into the room. His dark blue eyes glittered with an emotion she couldn't decipher. "I made the mistake of trying to be friends with everyone my first time undercover. Thinking if I engaged with enough people, it would give me the answers I needed. I was wrong. It was hard, knowing I was deceiving people for the greater good, so I learned to pare down." His gaze never wavered. "Focus on those who can truly benefit the operation. If you keep the mission in the forefront, you won't accidentally let your guard down."

His advice rankled. Like she had any intention of messing up. She'd trained for this, just like he had. "I was doing my job, Dante. Getting a lay of the land. Seeing who might have information that can work to our advantage. I know better than to get too close."

To you, or anyone else.

He held his hand up in defense. "Okay. I said my piece. I'll back off."

Her shoulder brushed his hard chest as she left the room, his spicy cologne tickling her senses. She ignored how her stomach fluttered, how her chest thumped. She needed some distance between them.

She stormed into the kitchen, hunting for a pen and paper to draw up a shopping list, needing to calm down. *He was only trying to help,* her inner voice taunted.

Logically, she knew that but didn't like being treated like a novice. Yes, this might be her first actual undercover operation, but she'd studied and talked to other cops in the field. It was almost as if Dante didn't trust her instincts.

Dante followed her. "I hit a nerve, didn't I?"

She slammed a drawer shut. Took deep breaths. She was overreacting. "Yes, to be honest, you did."

"Look, I was off base. You're a good detective, Ellie."

"Then treat me that way." She gathered her hair in her hand, pulling it off her neck. "I might make a few mistakes, but I would never do anything to put the op in jeopardy. There's too much at stake here."

A stillness came over Dante. "Right. Speaking of the promotion." He pinned her with his gaze. "Is that going to be a problem for us?"

Was it? She hadn't thought it would, but the reality of going undercover, fighting her infatuation for Dante now that they'd be living under the same roof and doing a competent job was a little overwhelming right at this moment. She needed to pull it together.

She dropped her hair over her shoulder. "Sorry. I know you were only trying to help."

"You are right, though. The promotion is hovering between us."

"Then we do our best work and the top cop wins."

"Sure. If you say so."

He was so exasperating! She wanted to argue the point, have him concede that she was a better fit for the position, but was she? Old insecurities hounded her, but she pushed them away. She had to remain professional until the end. Prove she could take on bigger responsibilities. Show the lieutenant she could handle a promotion. Become a sergeant on merit alone.

Her gaze fell on Dante's face. His dark blue eyes were shadowed. His lips firmly pressed together. Was he struggling, too? Worried he didn't have what it took to fill the sergeant position? Was the promise of the promotion going to destroy any kind of a relationship between them? And if so, what should she do about it? Because as much as she wanted the promotion, she also wanted Dante to think highly of her as a professional. Wanted him to be her friend. More, even. And wasn't that all confusing?

"How about we put talk of the promotion on

a shelf," Dante suggested. "Focus on the here and now. Get some food because I'm starving."

Her chest heaved with relief. "I'm hungry, too."

Dante lightened up, putting her back on an even keel. He then ruined her state of mind by saying, "We can do this, Ellie."

She swallowed hard. Nodded.

He grabbed the truck keys from the counter. "I sure hope you can cook, because other than my grilling skills, I got nothing."

Okay. They were back to bantering coworkers. "Don't worry. I'll make sure you don't perish."

"Is that a yes or a no on the cooking?"

"I can find my way around a kitchen."

"Good." His fingers hooked her arm, eliciting a shiver, as he tugged her to the door. "We'll get some steaks and I'll show you my way around a grill."

"Be still my heart."

He winked and her stomach dropped.

Professional, Eloise. Be professional.

CHAPTER SIX

DANTE LEFT EARLY the next morning to meet up with his contact, Ben, who had gotten him an interview at Battles Auto Repair. The plan entailed his contact playing up Dante's mechanic skills since he knew the shop owner, along with dropping the hint that Dante was willing to operate in gray areas of the law. The hope was that the owner would ask Dante to participate in any of the illegal activities Dante's contact suspected about the garage, leading Dante to answers about the auto thefts.

His cousin had just left, so there he was in the stifling business office with Rico Battles.

Rico, five foot nine, muscular, with a bandanna tied around his midnight-black hair, wasn't what Dante would call welcoming. "So, Dan, you just moved here from Jacksonville?"

"Yep. Got married and, let's just say, we needed to put some distance between us and her family. Ben and I are pretty close. He said he'd try to hook me up with a job."

"Been working on cars long?"

"Since I was fifteen."

"Can you change oil? Do a brake job?"

"Please. In my sleep."

"Rebuild an engine?"

"Any day of the week." *Thanks, Dad.*

"If I put you on the Ford engine we just took into the shop, you won't let me down?"

Dante cracked his knuckles. "Just show me where, man."

After long consideration, Rico picked up his application again. "Smith, huh?"

"I know, not very original. You'd think it was a made-up name."

Rico stared at him. Dante stared back, recognizing a power play when he was the target of one.

Finally, Rico spoke again. "Me and Ben go way back, so I'll take the chance. For now. By Friday, I'll let you know if you've got the job."

Dante rose and extended his hand over the messy desktop to seal the deal. A paper cup had tipped over, staining the invoices underneath. It had dried, the paper wrinkly, making Dante believe the cup had been sitting there for some time. Who ran a business without keeping paperwork in proper order?

"Thanks, man. I can use the work."

Rico jutted his chin toward the door. "Find

Mac. He'll show you the project I'm talking about."

"Got it." Dante reached for the doorknob.

"Wait up."

Squelching a frown, Dante spun around.

"You live on Orchard?"

"Yeah. Renting a place."

Rico looked down again. A sly smile curved his lips. "Three doors down from me."

"No way."

"Yeah." He tossed the application omto the disorganized desktop. If ever an office needed sorting out, this was it. Hopefully her organizational skills were a way to get Eloise on the inside. "I'll be looking for you around the neighborhood."

It sounded like a veiled threat, but Dante just grinned. "Newlywed, so…" He shrugged.

Rico laughed. "Get outta here."

As soon as Dante stepped into the garage, the familiar scents of oil, gas and rubber greeted his nose like a long-lost friend. A generator started up, its grumble echoing in the open bays of the garage. Dante's fingers itched to hold the tools of the trade again. Once he knew the job was locked down, he'd bring his own tools from home. It would prove his claim to be a mechanic since most purchased their own.

Two cars were already on lifts. In the back of the shop, a bald guy rummaged through a drawer in a tall red box, muttering as he tossed tools around, while another man, slight build with long, stringy hair, sipped from a cup.

"One of you guys Mac?" Dante called out before joining them.

The bald guy, muscular and rough around the edges, said, "Yeah. Who wants to know?"

"Rico sent me back here. Told me to get started on the engine rebuild."

Mac suspiciously looked him up and down. "Yeah? Since when?"

"Since about five minutes ago."

Stringy Hair sauntered over. "Stop givin' him a hard time, Mac. You know we're a guy short." He set his cup down, grabbed a towel from the pocket of his coveralls to wipe up before sticking out his hand. "Ramsey."

"Dan."

Ramsey nodded to the heavy engine hanging on the stand. "Rebuild, huh?"

"Guess I'm being tested."

Mac grunted and stomped to the office.

"Don't mind him," Ramsey said. "He's not very comfortable around new hires."

"Personal problem?"

Ramsey laughed. "The last guy who worked here ran off with his girlfriend, so yeah."

"That stinks." Dante held up the finger with his wedding ring. "Happily married. I won't be running around with anyone but my wife."

"Good for you." Ramsey looked around Dante. "No tools?"

"Wasn't sure the gig was a sure thing. I can bring 'em by later."

Ramsey nodded. "Word of warning. Mac don't share."

"Noted."

"But you can take whatever you need for now from my chest."

"Thanks." Dante walked over to the engine stand and rested his hands on his hips as he studied the piece of machinery. "Yeah. I can get this done."

"Like I said, we need help. We're starting to fall behind."

"Business must be good."

Ramsey tucked the towel into his back pocket and picked up his cup. "We've been lucky. Rico picked up overflow work from a dealership."

Score. "Which one?"

"Marcus King."

"The Car King of the South? He's got car lots all over the place."

"And we got extra work. Hope your wife don't mind you working overtime."

"If it turns into extra cash, she won't mind a bit."

Ramsey chuckled. "You said you just got married. Don't know many wives who would put up with her man not being home."

"Ellie's busy with her own job, so I don't see a problem."

"Sounds like you got a good one."

He did. Eloise had been all-in on this case from the minute Chambers had assigned them. Even went as far as a makeover. While he was floored, in a good way, by her change, that hadn't kept him from putting in his two cents about her role in the op. *Smooth, Matthews.* He appreciated her more than she knew. Needed to show her, he supposed.

"But also spoken from a guy with little marital experience," Ramsey scoffed.

"And you have some?"

"Been married four times."

Yikes. "Then I'll make sure not to ask you for advice."

When Ramsey just blinked at Dante, he thought he'd overstepped. Gone a little overboard in the new-guy camaraderie department. Then a smile split Ramsey's craggy face and he came up behind Dante to slap him on the back. "Glad to have you."

Dante smiled. "Glad to be here."

"Enough chitchat, ladies," Mac called as he stomped from the office. "Let's get some work done. We got a bunch of cars coming in this week."

Dante hunkered down and examined the engine again. His connection was right on target, suggesting he land a job here. Right now, he pondered the stained invoices. Did Rico's revenue stream come from another source besides regular auto maintenance from the general public? Cash flow that didn't involve receipts and detailed records? If so, the cars they worked on day-to-day were most likely their legitimate income. He'd have to discover if the cars coming from the dealership were off the books. By the end of the week, he hoped he had more information to pass on to Eloise. Or get her a job in the office.

Mac's booted feet appeared in his peripheral vision. He stood, raised a brow.

"You're overdressed for a mechanic," he griped.

Dante glanced down at his new indigo jeans and blue-and-white button-down shirt. "Hey, I thought this was just an interview. Had no idea Rico would put me to work."

"Make sure you show up in something less flashy tomorrow."

Flashy? Dante held back a snort. Compared

to Mac's grungy tank top and soiled blue pants and Ramsey's grease-stained jumpsuit, he did indeed look flashy.

"Will do," he called after Mac's retreating back, his mind back to the assignment.

Over breakfast this morning, he and Eloise had discussed the ramifications of him landing this job. She was up for infiltrating the shop if need be. Just thinking about her facial expression when she entered the messy office in the future made him chuckle. Not only was Dante expecting the shop to provide good intel, but if Rico hired Eloise to work in the garage office, the entertainment value would skyrocket. Rico wouldn't know what hit him after Hurricane Eloise cleaned up.

Either way, he liked the idea of having Eloise around. Not just at home, especially after the tasty omelets she'd prepared this morning, but here at work so they could compare notes and see if this place might actually have a tie with the theft ring. His gut was screaming yes and his connection's intel was spot-on. It was just a matter of time before they ferreted out the truth.

They. Together. A team.

He hadn't ever enjoyed working with a partner before, but with Eloise? This time was different. And if he was smart, he'd focus more on the op and less on her sweet perfume and sassy smiles.

It occurred to him that he had more at stake here than finding the bad guy.

THE MORNING DRAGGED ON.

First day on the undercover assignment and there wasn't much to do. Getting acquainted with her computer system after Dante left, Eloise had pulled up background information on Rico Battles. He had a record; petty theft in his early twenties. But the guy was thirty-five now and had been clean since. Married. Two children. Owner of Battles Auto Repair.

She collected any available information on the garage. Records showed that for the last two years, Battles had not paid his taxes. A lien had been filed against the company earlier this year, but removed when the amount owed had been paid in full, six months ago. Hmm. This was interesting. She dug around for another hour, but couldn't find the source of the money used to pay the tax bill. No loans. Hadn't filed for bankruptcy. But the lien was removed, and fines, penalty and charges were paid. Battles had come up with the money. But where? Or better yet, from whom?

A grisly old colleague she'd met her first year on the job had always repeated the mantra "follow the money trail." Good advice, but she couldn't find one. The sooner Dante got the job at the garage, the sooner the owner could be convinced that he needed her help and she'd hopefully have access to his records.

Afterward, Eloise read over the reports from previous car theft cases. Same MO in each case.

With a sigh, she went to the kitchen to top off her coffee, ready for a break. A movement in the backyard caught her eye and she looked out the window. A cardinal jumped from limb to limb on a nearby oak, its deep red coloring a bright giveaway in a sea of green leaves and brown branches spreading over the backyard like its own personal umbrella.

Last night, after grocery shopping and a quick dinner, Eloise had unpacked her boxes, but it had grown dark outside before she had a chance to investigate. In the bright morning light, she could inspect the backyard at her leisure.

She unlocked the back door, the upper-half window covered with white, puffy cotton curtains. Mug in hand, she stepped into a tropical paradise. A warm breeze greeted her, carrying a touch of damp earth, lightly touching her skin. Dressed in shorts, a short-sleeved blouse and flip-flops, she exhaled a breath.

The spring temperatures of Florida were made to savor.

A large stone paver patio ran the length of the house. Under the branches of the trees, mottled light filtered through the leaves onto a round wrought-iron dining table and four chairs. A grill, covered up against the elements, rested against the back of the house, under the kitchen window. A vision of Dante wielding a spatula, wearing a cooking apron while he grilled the steaks last night, flashed across her mind. She chuckled, remembering his running commentary as he cooked up dinner, surrounded by smoke and the mouthwatering aroma of barbecue.

A brick fire pit with four low chairs took over the opposite side of the patio. Very nice for entertaining, she thought, but the rest of the yard took her breath away.

Enormous palm trees towered over two corners of the fenced-in yard, the fronds swaying gently in the morning breeze. Fragrant flowers bloomed along the side of the privacy fence, a riot of colors and shapes. Eloise stepped into the rich green grass to investigate, her feet sinking into the thick, comfy sod. She noticed sprinkler heads scattered around the yard.

"That explains the noise I heard this morning," she said to herself, sipping from the second cup of strong coffee she'd brewed.

A sweet fragrance lured her deeper into the yard. "Jasmine," she whispered as she spied the spreading shrubs of green leaves and fragile white blossoms draped along the entire back fence. She reached out to run a finger over a petal, excited to know her favorite scent would greet her each morning, ushering back memories of her beloved grandmother, who had shared Eloise's love for the flower.

She studied the surrounding flora, recognizing the blue plumeria and hibiscus plants, but others had her stumped. Grammy Beth had small containers with bright pink-and-white impatiens on her screened-in porch, but that was the extent of Eloise's floral training.

Inhaling deeply, a sense of peace comforted her. Eloise had always loved the springtime. A time of rebirth. New beginnings. And the possible promotion? It would fall into that category, a much-needed boost to her career.

But what if Dante landed the job? What would it mean for them?

She shook her head, not knowing what to think of "them" together. Partners. A couple. *Stop*. This was an assignment. Dante had no inkling of her one-sided feelings for him, which in the end, if he found out, could be very embarrassing once they went back to the squad room.

Focus on the promotion, she reminded herself. At least that was a reality that could actually transpire.

A bird chirped overhead, a car door slammed somewhere in the distance. Since she'd started on the police force, she'd been on the run, never taking time early in the morning to sip coffee on the porch of her apartment and welcome the day. She hadn't realized all she was missing.

She turned to stroll back to the patio, her eyes lighting on the grill again. She couldn't wait until Dante showed off more of his mad grilling skills. But that would have to wait until he got home from work.

Supposing he got the job.

Glancing at her watch, she saw it was only nine thirty. If he hadn't come home by now, he must have been successful.

Taking one last sweeping glance of the yard, she was about to go inside when she heard a low voice.

"You come back here right this minute."

Eloise glanced in the direction of Mrs. Jamison's house. A spry, orange tabby jumped onto the fence. She kept her almond-shaped cat eyes on Eloise, flicked her tail and scurried down the top of the fence to jump into the yard directly next to hers.

"Pumpkin? Where have you run off to?"

Eloise walked over to the fence, trying to peer in through the slats. "Martha?"

"Oh, my dear," she heard. "I didn't disturb you, did I?"

"No, but I don't think Pumpkin will be returning soon. He took off in the opposite direction."

A metal jiggling sound came from the fence and suddenly a piece moved inward. Martha poked her head into the Smiths' yard.

"He's not exactly my cat, but he sure doesn't shy away from the food I leave out for him."

Eloise blinked. "How…"

"Janice and I sweet-talked Ted into putting a gate between our properties. Makes it much easier to visit."

She hadn't noticed a handle. "I just wasn't expecting the fence to move."

Martha chuckled. "It sure is nifty." She glanced at Eloise and her sunny expression sobered. "Unless you think I'm imposing."

"No. Actually, I think it's a wonderful idea."

Martha made her way to Eloise, cane in hand, squinting against the sun. "Admiring Janice's handiwork?"

"Talk about a green thumb."

"She spent many happy hours arranging her landscaping."

Eloise looked over Martha's shoulder. "And your yard?"

"Not as lush, but it'll do."

They walked to the patio. Eloise pulled out a chair for the older woman.

"I saw your husband out running early this morning," Martha said as she lowered herself to the cushioned seat. "He must be a health buff."

More a way to control nervous energy, Eloise thought, but said, "He takes his morning run seriously."

"And you don't join him?"

"Not if I can help it," Eloise said as she took a seat opposite Martha.

"You're the picture of health."

Eloise thought about the hours she'd missed at the gym recently. "This move has played havoc with both our schedules."

"Where is your husband, if you don't mind my asking?"

"Job interview."

"How about you?"

"I already have a job. Computer tech. I work remotely." Eloise chuckled at Martha's blank expression. "That means with a computer in the house, I can work from home."

Martha's face lit up. "So you'll be home during the day."

"As of right now." Eloise set her mug on the tabletop.

"Things are so different from when I was a young bride. I stayed home, took care of the house and, later, the children." A faraway look came into her eyes. "My husband, George, worked for the county. But that was many years ago."

"Where are your children?"

"Scattered about," Martha said with a wave of her hand. "They call every weekend."

Guilt settled heavily on Eloise's shoulders. She was pushing it if she called her folks once a month.

"How about you and Dan? Any plans for little ones in the future?"

Eloise swallowed hard. "Um, we're in no hurry. We still need to get used to living with each other day in and day out." True. Oh, so true.

"I enjoyed raising my three, but it isn't for everyone."

"Oh, I didn't mean I don't want any." Did she? It hadn't been a bullet point in her five-year plan. Not even a ten-year plan. "I just mean I'd like some time with Dan before the family grows."

Martha cocked her head, a knowing gleam in her eyes. "It was love at first sight, wasn't it?"

"Excuse me?"

"With your husband."

Had it been? Eloise wasn't sure. All she knew for certain was that one day Dante was in her orbit and, after that, she only had eyes for him.

"I suppose you're right, but how on earth could you tell?"

Martha sighed and sank back against the chair. "The whole short engagement thing, and when you talk about him, you become animated. You practically glow."

Sounded like a bad medical condition. She hoped no one else noticed.

"And you?"

"It took a grand gesture on George's part to finally convince me we were meant to be together." She heaved a self-satisfied sigh. "He was a very special man."

"It wasn't love at first sight?"

Martha shrugged. "Not exactly, but when you know, you know."

Unfortunately, Eloise understood exactly what her new friend meant. She'd run in a mud race because of Dante. How much worse could she have it for the guy?

A companionable silence fell over them. When Eloise glanced at Martha, the woman's eyes were closed. Had she fallen asleep? Eloise cleared her throat to test her theory.

Martha jerked. Her face turned pink. "Sorry, dear. I doze off easily these days."

"Are you okay?"

Martha rose, hand shaky on the cane. "Just the result of rising at 4:00 a.m."

Eloise wrinkled her nose.

Martha let out a crackly chuckle. "I should get back. Thank you for the visit."

"Anytime," Eloise said as she rose, as well.

She followed Martha to the gate. Once there, Martha turned. "Coffee tomorrow morning?"

Why not? The case had just started, she wasn't terribly busy and, honestly, she enjoyed Martha's company. "It's a date."

The gate closed behind her with a gentle snick. As Eloise turned to head back to the house, a blur of orange appeared on the fence, moseying his way back to the gate. "Hungry?" she asked, then laughed. She was talking to a cat? And what was worse, she could have sworn the feline nodded at her question.

At three, Dante walked through the garage door into the kitchen. Eloise was at the counter, thumbing through a cookbook she'd found in one of the cabinets, trying to decide what to make for dinner.

"Hey," he said, leaving his work boots in the garage.

She flipped the book closed. "How'd it go? Your thumbs-up text was cryptic."

"Passed step one. Rico put me to work— I guess like a tryout—then he'll give me his decision by Friday."

"They believe you're who you say you are?"

"After I fixed an engine no one could figure what was wrong with, yeah, I think I impressed the guys."

"Guys?"

"Got some names for you to run."

She nearly sagged with relief. "Thank goodness. My search into Battles proved interesting, but ultimately a dead end."

"In what way?"

She explained Battles's tax situation. "He got the money somewhere, Dante. And since I can't find the source, I'm betting it's illegal."

"I'd take that bet." He sauntered into the kitchen in his stocking feet and opened the refrigerator to extract a cold bottle of water. "Once you've got information on the employees, let's hope we have something solid to build on. Could you also check on Marcus King's dealerships? Apparently Rico made some kind of deal to handle overflow repairs from King's lots."

"That's odd. Don't they usually keep that kind of work in-house?"

Dante took a swig. "Usually. Most folks take advantage of the automaker warranty. But King does have a vast car empire. Could be legit."

Eloise rested her hip against the counter and crossed her arms over her chest. "When Parson's Auto Mall was robbed, I contacted other dealerships in the area. Everyone reported problems." Her mind clicked on a thought. "With as many locations as King owns, the odds of him having a problem with thefts would be significantly higher than a one-lot owner. Don't get me wrong, he's being hit, but not as severely as the other businesses."

Dante went quiet for a long moment. "You might be onto something. Using an outsourced garage can benefit a theft ring with their insider connections."

"And vice versa. If a dealership is a little shady."

Dante drained the last of the bottle and tossed it into the trash can. "Definitely an angle I'll keep an eye on. Good call."

Eloise tamped down her pleasure at his praise. She was doing her job, for Pete's sake.

"I know it's probably too soon, but were you able to learn anything else? Or get a feel for the shop?"

"First of all, the owner's office is a pigsty. Once I'm in I'll suggest he hire you to straighten out the mess."

"Aw, honey, thanks. We'll be working together. How cute."

He rolled his eyes. "Secondly, the man's record keeping doesn't look very effective."

"I can fix that."

Dante winked. "I have no doubt."

Her pulse rate shot up. Would she ever be able to control her reaction to him?

When Dante pushed away from the counter, Eloise didn't miss how his muscles flexed at the motion. "I'm going to take a shower and then we're going to get my tools and my baby."

Everything in her went still. "Excuse me? Did you say *baby*?"

"A 1970 Dodge Challenger I'm restoring for a friend. It will help with our cover story."

Right. A car. What was she thinking? That Dante had a child no one knew about? Eloise blew out a breath. Not that it mattered. If he had a child. Did it?

As Dante passed by, he nudged her shoulder.

She pushed him away, laughing. "Go take a shower."

"As you wish, my wife."

With a chuckle he strode from the room, leaving Eloise to catch her breath and rein in her daydreams. This crazy attraction had to end.

CHAPTER SEVEN

LOUD HEADBANGING MUSIC echoed off the walls in the garage as Dante, lying on a creeper, twisted an especially tight bolt on a shock absorber under the Challenger he'd hauled to the rental house. In the zone, he forgot about auto thieves and finding the culprits, instead dwelling on how the sunlight brought out the highlights in Eloise's long hair and that once this op was over it would be work as usual between them.

He'd finally got the darn shock loose when the music suddenly went silent.

"How can you think with all that noise?" floated a voice above his head.

Dante rolled out from under the car. "It keeps me focused."

Eloise shook her head, clearly stumped. "It gives me a headache. Not to mention what it must be doing to the neighbors."

He rose, grabbed a towel from the tool chest and wiped his hands. "Okay. What do you listen to?"

A faint tinge flooded her cheeks.

"Hey, AC/DC or Led Zeppelin isn't everyone's cup of tea."

"They're classic. And so are the artists I like." She pouted in such an un-Eloise way he couldn't hold back a smile. They'd spent time together all week and if he was being honest with himself, he was totally enchanted. It went beyond her physical makeover. He was finally getting to know the real Eloise, not the person she usually showed the world.

He tossed the towel aside. "What's up?"

"The block party starts in thirty minutes."

"Just need to get cleaned up," he answered, brushing dust from his jeans. He followed her into the house, admiring her lacy white top and pink shorts. He did not miss her business suits one little bit.

"So," he said. "About the music... You're a romantic?"

She shrugged, averting her face.

"I can appreciate a sappy love song once in a while."

Rolling her eyes, she tore a piece of foil from a roll to cover the brownies she'd baked. The chocolaty aroma still lingered, making his stomach rumble. *The advantages of having a roommate*, he thought. Homemade treats to satisfy his sweet tooth.

"Sure we have to bring the whole pan to share with the neighbors?" he asked, reaching around her to try to snag a square. The jasmine perfume and subtle scent of shampoo drifted over him.

She playfully slapped his hand. "We have to make a good impression," she reminded him.

Seconds later, Eloise reversed course and handed over a warm piece. It melted on his tongue. "Awesome," he mumbled around the brownie.

Eloise preened. A shocker, since she was usually stoic when working a case. What other hidden delights would he uncover the longer they carried on the assignment?

"That's it until we get to the party."

He licked his fingers, nodding at her in the process. Was he affecting her as much as she was affecting him?

"About that."

She finished covering the dish. "About what?"

"I have an idea to get more work hours at the garage."

She leaned her hip against the counter, giving him all her attention.

"I told you the garage building is run-down, but what I learned from Ramsey is that Rico has been purchasing new equipment. Lines up with what you uncovered about Rico's windfall to pay off his tax situation."

The first week undercover had flown by. Dante's gut feeling that Rico was up to his neck in illegal activity intensified each day. Having impressed Rico with his mechanic skills, the owner officially hired Dante on Wednesday. Cars came into the shop from King's dealerships, just like Ramsey had told Dante, but it was rather anticlimactic. Just repairs and back they went. Legit.

"Learn anything else from the guys?" she queried.

"Mac is tight-lipped about the business, even though he and Rico have had many closed-door meetings."

"Be careful around him," she cautioned. "I don't like the fact that he was arrested twice on assault charges."

"I will." That bit of information had made Dante supervigilant around the growly coworker. "At least Ramsey is clean."

"Is he?" Eloise snorted.

"He might engage in a little illegal overtime, but he's not so bad. At least he's freer with me than Mac, even though it took until Friday for him to mention some kind of specialty work. When I pressed him on it, he clammed up, but it was enough to know we're on the right track here."

Eloise's eyes flashed before she said, "The money is coming from somewhere."

"Obviously."

"We keep searching. And while you're uncovering things at the shop, I'll make sure I strike up a friendship with Rico's wife, Stella. Share some wifely insider info on our husbands."

Dante shivered. "Should I be afraid?"

"Very afraid," she said in a spooky voice, making him laugh.

It was just the first week, Dante reminded himself. He knew the guys weren't going to trust him right away, but keeping his sixth sense at bay made him antsy. He had to remain patient and wait for the opportune moment to gain more insight into the shady side of the business.

Now, it was time to move to phase two of the assignment. Attend the block party. Maybe plant some seeds of financial discord in their marriage in front of Rico. "I'm thinking we have a little spat in front of my boss today over money."

"You got the job. Why push for overtime?"

"Because I think that's when the illegal activities are happening."

She thought about it for a moment. He could just imagine the wheels turning in her head.

"Push the idea that I'm bugging you about money for, say…a second car, which makes sense since we don't have one."

He nodded. "I'll keep an eye on Rico. When he's in a position to overhear our conversation, I'll lead us in his direction. Ask you not to keep nagging me about getting a second job."

"Oh, dear. Are the Smiths in that much financial trouble?"

He couldn't hold back a chuckle. He loved how she asked questions about the Smiths as if they were a real couple.

"As of right now they are."

"You know it's because you spend too much money restoring your cars," she teased.

"Hey, a guy needs a hobby."

She laughed, a warm sound tinkling the air around him and making his chest squeeze tight. Yeah, she was getting to him.

"Just improvise," he said.

"Got it." She pushed from the counter. "Let's get moving."

After a quick shower, Dante had finished dressing in a T-shirt and cargo shorts when his phone dinged. A text from Dylan saying he wanted a quick video chat.

Barefooted, Dante crossed the tiny hallway

to the bedroom with the computers. "I need to make a quick call," he yelled to Eloise. Within a few minutes, Dylan's face appeared on the screen of his laptop.

"What's up, Dyl?"

"Mom bested me again."

Dante pressed his lips together to conceal a laugh. Mr. Serious hated to be bested. By anyone. But by their mother? Ten times worse.

"I missed her lunch date."

"How did that happen?"

"She told Kady she was going one place, but when I got there, there was no sign of her or the new guy. I found out later they decided to switch up their restaurant choice last minute."

"She's onto us."

Dylan nodded. "Yeah. She's pretty much refused to talk about the guy with Kady. That's bad for us because she loves Kady and they talk about everything."

"What do you want to do now?"

"Resort to a background check."

"Which none of us can do without getting into serious trouble."

"I discussed this with Derrick. He suggested we hire a private investigator."

"What about Deke? What does he say?"

If it was possible, Dylan's face grew even

more serious. "I wanted to call you, but knew you were setting up your cover."

At those words, his stomach tensed like he'd been kicked in the gut. "Is he okay?"

"Yes. I mean, physically he's fine. A close friend of his was murdered."

Dante drew in a bracing breath. His brother Deke felt things deeply and this news had to have thrown him off-kilter. "I imagine he's taking it hard?"

"Took a leave of absence. When I last spoke to him, he was planning to hike the Appalachian Trail. He needs to regroup. Clear his head. He said he'd go along with whatever we decide."

"Then I say we move to the next step."

"I'll let you know what happens. Take care, Pretty Boy."

Dante frowned and ended the call. When he rose to leave the room, he found Eloise loitering in the doorway, a smile curving her lips. "Pretty Boy?"

Great. He had some explaining to do.

A VERY UNUSUAL red stained Dante's cheeks, astounding Eloise. She'd never seen him blush. Or lose his cool. By the dangerous glitter in his eyes, she guessed he didn't like her hearing what his brother called him.

"Stupid family nickname," he muttered. "And don't you know it's not polite to eavesdrop?"

"I only came to remind you the party started five minutes ago."

"It's fashionable to arrive late."

"Ooh, someone's cranky."

Dante brushed past her to go into his bedroom. She followed, watching as he slipped into a pair of boat shoes. "You'd be cranky, too, if you had a nickname you hated."

"Like you haven't noticed you're handsome?"

He stared at her, clearly tongue-tied.

She chuckled. "Well, everyone else has noticed."

"I don't like being judged by my looks."

Eloise sobered. "I understand."

He snatched his wallet off the dresser and shoved it in his back pocket. "My brothers never take me seriously."

"Have they ever seen you at work?"

"No. They're all big-time law enforcement guys. DEA. FBI. Forensics." He paused a moment. "I can't even get promoted to sergeant."

Oh, dear. Seemed like this conversation had opened an old wound.

"They'd be impressed, I'm sure."

When he didn't answer, she moved to another topic. She knew all too well what it felt like not to have the support of your family, especially when you desperately wanted it. "What's up with your mom?"

At the change in conversation, Dante's entire body seemed to relax. "She's a widow. Recently started dating."

"I don't see the problem."

He sent her an incredulous expression. "She's dating."

"Did I miss the memo that states after your spouse dies you're not allowed to date?"

He pressed his thumb and forefinger against his eyes, as if warding off a headache. "It's weird. Thinking about my mom without my dad."

"I suppose."

He dropped his hand. "Wouldn't you be concerned if one of your parents started dating after the other passed on?"

"Um, I never really thought about it." That sounded terribly cold, even to her own ears. "We aren't very close."

He studied her for a drawn-out moment. "Sorry."

"No, it's okay. I don't have any siblings, either, but I'd love to have a family that gave each other nicknames and cared about each other deeply. It sounds nice."

He shot her a questioning look, then shrugged. *Resigned*, Eloise thought.

"I suppose it's not so bad," he allowed.

She laughed and punched him in the arm. "Buck up, Dan Smith. We have to go meet the neighbors."

He expelled a put-upon sigh. "If we must."

"It'll be fun. I can't wait to have our first argument."

That brought a smile, just as she'd intended. She hated to see one of her colleagues down in the dumps, Dante even more. He was always up, always full of energy. She wanted that guy back.

"Just don't leave me out of whatever happens."

"I won't." He bent at the waist and swept out his arm. "After you."

Captivated by his silliness, she collected the brownie dish from the kitchen and they left the house to join the revelers already gathered in the shady front yard of a neighboring house.

True to the kinds of block parties she'd observed as a kid, sawhorses closed off the road midstreet between the length of two driveways. Picnic tables were lined up for lunch, and another long table held the food. Tablecloths ruffled in the breeze. Kids ran around in the grass in front of one house, supervised by a man wearing a baseball cap, his generous stomach straining against his waist as he blew a whistle. Two younger men carried a large tin basin filled with ice to the side of the food table, where several people filled it with drinks. A festive mood permeated the air and Eloise found herself drawn in.

"This is just like I imagined."

Dante sent her a surprised look. "You've never been to a block party?"

"My parents don't like the outdoors, or socializing, very much."

"That's…different."

She flushed. "They're academics," she explained. Then realized how that sounded. "Not that all academics don't like to socialize. I guess I should say my parents only like to focus on their students."

"They never took you to parties?"

"No."

"How about amusement parks?"

"Never."

"Vacations?"

"We did the college tour the summer before my high school senior year."

He shook his head. "When we were younger, my brothers and I terrorized neighborhood parties. Derrick would hide firecrackers and then light them off at dusk, scaring little kids.

Deke fashioned bungee cords and sticks to make slingshots so we could launch water balloons, which were my specialty."

"And what about your other brother? Dylan."

"He was a cop even when we were kids, running around making sure no one got hurt or securing the situation so we didn't totally spin out of control. Or worse, he'd rat us out."

A wave of wistfulness hit her so hard her chest ached with longing. "It sounds wonderful."

"Yes. It was. Until we got home and my parents doled out punishments. But my dad later admitted he'd known all along what we'd planned and made sure things didn't get out of hand."

"You haven't hidden any water balloons around for today, have you?"

"No, but I confess it did cross my mind."

She laughed, feeling more lighthearted than she could ever remember. Was this what a real family felt like? Spending time together? Attending parties? Sharing memories? If so, she wanted it with all her being.

"Ellie, dear. Over here."

She followed the voice to find Martha sitting in a lawn chair in the shade, surrounded by other chatting people. Before long, she and

Dante were introduced to so many people she lost count.

"I won't remember all the names," she told Martha on the sly.

"We don't expect you to," Martha responded with a wink.

The crowd grew and soon everyone sat down to eat. It was like sitting at one long kitchen table with family. She stuffed herself with all kinds of homemade dishes, regretting it as the afternoon grew warmer and she became drowsy. To her absolute delight, Dante held her hand or rested his arm over her shoulders as they talked to people. Okay, it was make-believe, but she'd savor every minute of it to hide in her heart, recapturing the day once the investigation ended.

"Dan. Ellie," Betsy said as she tugged a man their way. "This is my husband, Steve."

Everyone shook hands, and before she knew it another couple joined them, then another. And then the questions began.

"How long have you been married?"

"We're newlyweds," Dante said, slipping his arm around her waist to tug her closer, wrapping her in the cocoon of his spicy cologne. She fought the telltale shivers she was sure would give her feelings away if Dante noticed.

"I remember those early days," a woman

said, grinning at her husband. "Every year we celebrate at the first place we met. Where'd you two fall in love?"

Eloise glanced at Dante. He met her gaze with a blank look. Oh, no.

"It would have to be at the park," Dante said.

"At sunset, right, honey?"

His expression warm at her answer, he said, "I'll never forget the sun setting and the last rays of light washing over the sky while you stood looking out over the water."

Hot tears gathered behind her eyes. How sweet. If only it were true.

"When are you starting a family?" Betsy asked, a knowing smile on her face.

"Whoa." Dante held up his hand. "We're in no rush."

Eloise ignored the sting in her heart. "Where's Baxter? He's such a cutie. I thought for sure he'd be on your hip again."

"With my folks." Betsy hooked her arm through her husband's. "We've got a free weekend."

Eloise blinked.

"You know. Getting someone to watch the kids so we can be together without interruptions."

"Makes sense," Eloise replied, not sure how

else to respond. She hadn't been in any serious relationships to need together time, let alone a breather from children.

"You two don't have to worry about that right now, but once the kids come? You can't wait for couple time."

Dante squeezed her. "I think we're good."

As the group began to dissipate, Eloise swallowed. All of this seemed so...normal. She'd miss this when she went back to her old life.

As if sensing the direction of her thoughts, Dante leaned over to whisper, "Rico's off by himself." His breath tickled her ear and the shivers she'd been holding back threatened to let loose. "He's on the phone. Let's wander over in that direction."

She pulled herself together. *Right. Work.*

He took hold of her hand. "Let's go." They slowed their gait as they neared Rico.

Dante started the conversation. Lowered his voice for only Rico to hear. "You know we can't afford a second car."

"Then how am I supposed to get around during the day?"

"I told you to drop me off in the morning."

She threw up her hands. "You know I can't. That's when my clients are sending work orders."

"So save up your money."

"I pay all the household bills as it is."

They stopped a few feet from Rico, who had ended his call.

"We had it pretty good in Jacksonville. I had money coming in all the time, then you—" Dante stopped to finger quote "—wanted to get away."

"Don't blame me. You wanted to move away from my family as much as I did."

"Then stop whining about finances."

"And if I don't, who will?"

With a very slight nod of his head, Eloise got the message. She glared at him, then stomped off. All they had to do was wait and see if Rico took the bait.

DANTE LACED HIS fingers together and rested his hands on the top of his head, watching Eloise stomp away. She'd do well in theater if she had a mind to act.

"Hey," Rico said as he sauntered over. "Trouble in paradise?"

Dante dropped his hands. "Sorry you had to hear that."

"No big deal. Stella and I fight all the time."

"We weren't exactly fighting."

"I overheard the word *money*." Rico slapped Dante on the back. "You were fighting."

"Ellie wants me to get a second job. I told her I like working for you and don't want to blow a job I just started." He shook his head, pulling a perplexed expression. "I don't know what happened? We got married, and bam, it's all about the money. Back home it didn't matter. I had a sweet deal with the guy I worked for. Now…"

He let his sentence trail, hoping Rico would pick up on it.

"What kinda deal?"

"I shouldn't really say."

"Look, your cousin told me you liked to do things off book when he suggested you for the job."

Dante grimaced. "That sounds really bad. I don't want you to think I'm a crook."

"No, but you got ambition. I see it by the way you hustle to get repairs done."

"Ramsey's been good about giving me extra cars to work on when they come in from the dealership." He paused. Waited. "If I don't find something soon, my wife will keep riding me on the issue."

Rico's eyes narrowed. Was he thinking or trying to decide if Dante was on the up-and-up?

"Ramsey likes you. Says you fit into the shop."

Dante laughed. "And what does Mac say?"

"Mac is suspicious of everyone. But he doesn't have a quota to meet like I do."

Dante raised a brow. *Bingo.*

"You into working some overtime?"

"Are you kidding?"

"I have a special deal with a friend. On the down-low. At night. Think your wife will have a problem with that?"

"I don't care if she does, as long as she quits nagging me about money."

A little boy ran up to them, locking his arms around Rico's legs. "Daddy. Come play."

Rico smiled down at his boy, pride in his eyes. "You got it, son." He disentangled the boy from his legs. "We'll talk Monday," he told Dante, then pierced him with a threatening gaze. "Not a word. To anyone."

Dante held up his hands. "Hey, no way. I appreciate the shot."

As Rico passed by, he leaned toward Dante and said in a low voice, "Good, 'cause I'd hate to tell you what happens if you cross me."

"Message received."

Rico took off with his son. It was all Dante could do not to fist pump the air in victory.

Searching for Eloise, he found her talking to Rico's wife, Stella. He was impressed. Apparently Eloise didn't waste time. He waved at her, and after agreeing to a shopping date, Eloise was beside him.

"How'd it go?" she said in a low voice.

"I'm in."

A smile that made him feel like a hero spread over her lips. The sun had pinkened her skin and her hair shone in the sunshine. After the victory and having spent the day in close proximity to Eloise, he wanted to kiss her.

The thought shocked him to his core. Kiss her? He'd been dealing with this new attraction, but to take it a step further? Too much too soon.

"I knew you could do it," she said.

"Saying I'm sneaky?"

"In the best way." Her grin grew bigger. "I made inroads with the wife."

He threw his arm over her shoulders and tugged her close, one part undercover, the other part pure selfishness. It was like they fit together, something he'd never experienced with another woman.

"Looks like we're moving ahead with the case. I'll catch this guy soon enough," he said as they strolled back toward the milling crowd.

Eloise's shoulders went stiff.

"You okay?" he asked against her ear, inhaling the jasmine that always flitted about her.

"*You'll* catch the guy?"

"Sorry. *Us.* Slip of the tongue. It won't happen again."

Her stern expression telegraphed it had better not.

CHAPTER EIGHT

A LITTLE MORE than a week later, Dante slipped out of the shadows down the street from the auto garage and into the idling truck. It was after 1:00 a.m. Tuesday night—his "extra" shift was over—but he and Eloise still had detective work to do.

"Did the guys give you a hard time about your ride?" Eloise asked from behind the wheel, waiting for Dante to take a seat before easing the truck forward.

"Nah. Told them I had it under control." He pointed to the far end of the block. "Park down there. There's a guy we need to follow."

Due to the dashboard glow, Dante couldn't miss Eloise's outfit. One brow rose in surprise. Her hair, wavy and spread over her shoulders, framed her face. Her dress, a little black number from what he could see in the limited lighting, had him wondering just what other surprises she kept locked away in her closet. "Did I pull you away from a party?"

She tugged the skirt hem that wouldn't

budge past midthigh. "You texted while I was out with the neighborhood girls. They know how to have a good time." She eased the truck to the curb, making sure to evade the halo of light from the nearby streetlamp, and cut the engine. The normally busy street was notably empty, the other businesses on the block having closed for the night. Buildings were dark, with the exception of outdoor floodlights. The truck motor knocked a few times as it cooled down. Silence, like a blanket, settled around them.

Eloise twisted in the seat to face him, struggling to keep the dress at a modest length, revealing shapely legs. With a huff, she grabbed a wrap draped over the seat back and spread it over her lap.

Dante chuckled. "How's that going?"

"Slow, but the more I hang around Stella and her friends, the more I pick up tidbits. Mostly about Rico, since nothing in Stella's life seems to be a secret." She finished adjusting her wardrobe malfunction with a put-upon sigh. "How about you? Your text wasn't very detailed, but *news* sure caught my attention."

Dante rubbed his hands on his jeans, controlling the rush of excitement he'd managed to contain since discovering this new lead. He'd been working the late shift four nights now, champing at the bit to gain some insight on the operation, and tonight was the first time he'd overheard any useful information.

"I had to send it fast while no one was watching. I figured you'd understand the urgency by using the code word. We were extra busy tonight and I didn't want Mac to notice. He still doesn't trust me."

"Give it time."

He heard the humor in her tone and smiled.

"Guess everyone doesn't appreciate my charm."

She pierced him with an earnest gaze. "What did you learn?"

Dante glanced in the side mirror. No sleek Porsche leaving the garage yet. "Rico's friend showed up tonight. Slick suit, air of money. He and Rico disappeared for a while, but later came back while we were finishing up. There were more cars to work on than usual tonight. Much higher end."

"But you still did the same work as the rest of the week?"

"Yeah. I suspect Mac is changing the VIN plates while Rico has me fiddling around with engines. I took as many pictures with my phone as I dared without arousing suspicion."

"Good. I'll add them to the computer database at home."

At home. Still sounded weird when either of them said the words.

They'd settled into a routine of sorts, but his work hours had changed. He went in at noon, did the legit car repairs until dark. Later, high-end cars arrived so they could replace the VINs and any other modifications Rico requested. When he saw Dante's magic at tuning an engine, he'd had Dante work strictly on the high-quality motors, but Dante figured out what was going on. Like Eloise said, time would decide if Rico would trust him enough with the VIN replacement. In the meantime, he still needed to get Eloise more involved in the business. On location, if possible. He had an idea but the right time to approach Rico hadn't presented itself.

Eloise rolled down the window. Damp night air rushed in, followed by the scent of wet earth and warm asphalt. "Who is this guy?"

"Not sure. Goes by the name Greg. I stayed out of his sights so he wouldn't notice me, but managed to take a picture of his car tag. I'm hoping you can find out more on him." He pulled out his phone to scroll through the gallery. "He's a player, but I don't think he's the top guy."

"What makes you think that?"

"He told Rico the boss wanted to up his quota."

"His boss. So we're still looking for the head of the ring," she confirmed before a frown wrinkled her brow. "Why are we pulled over here?"

"Like I told you, the cars are dropped off, one after another. We do the work, but when I leave, they're still in the lot. Gone the next day. Tonight I heard Greg mention something about a car carrier. If my guess is right, the more expensive cars will be loaded up and taken away. We follow and find out."

"Makes sense. And these high-end cars?"

"Mercedes. BMW. Jaguar. Not the usual makes we handle during the day."

Eloise glanced into the rearview mirror. He followed suit. Still no movement. He glanced at his watch. "Close to one thirty now. There's no telling when we'll see some action."

"Then a stakeout, it is." Eloise removed her seat belt, then scrambled around to rummage the back seat. "I wasn't sure what tonight would hold." She tugged out a bag and settled back, placing it between them. "I stopped for some supplies."

Dante opened the bag, trying to make out the contents in the darkness. "Water bottles. Crackers. Beef jerky?" If the cab hadn't been shrouded in dark shadows, he imagined he'd find his partner's face a crimson shade of red at his question. Eloise seemed to always second-guess herself, which he found surprising since she really impressed him by having her act together.

"Since we never discussed it, I wasn't sure of your favorite go-to food for a stakeout. I have limited experience, and I'll admit, I never like to eat at times like this."

Dante peeled open the jerky. The aroma of spiced meat filled the cab. "Nerves?"

"Yes. I've heard other officers talk about the adrenaline spike. I want to be prepared."

"Hopefully you'll experience it tonight." He took a bite of the stick and chewed. "Thanks. I was hungry."

"I thought about stopping for coffee but figured we didn't need any unscheduled bathroom breaks."

He chuckled. "As much as I'd love a cup of caffeine, I agree."

Dante polished off his dinner in no time, taking a sip from his water bottle. "So, we have time to kill. Fill me in on your night."

She turned toward him again, noticing a sheepish expression on her face as his eyes adjusted to the darkness.

"Stella and her friends are way out of my league."

"Meaning?"

"Shopping. Long lunches. Spa days. Sometimes dancing, like tonight."

"Sounds like fun, but don't they have kids? Who takes care of them?"

"Nannies, it sounds like. Stella mentioned that Rico hit the mother lode. Seems she's made it her mission in life to spend all the money he brings home."

Dante shook his head. "Trust me, she isn't seeing it all."

"What makes you so sure?"

"Safe in his office. I've seen cash inside."

"Well, whatever he gives her is making her happy. Thankfully she knows the Smiths don't make a lot of money because even though she's adopted me into her group, and insisted I shop with them, she understands when I leave a store with one bag to her five."

"Any intel on the women?"

"No red flags. Stella is the leader. I get the impression they're all childhood friends. No one stands out."

He nodded his head toward her. "Where were you tonight?"

"A new club. Twilight. It just opened and Stella's been dying to go. There were lots of

women, few husbands and many male employees. Let's just say I was glad to call it a night.
Things were getting out of hand."

"Not your scene?"

She shuddered. "Never in a million years."
She paused. "Not that I'm boring or anything."

Dante checked the mirror again. "Didn't say
you were."

"I just don't understand throwing someone's
hard-earned money around for…whatever
those women find pleasurable."

"It's not their money so they don't care."

"I suppose. It's just not my idea of a good
time."

Dante opened the box of crackers. "And
what is?"

Eloise laid her head against the seat rest.
"Spending time with people I enjoy. Reading." A smile curved her lips. "Filing reports."

"Why am I not surprised." He bit into a
salty square and crunched.

"I don't have a wide circle of friends, but the
ones who are in my life are important to me."

"Same here."

She turned her head toward him. "Not a lot
of friends, either?"

"Nope." He took another bite.

"I didn't expect that."

"Why?"

"You seem like the popular guy."

"I'm like you." He shrugged. "I'd rather have close friendships than lots of acquaintances."

"And your family?"

Dante pictured his mother. His brothers. Smiled. "Love them all, even if they treat me like the annoying younger brother I probably am or was."

Eloise stared out the front window. "Someone has to be the youngest and therefore the picked-on one."

"It gets old once you grow up." Dante tossed the box into the bag. "You mentioned your folks. Not close to them?"

"No." Her voice sounded so tiny. He wondered what her childhood had been like. Decided to go ahead and ask when an eighteen-wheel car carrier, lights flashing, turned into the street. They both ducked at the same time so as not to be noticed in the headlights, their heads close enough to touch.

Eloise's jasmine perfume surrounded him. Lured him closer. He inhaled, savoring the scent of the intriguing woman. She was smart, pretty and read him really well. He'd never had that vibe with a partner. Until now.

The semi rumbled by but they kept their heads down until it was safely behind them.

He lifted his head, as did Eloise, and their eyes met. Dante's pulse picked up. This close, he could feel her breath on his cheek. And admitted to himself he was in deep water as far as Eloise was concerned, because the attraction he was supposed to quash was growing stronger every day.

It took everything in him to move away from heaven, from Eloise, and focus on the reason they were in these tight confines to begin with.

WAS HE GOING to kiss her?

Eloise blinked. The op and the cool night air, combined with the close confines of the truck, faded as she held her breath. Waited. Wished.

Then the semi brakes screeched in the distance, pulling her from the magical haze.

"Ah, looks like we have action," Dante said, his voice strained.

Eloise blinked. Right. Action. The job.

Had she really wanted him to kiss her? Right now? In the middle of a stakeout? Yes!

With that revelation, she sat up, straightened her dress and hair. Dante was intently peering out the back window.

"The guys are pulling a ramp from the truck." Eloise turned in her seat to see what was going on. Bright red lights flashed on the semi. The sudden quiet seemed deafening after the loud semi engine shut down. Moments later a car moved up the ramp. Followed by another and another.

"Looks like your hunch was correct," she stated the obvious.

Dante sent her a cheeky grin. "Don't you love our plan?"

Sure, if she had an idea of what the plan was. With Dante, anyway. The job, she could figure out. Her feelings for the man seated next to her, all kinetic energy and edgy excitement, were still part of a process she didn't have any answers to. For a woman who went by the book, not having any kind of guidelines to go by in the romance department was frustrating.

Within thirty minutes the cars were loaded and the driver jumped back behind the wheel. Eloise recorded the entire exchange with the PD digital camera Dante insisted they keep in the truck for moments like this.

"Let's go," Dante said. "We can't go by the repair shop, so head out to the main road. We'll follow once they make it around the block."

Starting the truck, Eloise calmed her shaky hands. They were closer to getting answers and she had to admit Dante's enthusiasm was contagious. Stepping on the gas, she wished she'd thrown flats into the truck but she hadn't been thinking. High heels were not her idea of professional footwear, but Stella's invitation had come last minute and, in her haste, Eloise hadn't thought ahead to a possible stakeout.

Pausing at the stop sign at the end of the street, she waited until the huge car carrier pulled out a few streets down. She eased onto the main road, merging with the couple of cars still out this early in the morning.

"Slow down," Dante warned. "The Porsche is following the semi."

Eloise fell back, tailing the sports car and carrier.

Laser focused now, they traveled five miles in silence before turning into an industrial park. Again, Eloise trailed, keeping her nerves in check while slowing down until the semi pulled into the empty parking lot of a large warehouse. She cut the lights and pulled over onto the grass shoulder, far enough away not to be noticed, but with an unobstructed view to monitor the activity and take pictures to record movements.

A man jumped out of the sports car, unlocked a glass door and disappeared inside the building.

"Greg?" Eloise asked.

"Yeah," came Dante's terse reply.

The warehouse in front of them appeared newer than the others in the park, which had a general run-down feeling. A minute later, a huge garage door opened while the semi driver readied the cars for removal. The stark warehouse lights were bright in the night, revealing other cars parked inside. It took another thirty minutes to off-load the high-end cars. Once Greg closed the large doors, he and the semi driver appeared again. Greg walked the driver to his truck, slapped him on the back and watched the driver swing into the truck cab. As the semi roared to life, Greg stepped back, then fished something out of his pants pocket.

"Looks like he's getting a phone call," Dante observed.

The truck moved slowly down the road, leaving Greg behind to carry on an animated conversation. He paced, raised his hand, then finally ran to his car, jumped inside and peeled out of the parking lot.

Dante turned to Eloise, a smile spreading over his lips. "No way. Did he forget to lock the front door?"

Eloise shook her head. Actually, she wasn't surprised. She'd worked enough property theft cases to realize criminals did strange things. "Sure looks that way."

Dante barked out a laugh. "Let's hang out a bit longer, in case he realizes his mistake and comes back."

"Do you think anyone else will drive by? One of Rico's guys?"

"I doubt it, but we can't be too sure. Usually when we've finished for the night, Mac and Ramsey head right home. I always leave before Rico. There's no telling what he does afterward."

Fifteen minutes later, there was no additional traffic. "Let's roll," Dante said, slipping out of the truck.

Eloise followed, pulling her hair back into a ponytail with the clip she'd thrown in her tiny evening bag. She also carried the camera to document the cars inside.

"You aren't going to break your ankle in those things, are you?" he asked as they shuffled through the grass to the dusty road.

Eloise glanced down. The black heels were stylish on a dance floor, but not so much running across asphalt. "I'll be fine."

Dante shook his head. "Must be a woman thing."

She held back a grin.

They stayed to the fringes of the parking

lot, working their way through the shadows to the building. A bird cried out a warning. In the distance, Eloise could hear cars zooming down the main road. She broke out in a light sweat. The humid spring night was not meant for running around in a clandestine mission wearing an evening dress.

Dante stopped, hunkered down. "The outside lights are a problem, but the only place I can see inside is through the glass door."

He waved and they streaked across the lot to the building, backs to the wall as they worked their way to the door.

"They must be using this place for storage," she surmised.

"Until they move the cars again? Or do they keep them here awhile?" Dante wondered out loud. He pulled his phone from his pocket. "I've got a flashlight app. Maybe it'll give us more light."

"While you try, I'm going around the building."

He glanced her way, his face serious. "Be careful."

"I can take care of myself," she said, jogging off.

Rounding the corner, dark shadows covered her movement along the length of solid wall. No doors or windows. She gingerly stepped along the sparse grass. A crash, like a garbage can tipping over, startled her. Her hand flew to her chest. An animal scavenging for food? She shivered and hurried on.

As she crept to the back, she spied metal stairs leading up to a door on a much higher level. Not wanting to exclude any possibility, she climbed the stairs. Heart pounding, she gripped the cool metal with damp palms as she drew closer to the landing, trying to keep her shoes from echoing in the still night. Once on top, she hurried to the door. As she expected, the entryway was locked. There was a half window in the door. Eloise peered inside the warehouse and let out a gasp.

Hurrying back down the stairs and around to the front, she moved as fast as she could without turning an ankle. Once at the office door, she hesitated. Taking a deep breath, she grabbed the handle and pulled, stepping inside to seek out Dante, who was roaming around the warehouse.

"Are you crazy?" she hissed.

"What?" He tried for innocence but couldn't pull it off. "The door was unlocked. I was afraid a thief might be inside so I decided to perform a business check. You do realize this could be a high-crime area."

"Could be?" she huffed. "And getting a warrant didn't cross your mind?"

"Not when I sensed positional danger."

She rolled her eyes. He had a point—a business check fell under their purview, even if the motivation was a bit shaky.

"I just wanted to get an idea of what was in here." He nodded toward the inventory. "All high-end cars."

She had to admit, she'd been curious, too.

"This isn't the end run, I'm sure of it," Dante continued. "At some point, these cars must be moved somewhere else. But where?" He looked at her, no doubt seeing the frown on her face. "Don't worry. When we get that far along, we'll be sure to do things by the book."

Okay, it made sense, but it went against Eloise's grain. She didn't like playing fast and loose with the law, but saw Dante's point. And they were undercover to acquire information.

Mind made up, she inspected the huge area. The door she'd noticed from the back side of the building opened onto a sort of catwalk that circled high above the cavernous space. No other offices or side rooms. Other than that, only cars filled the warehouse.

"Who steals all these expensive cars and doesn't have an alarm system?" she asked in a low tone.

"Thieves who plan on moving the merchandise soon?"

As she walked around the beautiful vehicles, the faint scent of gasoline and damp concrete tickled her nose. The overhead light reflected off the perfect paint jobs. She noticed something off near the bottom of one car body and bent down to get a closer look.

"Is someone repainting the cars?"

Dante joined her, squatting down to check. "Good eye."

She tried not to beam. She was doing her job, after all.

He rose. "You go that way." Dante pointed to his left. "I'll go the other and we'll meet in the middle."

She took off, snapping pictures of cars. "There are no plates," she called out.

"I noticed that earlier. Must have been removed when the cars arrived at the shop."

"Rico has them?"

"I'll have to find out."

After taking a few more pictures, she met up with Dante. "No license plates and they changed the VINs. There's no way I'll be able to trace where they came from."

"We'll call Chambers. Have him put a surveillance detail on this warehouse." He took another scan of the room. "Let's check the office."

The room was empty except for a solitary desk and a landline phone. Eloise lifted the receiver. "There's a dial tone."

"Then there has to be a number leading to someone who owns or rents this place." He checked his watch. "Let's get out of here."

"You don't have to tell me twice."

As they moved together toward the door, a squealing, followed by lights, flashed into the parking lot.

Dante muttered under his breath. "Greg must have realized he didn't lock up."

They were blocked. The only way out would lead to their discovery.

Thinking fast, Eloise said, "This way." She grabbed his shirtsleeve to drag him back into the warehouse. Pointed to the metal stairs. "We can get out up there."

He nodded. They both ran for the stairs and climbed up, sprinting down the catwalk to the exit. Dante had the door open and they made it outside just as Greg arrived inside. Eloise gently closed the door and huddled beside Dante, watching through the window. Greg made a circuit of the warehouse, made sure all was okay, turned off the lights and left. From their perch on the landing, Eloise could hear his car start up and drive away.

She sagged against the building, tugging the camera strap over her shoulder. "That was close."

Dante winked at her. "And fun."

"Right. Almost getting caught and blowing our cover was fun?"

"Beats sitting in the truck doing nothing."

He had a point, even if she didn't like it. Her heart felt like it was going to beat right out of her chest.

Dante made sure the door was locked again before leading the way down. Near the bottom, Eloise moved so quickly that her heel caught and she lost her footing. Dante had just turned to gauge her descent. His fast reflexes caught her before she could tumble into the grass. She didn't hit the ground, but she did end up in his arms.

They both froze. Dante's hands on her waist, hers gripping his upper arms. By the light of the moon hovering in the clear night sky, Eloise watched Dante's gaze search her face before moving to her lips. Her breath caught.

"Back in the truck," he said, voice low and husky, "I wanted to kiss you. Looks like fate has given me a second chance."

He lowered his head, gently touching her

lips with his. She lost all rational thought as she returned the kiss. His lips brushed hers, once. Again and again. His spicy scent made her dizzy. Her fingers tightened around the soft fabric of his shirt. She wasn't sure how long the kiss went on. Would have let it go on forever if Dante hadn't pulled away.

"I...probably shouldn't have done that," he muttered, putting space between them.

She opened her mouth to respond, but what could she say? No, he shouldn't have kissed her, not on the job. Wasn't it an unspoken rule that you didn't kiss your partner on a stakeout? But she'd wanted him to. Was glad he did. Now what?

He cleared his throat. "It's one thing if we kiss for the sake of the cover, in front of people who think we're married. I don't have an excuse for this moment."

Covering her reaction to his kiss, she straightened her shoulders. "You're right. We don't."

His brows angled. He kept his mouth shut, making her wonder what he was thinking. Certainly regretting his actions. His chagrined look confirmed it.

When he didn't say anything else, Eloise stepped back, tottering on her high heels. He reached out to grab her but she held him off. "I'm fine."

Dante ran a hand over his hair. "Eloise—"

"We should get back. Write up our report while the events of tonight are still fresh in our minds."

"Right. Report."

Still, she lingered. He shoved his hands in his pockets and started to walk.

She blinked rapidly. They needed to move, not hang around and chat about their feelings. What if the thieves came back and found them? They couldn't take the chance.

When they reached the front of the building, Dante scanned the surrounding area before waving her forward. "Clear."

They jogged back to the truck, jumping inside. Eloise caught her breath, reached out to turn the key she'd left in the ignition. Dante's hand caught hers in midair.

"What just happened back there... Is it going to be a problem?"

She searched his face for any tip-off to what he might be feeling. All she could see was his cop face, straightforward with no emotion.

Swallowing hard, she said, "Let's chalk it up to adrenaline. We're professionals, Dante." *Professional. Right.* "We won't let a slip like this happen again."

He nodded and turned to look out the window.

Embarrassment flushed her cheeks. Thank goodness it was dark so he couldn't see her mortification. She started the truck and steered in the direction of home, wondering how on earth she was going to face him at the breakfast table tomorrow, acting like he hadn't just altered her world.

CHAPTER NINE

THE FOLLOWING MORNING, Eloise hitched a breath before entering the kitchen. Dante sat at the table, an empty plate before him, scrolling through his phone. How did he manage to look so handsome after only a few hours' sleep? She'd intentionally walked past the mirror without looking when she rose this morning.

Dante set the device down and gave her his full attention when she tossed a file on the table.

"Your guy is Greg Reed. He's got a sheet. Juvenile record. He's kept his nose clean for the past fifteen years."

"More like he just hasn't gotten himself caught." He opened the file and read. "Auto theft. Petty theft."

"He was working solo back then. Maybe he feels safer having a boss, or a network, to work with."

"I don't know. He was pretty cocky, strutting around and barking out commands. I could tell Rico was ticked but managed to hold it in."

"Maybe Rico doesn't want to upset the ringleader?"

"That would be my guess. He might not like Greg around, but Rico's in too deep now. He'll put up with this guy as long as the money is rolling in." Dante closed the file. "Any luck on the warehouse?"

Blinking the grit from her eyes, Eloise adjusted her glasses, then turned and poured herself a mug of coffee. The rich aroma did little to energize her. Leaning against the counter, she answered, "No luck there. I only found a numbered corporation as the owner and kept digging deeper, but got nowhere. Once I reached a dead end, I wondered if it's a front for a dummy corporation. I'll keep searching."

"I called Chambers this morning. He said he'd station a surveillance team outside the warehouse."

Taking a few steps across the room, Eloise sank down into a chair across the table from him. "If we can find the location where the cars are being shipped next, it would certainly go a long way in revealing who is in charge." She sipped the coffee. Winced at the industrial-strength potency.

The corner of Dante's mouth angled down. "Sorry. Not my best pot of coffee."

She set the mug on the table and ran a hand through her messy hair. After last night's adventure, she'd tossed and turned, finally rising well before dawn to power up the computer and start her searches. Still dressed in an oversize sleep shirt and yoga pants, she wasn't exactly at her best after little sleep.

Dante nodded to the stove. "I scrambled some eggs if you're hungry."

Hungry? After last night? Hardly. "I'm fine."

A heavy silence settled on the room.

"Eloise, about last night."

She held up a hand. "We're good. There's no need to rehash our lapse of judgment."

He flinched. "I need to explain."

This she couldn't wait to hear. He'd kissed her, then quickly apologized. Obviously, he'd decided she wasn't worth the trouble.

"Look, I stepped over the line."

She held her tongue.

"My brother warned me about this. Working closely together, that is. That line between the job and personal feelings being blurred. I'm the guy everyone accuses of being impetuous. Jumping in before considering the consequences. I don't want that for us, Ellie."

She closed her eyes. She'd never admit it, but she loved it when he shortened her name. Ellie sounded playful, fun. Unlike nose-to-the-grindstone Eloise.

But Dante was correct. He was labeled the loose cannon. And since most of her colleagues considered her by-the-book all the time, she understood the weight, and resentment, of carrying an identity others saddled you with.

Releasing a sigh, she asked, "What do you want?"

"To finish out this case. Then maybe we can figure out where we stand."

She met his gaze head-on. "Where we stand?"

"Personally."

It took everything in her to control a shiver. His eyes were dark. Heated. But he was right. Neither of them could risk crossing the line. After they closed the investigation? That was a different story.

"About that kiss," he clarified.

"I know what you were referring to." She paused, wanting to ask, *What about what I want?* but had come to terms with the fact that they were on a job. There were expectations and duties to uphold. This was their real purpose, not playing at being married. The case needed to be wrapped up and personal feelings had no place in the middle of an op.

Too late, Ellie, the part of her who didn't hide her feelings taunted.

Dante leaned forward in his seat. "If our superiors get wind of us becoming...closer during this op, do you think any of them will condone it? No. Then we can both kiss the promotion goodbye."

Her breath stilled in her chest. The promotion. Last night, she'd been so topsy-turvy over his kiss, all thoughts of the sought-after promotion had flown from her mind when his warm lips brushed hers. It wasn't until she'd gotten home that the gravity of their actions hit her. She could have blown all her hard work for a few moments of paradise. And to make matters worse, she'd so easily kissed him back. While her feelings for him were accelerating, he seemed to be backpedaling, considering last night's conduct a big mistake.

She cleared her throat. "I know all this, Dante. I agree. We take a step back." Even if she wanted to throw caution to the wind, she couldn't. She wanted the promotion as much as Dante. If they continued down the road they'd started last night, neither of them would accomplish their goal. "We forget about what happened. Keep up the married-couple ruse until the case closes. Find out which one of us makes sergeant."

He reached across the table to place his hand over hers. "I'm sorry, Ellie. I wasn't thinking."

Neither had she. Now she had to abandon any personal feelings and wishful what-ifs. What a crazy idea, that Dante would want to have anything more than a working relationship with her.

"Don't apologize. I wanted to kiss you as much as you wanted to kiss me. You're right. It was ill-timed and thoughtless. We need to move forward."

He nodded, but in the last moments, she'd been unable to read his eyes. Had he put up a wall? Fine, then she would, too.

"I need to get ready for work." He rose, carried his dish and coffee mug to the sink, rinsed them off and placed them in the dishwasher. He stopped right next to her before leaving. "You sure we're okay?"

Ignoring the scent of his tantalizing cologne and the warmth of his body, she nodded firmly. "Absolutely."

He sent her a questioning look, then left the kitchen.

Eloise sat in silence, blinking back the moisture gathering in her eyes. The refrigerator motor kicked on, rattling with a mechanical hum. Grabbing her mug, she headed out back, away from Dante and the sting of his rejection.

Stepping onto the patio, she covered her eyes against the late-morning sun. Birds chirped a cheery song overhead. "Quiet," she muttered, then dropped into a chaise longue, placing her mug on the table nearby. She crossed her arms over her chest and closed her eyes. Maybe she could finally fall asleep. Put the discussion with Dante out of her mind for good.

Just as she was dozing off, a creaking sound stirred her. She cracked one eye open to see Martha, covered dish in hand, slowly making her way across the grassy stretch of yard to the patio.

"Oh, my dear. I hope I didn't wake you."

Eloise linked her fingers and raised her arms over her head to stretch. "I've heard sleep is overrated."

Martha laughed. "I see you've been spending time with our sassy Stella."

"Guilty as charged."

Martha placed the plate on the outdoor table. "I baked cookies. When you didn't stop by for coffee this morning, I decided to drop them off. Thought your hunky husband might like them."

"Hunky?"

A becoming blush swept over Martha's face. "As if you haven't noticed."

Oh, she had, much to her detriment.

"Have a seat," Eloise invited.

"Don't mind if I do." Martha, hand gripping her cane, made her way to the chair closest to the chaise. "Beautiful day."

Eloise shrugged, took a sip of her cooling coffee and grimaced. She needed to dump Dante's sludge and make a new pot.

"Something troubling you, dear?"

Eloise cocked her head. Was it obvious?

"Those circles under your eyes give you away."

Eloise met Martha's concerned gaze and her heart sank. Oh, how she wanted to confide the truth to someone. She was in deep water and felt like the riptide was carrying her farther and farther away from the safety of the shore. She didn't have any close friends to talk to, couldn't tell Brandy about her conflicted emotions or word would get back to the station. Her parents would most likely brush her off. But here sat a woman Eloise felt herself growing closer to, offering a chance to unburden her heart. Did she dare?

"This marriage thing is a lot harder than I thought it would be."

"Oh, Ellie, marriage is a lot of hard work.

No couple makes the perfect partnership right away. It takes time and you're just starting out."

Eloise nearly choked at Martha's words. Partnership? The sweet woman had no idea.

"I'm not being foolish, Martha. I get that things don't gel overnight."

"George and I were married for over fifty years when he passed. A day didn't go by that I learned something new about the man I'd lived with for most of my life."

Fifty years? Eloise couldn't imagine being in love for that long, but had to admit she saw happy couples in loving marriages every day. Even her parents had a good life together. It was dealing with an unwanted daughter they had problems with.

Martha pierced Eloise's gaze with hers. "That's not to say it was all fun and games. We had years where things didn't go right, but we kept the lines of communication open. That's important."

Yes. Like Dante reminding Eloise they couldn't cross the line in this work relationship. Before this case, no one would have had to warn her of the pitfalls of doing so. Yet here she sat, dwelling on those blurry lines and nursing a bruised heart as a result.

"I suppose I have to work on my patience."

"Oh, dear, this is just the beginning. Wait until little ones come along."

Eloise couldn't fathom that far ahead. She was still trying to wrap her mind around one kiss. "Please, don't rush me."

Martha laughed. "Nothing worth having is easy."

"Trust me, nothing about Dan is easy."

As if on cue, Dante sauntered outside. "Did I hear someone say my name?"

Eloise controlled an eye roll.

"I was just telling your wife that I made cookies." Martha pointed to the dish. "For you."

Dante placed a hand over his heart. "What did we do to deserve you for a neighbor?" He leaned down to peck a kiss on the older woman's pink cheek, then lifted the dish to sniff the goodies under the covering. "Chocolate chip?"

Martha grinned.

"My favorite."

Eloise had to admit, she was as smitten with Dante as Martha, so she needed to send him off before she forgot her vow to remain professional. "Time to leave?"

Dante's dark gaze met hers. "It is. See you later."

Eloise nodded as Dante took the dish inside with him.

The birds sang overhead and squirrels chattered as they jumped from one tree branch to another, foraging for food. Eloise took another sip of coffee, shook her head and set the mug down.

"You know you can talk to me whenever you need to," Martha said, her voice steady. "I won't judge."

Eloise couldn't meet her gaze. "Why would you judge?"

Martha looked at the kitchen door, then back at Eloise. "You're newlyweds. Your husband just left for work. And there you sit, without jumping up to kiss him goodbye."

Oops.

"I, ah…"

"And by your earlier comment about not being sure about the marriage, it doesn't take much to put two and two together."

Pushing herself up, Eloise swung her legs over the chaise. Time to nip this in the bud. "Blame it on the late night out."

"You don't want to talk? I get it. But can I give you a piece of advice?"

"Sure."

"Even though Dan is working a later shift, you might want to spend more time with him than with Stella and her gang. What seems like fun now won't last, I can promise you that."

Under normal circumstances, Eloise would have agreed wholeheartedly. But she had the op to consider. Still, she didn't want to come across ungrateful. "I will take your advice under advisement."

"Good."

"Now that we have my married life settled, what are you up to today?"

A sly twinkle shone in Martha's eyes. "Actually, I stopped by to see if you were free this afternoon. I have some errands to run and wondered if you'd drive."

"Dan took the truck."

Martha waved her hand. "I have a car in the garage."

Surprise had Eloise gaping. "You drive?"

"Not any longer, but my son insisted I keep the old rattletrap. It comes in handy when I talk—er, I mean, ask someone to drive me around."

Eloise grinned. "Then it would be my pleasure. What did you have in mind?"

"My craft group meets every other week. I need additional yarn for a project I'm working on." The light still glimmered in her eyes. "You know, you should come join the group. There are some young women your age who are settled into their married lives. You would enjoy their company."

"Are you trying to save me from the scandalous lure of the nightlife?"

"I am."

Eloise laughed. "As it happens, I worked early this morning, so I'm all yours. We can go grab a bite for lunch if you'd like."

"I'd consider it an honor." Martha rose a little unsteadily. "And you should seriously consider taking up a hobby."

Eloise threw up her hands. "Okay, you've convinced me. Let me take a shower and get dressed. I'll meet you in…thirty minutes?"

Martha was already making her way across the lawn. "It's a plan."

Shaking her head, Eloise picked up the mug and carried it inside. This is what she needed. Girl time. Some distance from Dante while she made strides in regaining the professional attitude she had before this undercover op ever started.

"DAN. MY OFFICE."

Rico's voice carried over the din of the repair shop. Looking up from the engine he was taking apart, Dante saw his boss standing in the open door to his office. He tossed the wrench, with a little more force than necessary, into his toolbox, grabbed a towel and strode Rico's way.

"What's got you in a mood?"

Dante heaved out a sigh. "Married life."

Rico chuckled. "Lemme guess. Trouble in paradise?"

"You could say that."

An electric drill whirred, drowning out the conversation for a moment. Ramsey inspected the undercarriage of a car raised on a lift. Nearby, Mac slammed a hood closed. Oscillating fans mounted on the walls battled the heat of the afternoon. The prevailing scents of oil, grit and rust grounded Dante.

"Heard your wife went out with mine last night."

"Yeah. Don't get me wrong. I don't mind Ellie having friends. It's just…"

"Just?"

Dante glanced over his shoulder. "Mind if we talk where the guys can't overhear?"

"Sure." Rico waved him into the cramped office. Inside, the stifling heat enhanced the greasy aroma of French fries sitting on a paper wrapper.

Once again Dante didn't know how the guy worked in this jumbled mess. Papers were strewn over the desk, the trash can overflowing with empty coffee cups and soda cans. He was surprised a family of rodents hadn't taken up residence in here.

"So, your wife's a little uptight?"

Dante stopped in front of Rico's desk. "What makes you say that?"

"Stella. She mentioned Ellie isn't comfortable with all the shopping and nightlife."

Grateful for the direction of the conversation, Dante took advantage of the opening. Running a hand over the back of his neck, he said, "It's not that she's uncomfortable. It's the money."

"Still harping about that?"

"I feel like it's all we talk about. Even with the extra work you've thrown my way."

"I thought she has a job."

Dante dropped his hand. "She does, but her hours just got cut back."

"Bummer."

"Yeah." He shifted his stance. "Listen, you didn't call me in here to talk about my family problems."

"Right." Rico riffled through a mountain of papers. "I need you to run out for some car parts."

"Now? Dude, I'm in the middle of a rebuild. Got engine parts scattered all over the place. Can't Ramsey do it?"

A scowl wrinkled Rico's brow. "You're the new guy. Honor goes to you." He rummaged around the desk until he found the list and handed it over.

As he took the paper, Dante realized this was the opportune moment to suggest bringing Eloise in. "You gotta be kidding me. Last place I worked we had a parts runner."

"I had one, too."

"What happened?"

"I started making more money and she decided to shop instead of work." Rico shook his head as if the burden of making lots of money was his alone to bear.

"Stella?"

Rico nodded. "She organized the office. Ran errands." Rico's countenance fell as he gazed around the room. "Kept things under control."

"No offense, man, but you need some help here."

Rico sighed. "Been putting it off, but you're right."

"Hey, I don't want to sound out of place, but how about hiring Ellie? She can run around for parts. Plus, her office skills are pretty good. Her desk is so tidy it's ridiculous."

Rico narrowed his eyes.

Too much? Dante backed off. "Hey, it was just a suggestion."

"No, it's okay." Rico sank into his battered

leather chair. "You wouldn't mind having her around?"

"No. I mean, despite a couple of problems—" like kissing her when he shouldn't "—we get along pretty good."

"I would like to free up some time for other projects."

Yes. He's warming up to the idea.

"You'd be doing me a big favor," Dante went on. "If Ellie can get some extra hours, maybe she'll lay off the money discussions."

Rico leaned forward, resting his elbows on the desk, a warning crossing his face. "This is work. No hanging around her and not getting any repairs done."

Dante held up his hand. "No worries."

"Then yeah, bring her in with you tomorrow. I'll talk to her and we'll go from there."

"Thanks. You won't regret it."

He flashed the enforcer expression Dante recognized as Rico's way of making a point. A threatening point. "Don't make me, then we won't have any problems."

Not pushing his good luck, Dante held up the list. "I'll be back soon."

Rico waved him off. "Go."

Doing everything he could not to let his pleasure show, Dante weaved through the cluttered garage to pick up his truck keys from his rolling tool cart. He'd been hoping to get Eloise closer to the action. Rico was either tired of working in that pit of an office, or he was warming up to Dante. He'd take the victory.

His good mood sobered when he thought about telling Eloise the news. She'd be happy to be more involved in the op than just relegated to computer searches. But going forward, Dante had to make sure he kept his word like he promised this morning. No more crossing the line, no matter how much Eloise tempted him. What was it about that woman that made him want to throw away this chance of moving up the ranks? Because that's exactly what he'd be doing. Since he'd decided to work harder toward that promotion, it seemed like Eloise became more attractive than ever before. Or had he just never admitted to himself that he was interested in her?

And what about her goals? She wanted the promotion just as much as he did. So yeah, he had to be on guard now.

Closing his eyes, he recalled how soft her lips were when he brushed against them last night, how her lip gloss tasted of strawberries. How her brown eyes had turned a shade darker when he moved in for the kiss. He craved her scent, like exotic flowers blooming at dawn. When had he ever waxed poetic about a woman before? Never. That's how he knew he was in trouble.

Eloise agreed they'd made a mistake. Was more than clear that it could not happen again. Still, he had to wonder. He never expected Eloise, by-the-book and professional, would ever lose her composure with him. He wasn't exactly the kind of guy someone gave up a promising career for.

Shaking off his regret, he headed to his truck parked at the side of the building. He bit back a retort when Mac blocked his way.

"Where you off to?" the big, bald man challenged.

"Parts run."

"That it?"

"Where else would I go?"

He moved in closer, making sure to let Dante know he had no trouble invading his space. "Not sure. Haven't decided about you yet."

"Doesn't really matter what you think. Rico makes the decisions around here."

"And you intend to get on his good side?" Mac barked out a laugh. "Good luck with that."

"What's that supposed to mean?"

Ramsey ambled over, a greasy carburetor

in his hands. "Mac likes to think he's second in command. Ignore him."

Mac cut his coworker a dirty look. "You need to butt out."

"And you need to remember your place."

What was going on here? The tension between the two men was palpable. And since when had Ramsey become confrontational?

Taut seconds played out until Mac huffed and returned to the car he was tuning. Ramsey's easygoing demeanor emerged. "Don't mind him."

"I won't." Dante frowned. "Thanks?"

Ramsey chuckled. "Got your back."

"I'll be back soon," he said, then took off to get the parts his boss needed. As he approached his truck, he noticed Rico walking to a small brick building behind the shop. How had he slipped by without Dante noticing? Rico pulled out a set of keys to unlock the door of the structure Dante had noticed before. What could be in there? The real center of the business? Because his office certainly wasn't it.

Rico disappeared inside and Dante got moving. With Eloise working with him, maybe they'd be able to figure out a way inside. Discover more about the car theft ring. Finally get some evidence they could use in an arrest.

Once he was on the road, he pulled out his cell and called Eloise. "Guess what, honey. I just got you a job."

CHAPTER TEN

ONE SNIFF OF Rico's office and Eloise took a giant step backward.

The tall, olive-skinned man with dark hair and equally dark eyes had the grace to grimace. "Before you say anything, I know. This place has gotten out of hand."

Eloise tried not to gape, but really? No wonder Stella was no longer working for her husband. If she'd had to put up with the noxious odor when she worked here, his wife deserved all her recent shopping trips and spa days.

"It's not so bad," Dante said beside her.

She shot him an *Are you kidding me?* look, then focused on her new boss.

"When Stella decided to stay home, I kind of let things go," Rico explained.

Not sure how to reply nicely, she stepped into the small room to get her bearings. The trash cans overflowed with old food wrappers and what else she didn't want to imagine. Just like Dante said, the desk was loaded with papers, which actually spilled over to the top of the filing cabinet. File folders had been set on the floor and an ancient computer sat in the corner, turned off. By the sheer volume of paperwork, Eloise wondered if Rico even bothered with the machine.

Rico gathered the mess on the filing cabinet and dumped the pile on the already overflowing desk, then set a small fan on top of the metal cabinet and turned it on. "Sorry it's hot in here. The wall unit is on the fritz." He turned to her. "Dan tells me you should have this place in tiptop shape in no time."

No time? She wasn't sure, but said, "We'll see. I should get started."

"And I need to get back to my work for the day," Dante said, winking before making his way to a red sports car with the hood up. Eloise knew his gesture was for show, but couldn't deny the tendril of pleasure.

"Any questions?" Rico asked.

"Not at the moment."

He fished a plastic bag from the corner and tossed it to her. "Work T-shirts."

She pulled one out, read Battles Auto Repair silk-screened on front, noticed the large size and held back a sigh.

Rico inched to the open door. "If you need me I'll be out back."

She raised a brow.

"I have another office."

"Oh, my." Eloise placed her hand over her chest, going for overwhelmed instead of curious.

"It's in better shape," Rico said, his deep voice gruff.

"Good, because I won't be able to get to that one for—" she scanned the room again "—a while."

"No."

"No?"

Rico's expression turned scary serious. "The building out back is off-limits."

By his reaction, it was clear the office out back was where the real information lay. Now all Eloise had to do was figure out a way to gain access.

"Oh, okay." She lifted a few papers from the desk. "If you change your mind, you know where I'll be."

Rico nodded.

"And, Mr. Battles?"

"Yes."

"Thanks. For the job."

He cleared his throat. "Sure. Just don't make me regret having you and your husband under one roof." His gaze narrowed. "What with you being newlyweds and all."

She grinned at him. "We can behave."

With a grunted response, Rico beat a hasty retreat.

Squaring her shoulders, Eloise surveyed the room. For all her organizational skills, she had no idea where to start, but for the sake of the investigation, she'd better figure it out soon.

"These might help."

Eloise swung around to find a skinny man with stringy hair tossing a box her way. She grabbed it. "Trash bags?"

"You'll need 'em." With a chuckle he held out his hand. "Ramsey."

Shaking his hand, she said, "Ellie. Dan's told me about you."

"All good, I hope?"

"So far."

He chuckled. "Dan's good people."

"I think so."

Returning to the task at hand, she decided to start by emptying the garbage first. The room immediately smelled better. Finding more garbage littered here and there, she filled another bag and then hefted them to the Dumpster. On her way back, a bald guy stopped her. Had to be Mac.

"Since you're tidying up…" Mac tossed her a dirty work towel.

She caught it.

"You can figure out where that goes."

"Then so can you." And she tossed the dirty rag back to him.

Figuring he'd tell her off, she was surprised when all he did was let out a big belly laugh. Yeah, she didn't like Mac at all.

In the office, her stomach sank at the amount of work that awaited her. Pushing back the sleeves of a cute peasant blouse she'd worn today—mistake—with skinny jeans, she checked the filing cabinet for a place to store the papers. Not much help since she ended up adding the haphazardly stuffed paperwork in the cabinet to her collection on top of the desk. Two hours later, three neat piles replaced the earlier disaster: shop work invoices, vendor bills and what she deemed miscellaneous.

It was the miscellaneous pile that caught her attention. Making sure everyone in the shop was busy, she slowly read through each page. The documents varied from bank notices to insurance reports. She pored over each one, searching for something out of place. Just before she reached the bottom, one page stood out.

The bold letterhead declared Griffin Enterprises. She lifted her head. Why did that seem familiar? She racked her brain, but couldn't find the connection. Yet for some reason the name stood out.

The contents were random numbers and dates. She couldn't risk taking the time to decipher it here, so she snapped a quick picture with her phone, then continued scrutinizing the rest of the pile, but nothing jumped out.

Moving to the filing cabinet, she straightened the drawers stuffed with folders. In alphabetical order, each folder was recorded with a neatly printed name. The writing looked female, most likely Stella's work. How far back did the information in each file go?

She had her answers soon enough. Most files hadn't been updated in six months, which pretty much lined up with the piles on Rico's desk. Curious, she fingered through to G and found a vague file heading: GE. She pulled the folder. Empty.

"Shoot."

Quickly returning it, she checked for any files on Marcus King. Just a few random receipts. Nothing to tie the two men together besides the legitimate side work, which would have been way too easy.

Going back to square one, she patiently read the contents of each folder, but found much of the same garage business. Well, at least she had one name to go on.

Glancing around, she groaned at the folders on the floor. "Not today."

Ready to discuss her neat piles with her new boss, she looked over her handiwork, hands on her hips. "Not bad."

Her gaze settled on the computer and, out of curiosity, she switched it on. The old thing took forever to boot up. Once the main page popped up, she hunted for a VIN replacement program, with no luck. No surprise, really. What did she expect? A flashing icon leading her to illegal activity? If there was anything fishy going on, Rico kept the info stored elsewhere.

It didn't take long to find the business program for the auto shop. She fished out the invoices she'd found around the office and began to enter information.

"What are you doing?"

She glanced over her shoulder to find Rico in the doorway. "Entering invoices."

"Did I tell you to do that?"

She rose. "I thought it would be helpful. Some of these go back a few months."

He stepped farther into the room. "I've gotten behind. Don't have the patience to enter numbers."

"Since I work on computers for my other job, this is a piece of cake."

"Really. You don't mind data entry?"

"Not at all."

He waved his hand toward the computer. "Okay, then. Carry on."

He turned to leave but Eloise stopped him. "I do have a few questions, if you don't mind."

With a look of impatience, he nodded. "Shoot."

She pointed to the miscellaneous pile on the desk. "I wasn't sure how to file or categorize this group of papers."

Rico riffled through them, a frown creasing his brow. "These are just some old things that got mixed up here. I'll take them out back."

"Is there anything else I should be aware of that belongs out back?"

"If you aren't sure, bring it to me."

An opening she could use to investigate the other office. Success had her heart racing. "Gotcha."

He took the papers and left. She'd made a good dent in the invoice pile when Dante stuck his head in the office.

"Anything?" he asked, voice low.

"Not yet," she mouthed.

He nodded and said with more volume, "Looks good in here."

Eloise stretched, a grin curving her lips. "I'm surprised I made this much headway."

"I'm not." He lowered his voice to a pitch only she could hear. "I've seen your desk at the department."

"And?"

"Nothing. You have great organizational skills."

"Thanks?"

"It was a compliment."

"Sometimes I'm not sure with you."

"And sometimes I tease you too much." He glanced at his watch. "It's quitting time for you. Want to grab dinner during my break?"

"Sure." She powered down the computer and set the work she'd continue tomorrow off to the side.

"Shouldn't I tell Rico I'm leaving?"

"Yep." He sent her what she'd deemed his supersecret-undercover grin that not only conveyed undercover code—*yes, go see what the boss is up to and report to me*—but sent cascades of shivers across her skin. "And it just so happens he's out back."

"Imagine that." She grinned.

Making her way through the stuffy garage, Eloise took a deep breath once she stepped outside, controlling a rush of anticipation along with the pulse-pounding aspect of police work she shared with Dante. Knowing answers might lie ahead. Drawing one step closer to figuring out the puzzles of the case. She balled her fists together to calm down.

The heat of the day had passed; the temperature had dropped and the air was fresh and welcoming. After being stuck in a small office, her nose bombarded by stale food, oil and car parts, the refreshing evening air revived her. Following a worn path through the scraggly grass scattered around the lot, she came to a brick structure. There were no windows, one door and a humming portable air-conditioning unit sticking out of the wall. She knocked on the door. Once. Twice, before it swung open.

"Huh?"

"Sorry to bother you, Mr. Battles. I wanted to let you know I'm leaving and will finish up tomorrow."

"Let's get one thing straight," he said.

Oh, no. I shouldn't have come back here.

She tugged her purse strap tighter over her shoulder. "Yes?"

"Call me Rico."

She eased out a breath. "Right. Rico, it is."

Over his shoulder she could partially see into the room. A more updated computer system streamed information over a large screen. This was definitely the hub of Rico's business. And the system to which she most needed to gain access.

"See you tomorrow," he said, already closing the door.

"Yes."

Returning to the shop, Dante met her on the way. "What do you say we grab a sandwich? Then you can bring me back here."

She raised a brow in question. His barely perceptible nod gave her the heads-up. *Not now.*

"Sounds good to me."

He took her hand, eliciting another shiver, waving to his coworkers with the other. "Going to have dinner with my wife. Later."

Ramsey grinned. Mac glared.

"Do those two have any different facial expressions?" Eloise asked under her breath.

"No. That's pretty much it."

At the passenger door, he dropped an unexpected kiss on her lips. Her breath lodged in her throat and her eyes went wide. When he pulled away, she started to ask him what he was up to, but he placed a finger against her lips to hush her.

"Can't resist giving my wife a kiss."

Right. His wife. The cover.

Sheesh. She needed to remember that.

IT ONLY TOOK a few minutes to drive to a nearby sandwich shop, but the silence in the truck made the ride seem five times longer. Okay, he'd told Eloise no more kissing but they still needed to maintain their cover.

"You mad at me?"

She blew out a sigh. "No. I realize you kissed me for show."

Or not.

"You just caught me off guard."

His fingers tightened on the steering wheel. "Sorry. Seemed like a good time."

"I agree. Mac is waiting for you to make a mistake so he can pounce."

"True. He still doesn't trust me."

"I suppose that's good. Supports your role."

Dante shot her a sidelong glance. "What did you say to him? He came over and clapped me on the back. Said he didn't envy me being married."

"I simply reminded him to look after his own laundry."

Dante chuckled. "Good for you."

She shrugged. "I never liked people who assumed things about others, especially women."

"Me, neither. My mom was always big on being respectful, especially to women."

"She sounds wonderful."

"Yeah. She is."

"Any luck finding information on her new boyfriend?"

"Dylan hasn't gotten back to me. I'm assuming he either hasn't learned a thing, or he did and took care of it."

"Without filling you in?"

"If necessary."

"Sounds like you and your brother are a lot alike."

He stopped at a red light and turned his head to her. "Why would you say that?"

"You always take care of a situation immediately. Good or bad. I imagine if your brother has confronted your mom without telling you or your brothers, that means he's sorted out the matter."

"Huh." He never would have pegged him and Dylan being similar, but as Eloise pointed out, Dylan did have a knack for taking over without first running it by his superiors. Isn't that exactly what Dylan had done in Cypress Pointe when he had a lead on a notorious drug dealer? He'd gone undercover at the florist convention to dig up intel. And his hunch was right. In the end, he caught the bad guy and got the girl.

"I never looked at it that way."

"You should."

Traffic moved along and he pulled into a full parking lot. He found a spot and parked. Before Eloise could exit the truck, he placed his hand on hers. "Thanks."

"For what?"

"Seeing the similarity. Trust me, no one in my family would ever have noticed it."

"I'm not family," she said as she opened the door.

True. But wouldn't it be nice?

Once inside the crowded shop, they placed their orders. The yeasty scent of freshly baked bread made his stomach growl. Taking a seat at a table in the corner, Dante noted the excited expression on Eloise's face and hoped she'd found evidence they could use.

Eloise glanced over her shoulder, then leaned closer to the table, her voice low. The din of the busy shop kept the conversation private. "I found something but I don't know what it means."

The kick of adrenaline shot through him. "Go on."

"Most of the paperwork in Rico's office has to do with the shop. Legitimate work. But I found a paper with Griffin Enterprises letterhead. Sound familiar to you?"

He thought for a moment. "No."

"The second I saw the name I knew I'd seen or heard it somewhere, but I can't pinpoint the source. When I get home tonight I'll search."

"Think it might be the lead we've been hoping for?"

"We'll see."

He grinned. "Never like to get ahead of yourself, do you?"

"No. I prefer hard facts."

A server came to the table to drop off their orders.

Dante lifted his roast beef and Swiss on a crusty roll and before taking a bite asked, "Anything else?"

Eloise lifted the top half of her bread, added mustard to her turkey from the bottle on the table. "When Rico opened the door to the building out back, I could see a very sophisticated computer system running. He insists he doesn't like working on them—I mean, have you seen the dinosaur in his business office? Anyway, he has to know a thing or two about the computer to get around what I glimpsed on the screen."

"We need to find a way inside?"

"Yes. He warned me away from the building, but did give me an opening when he said I could bother him with questions." She grinned at him. "Tomorrow I'll have questions."

"And maybe more information about Griffin Enterprises."

She placed the bread back on her sandwich, then tapped a finger on her temple. "It's right there, but I can't place it."

"It'll come to you. Don't force it."

She took a bite of her sandwich and chewed. He liked watching her, the dainty way she ate or how her eyebrows angled when she was engrossed in a book. He'd caught her seated in the armchair in the living room a few nights ago, glasses on, reading a thick book. He silently stood out of the way, taking her in. Wondered what a real life with her would be like. Shook off his fancy. She needed someone more grounded than him. More serious.

Living with her was different than he'd expected. She wasn't bossy or critical of his housekeeping skills. He'd laughed when she thanked him for putting his dishes in the dishwasher when he was finished eating. What had she expected, that he was a slob?

"Have you ever had a roommate?"

She blinked. Swallowed. "No."

"I didn't think so."

She set the sandwich down. "Where did that come from?"

"Since living together, you thank me for doing little things around the house. Like you're surprised."

"I...um. Should I not say anything?"

"No. I like it."

He smiled at her befuddled expression, then resumed eating. They'd just finished when he reached across the table and linked her hand with his.

"What—"

"Ramsey just walked in," he said, voice low.

Instead of turning toward the door, Eloise tightened their grip. "What do you suggest?"

"Act like newlyweds?"

That is how Ramsey found them when he sauntered over, smiling at each other.

"Hey. Didn't know you two were coming here."

Dante looked up. "Ramsey. It's nearby."

As Ramsey greeted them, Dante didn't miss the strange light in his eyes.

"Care to join us?"

"Nah. I can see by the bread crumbs that you two are finished eating. I'll place an order and take it back to the shop." He smiled. "See ya."

He went about his business while Dante rose. "Let's get out of here."

She nodded and they hurried back to the truck.

"What's with the look?" Eloise asked as soon as they were in the cab.

"I don't know. I feel like Ramsey intentionally followed us."

"Why would he?"

"Don't know. Like you said, it's there—I

just can't put a finger on it." He started the ignition. "Listen, why don't you drop me off."

"You don't want the truck?"

"I do, but I want them to see us together like everything is normal. Then later when you pick me up, we can run by the warehouse again."

"It's not too soon?"

"Call it a hunch, but something feels off. Rico's been edgy all day and Ramsey... There's a gleam in his eyes I haven't seen before."

"Noted. I'll pick you up later."

Once back at the shop, Dante stopped the truck by the curb. He jumped out, holding the driver's-side door open for Eloise when she came around the vehicle. Before she could climb inside, he placed his hands on either side of her face and gave her a long, thorough kiss. Later he'd claim it was for show, but really, he needed this.

When he pulled back, Eloise slowly opened her eyes. "So, um, call me when you're ready for me to get you."

He planted another kiss on her lips, then walked backward to the open bay door, giving her a thumbs-up. Once she'd driven away, he turned. Mac stood behind him, arms crossed over his beefy chest.

"Really?"

Dante grinned his most charming newly-wed grin, then hurried off to work.

The hours passed by slowly. No VIN work tonight from what he could tell. Ramsey kept his distance but Dante felt the man's eyes on him when his back was turned. He'd have to get Eloise to dig deeper into this guy's background.

Just after midnight, Rico told him to head home. He called Eloise and she arrived fifteen minutes later.

"Are the others leaving, too?" she asked, pulling away from the curb.

"I think so."

"Should we still go by the warehouse?"

"Yes. Like I said, something is off."

When she arrived at the industrial park, Dante pointed to a parking area across the street from the warehouse containing the stolen vehicles. "Park in between those cars over there."

Eloise pulled into the lot and killed the engine. The taut silence in the cab bugged him, especially since they weren't tailing a suspect this time.

"Are we going to check it out?" Eloise asked.

He held up a hand. "Just a minute."

While they waited, she scrounged behind

the seat and pulled out a pair of binoculars. Handed them to Dante.

When he took them, their fingers brushed. "I'll bet you were a Girl Scout."

"I wish," she muttered under her breath.

Sure enough, a familiar car came down the main drag, slowing as it neared the warehouse. Dante lifted the binoculars. "Ramsey."

As they watched, Ramsey's beater rattled into the warehouse parking lot and halted close to the building. He opened the door and stood next to his car, surveying the area. After a few minutes, he got back inside. Drove to the end of the lot. Before turning on the main road, he sat there, idling. Scanning the lot he and Eloise were in?

Dante held his breath, ready to duck if Ramsey pulled into the area where they were hiding. Long moments passed, then Ramsey pulled out and drove back down the street.

Eloise blew out a breath. "That was close."

"When I first started at the garage, I didn't think Ramsey was a problem. Now? I'm not so sure." He turned to see her pretty face in half-shadows. She had that intense look about her. She was a lot tougher than she gave herself credit for. An intoxicating mix of strength and femininity he found increasingly attractive.

"We can't chance checking the warehouse tonight. We'll try again later."

As if reading his mind, Eloise said, "In the meantime, I'll dig deeper on Ramsey."

He nodded. Met her somber gaze. Something shifted. In the air, or him, he wasn't sure. All he knew was that they were in sync, more in tune than he'd ever been with any woman in his life. More than any other person, for that matter. The fact warmed and scared him at the same time. He didn't ever want her to regret teaming up with him.

CHAPTER ELEVEN

SATURDAY MORNING, A group of chattering women sat around Eloise's living room, gossiping and drinking coffee. Martha had been scheduled to host the craft group last night, but a few days earlier she'd confided in Eloise that she was feeling tired, and talked Eloise into moving the meeting to today at her house. She'd argued against it, not sure this was a smart move in light of her real purpose—catching criminals—but Martha wouldn't take no for an answer. And honestly, Eloise couldn't resist her. Dante had assured her it would be okay, but Eloise wasn't sure.

Standing in the kitchen doorway, she observed her guests. It felt odd, having women over to her place. With her focus always on work, she'd never had any real friends, except Brandy, but even their friendship was relatively new. There were never late nights at her apartment, sitting around with girlfriends drinking wine and telling stories. Eloise had always been the odd woman out, in high school through college, until landing a position on the police force, and even then, she still held back. Witnessing the comfort level of the ladies here today, she keenly realized she'd missed out on the opportunity of wonderful camaraderie with others. The shame of it was that, once the case was over, so would these new friendships.

"Dear, you seem a very long way from here," Martha said as she carried a tray of warm muffins, right out of the oven. The scent of blueberries and sweet spices made Eloise's tummy grumble.

Shaking off her thoughts, she grabbed hold of the oven mitts and transferred the tray from Martha to herself. "Sorry. Just thinking, when I should be enjoying everyone's company."

"You act like this is the first time you've entertained."

"It is."

"Since you've been married?"

"No. First time ever."

Wide-eyed, Martha leaned against her cane. "You've never had friends to your house?"

Eloise felt her cheeks heat. "I don't really have many friends. Only one, really." But Eloise couldn't invite Brandy here today.

"Surely you had girlfriends over when you were younger. Sleepovers, perhaps?"

"My parents weren't big on having people at the house."

An understatement if there ever was one. Sylvia and Jonathan Archer were either at the college teaching classes or in their offices. And when they were home, they liked it to be just the two of them, with Eloise tucked away in her room.

"Then it's a good thing you moved to this neighborhood," Martha said. A grin flashed across her face, like she'd come up with an idea. "You know, you should host the craft group every time it's my turn."

"Martha, I don't want to overstep."

"I'm just not up to readying the house for guests these days."

An alarm triggered in Eloise. "Are you okay?"

Martha waved away her concern. "Just getting old. If you take over, I can visit with the ladies and you can do all the work."

Eloise laughed. "I should have known you had an ulterior motive."

"When you get to be my age, you can make all the excuses you want."

"Agreed."

Eloise followed Martha into the living room, setting the tray on the coffee table. While Martha sank into the comfy armchair, Stella eyed the goodies with an evil eye. Yes, Eloise had invited the boss's wife and, to her surprise, Stella showed up. Eloise had invited Stella on a whim when they ran into each other at the grocery store. She'd explained the harrowing ordeal of cleaning Rico's office and Stella was suitably embarrassed, enough to make sure she couldn't turn down the invitation.

The second part of Eloise's plan hinged on the two women comparing notes about Rico's untidy office, hoping to learn more about the operation at the auto shop.

"Ellie Smith, you've seen all the hard work it takes to go to the spa and buy new clothes. Now you want to sabotage me with that calorie-laden muffin? I won't fit into my new outfits."

Betsy from across the street, blonde and perky to Stella's dark and exotic eye-tilt, chimed in, "You can always work out with me."

"Do I look like I exercise?" Stella shivered. At ten in the morning, she was in full makeup and a trendy outfit with high-heeled shoes, compared to the other casually dressed women. Eloise had settled on shorts, an off-the-shoulder shirt and sandals.

"If you want to keep wearing those clothes," another woman, Marie, piped in, then took a big bite of a muffin. This led to good-natured banter and a promise by Stella to consider a trip to the gym.

Martha clapped her hands together. "Now, ladies. Let's get started." She leaned over the basket at her feet. "I understand most of you are novices when it comes to knitting."

Eloise held back a groan. Despite purchasing skeins of yarn and supplies during her shopping trip with Martha, Eloise still hadn't mastered the technique, no matter how many times she watched a tutorial on YouTube.

Stella's long fingernails snagged on the unraveled yarn in her lap. "I don't see the appeal," she groused as she tried to roll it into a ball.

"Stella, dear, you spend too many hours shopping," Martha gently scolded. "Why not sit back and make something of your own?"

Holding up a long length of yellow yarn, Stella said, "Because buying already made is easier."

"But not as much fun."

Eloise, who had already wound her yarn of variegated shades of blue into a ball, tried to maneuver the needles. "We can do this, Stella. After all, we've both tackled Rico's office."

Stella snorted. "I got tired of yelling at him all the time. Truthfully, the office was my domain when I worked there. It wasn't until he started pulling in extra work that he sent me on my way, extra cash in my pocket." The woman's exotic eyes barely hid a sheen of hurt. "I'm not complaining, but if I didn't know better, I'd think my husband was trying to get me out of the way."

Hmm. Rico had cause to prevent his wife from working at the office. If he went so far as to throw cash at Stella as a way to keep her busy, Eloise wagered Stella had no clue why.

Listening intently to Martha's instructions, Stella muttered under her breath.

Not wanting to push the conversation about the auto shop, Eloise focused on the task at hand and slowly got the hang of it. She should make Dante a scarf, not that he'd probably use it here in Florida, but it was the thought that counted. As she listened to her guests talk about their lives, husbands and children, a pervading sense of shame made her uneasy.

These women were fast becoming her friends. Yet here she sat, a fraud. And worse, her actions would definitely hurt Stella. Yes, her husband may be a criminal, but Eloise never got the impression Stella was involved in his activities. The earlier thread of their conversation confirmed this. Dante had warned her to distance herself emotionally, but how could she do that? She needed to spend time with the neighbors to keep her cover, but these were good people. She liked them. Especially Martha.

She'd miss sharing early-morning coffee with her elderly neighbor when she went back to work at the department. She and Martha talked easily about any topic. Eloise had revealed a bit of her unhappy childhood and was rewarded by Martha's concern and assurance that Eloise had turned out just fine. They'd grown close in such a short time and Eloise cherished spending time with a woman she was quickly coming to think of as family.

And what of the others? She wouldn't see Betsy running after little Baxter in the yard. Wouldn't go shopping with Stella, but then again, if Rico was in as deep as Dante thought, Stella wouldn't be engaging in any more high-end shopping trips, anyway. And what about their kids? What would happen to them?

If the ache in her chest was any indication, maybe her own parents not encouraging personal relationships hadn't been such a bad idea. She was starting to feel part of a circle of friends, and once the investigation was over, she'd be alone, like she'd always been.

Hot tears blurred her vision. Trying to blink them away without anyone noticing, she looked up and met Martha's gaze. Compassion sparkled in the other woman's eyes. What did she know? And how could Eloise hide her emotions from this kind woman?

"I'm going to make some more coffee," Eloise announced, abandoning her knitting needles and yarn to escape into the kitchen.

Once away from curious eyes, she rested her hands on the counter and took deep breaths. Gaining control, she dumped the old grounds from the basket and proceeded to fill a clean filter with scoops of fresh coffee.

"Is something wrong, dear?"

Eloise angled her back to Martha, closing her eyes. Now what did she do?

"It's nothing."

"Sure seems like something to me."

Eloise could hear Martha crossing the room. "Are things okay with Dan?"

Briskly wiping her eyes, Eloise turned. "We're fine."

"His odd hours aren't bothering you?"

"No. I get to spend mornings with him."

"Then what is it?"

"I…" She turned, waved her hand in the direction of the other room. "You've all accepted me so easily."

"Why wouldn't we? You're a very special woman."

No, I'm not.

"What if I can't live up to your friendships?" she questioned, guilt hounding her.

"You already passed the test by opening your home to us *and* getting Stella to a neighborhood function that doesn't require hours spent in the mall."

The knife in her heart twisted. "I don't want to disappoint you."

Martha moved closer, placed a comforting hand on Eloise's arm. "I suspect there's more going on here."

Throat clogged, all Eloise could do was nod.

"My dear, don't worry about what others think. You must be true to yourself."

Did her truth only consist of the job? Getting the promotion? What about these women? What about her growing feelings for Dante?

When she'd first been given the assignment, her focus had been all about apprehending the bad guys. That was the part of law enforcement that gave her satisfaction—getting criminals off the street. To protect and serve. But in serving, she was deceiving these good people, the ones who deserved her full protection.

If anything, going undercover magnified her goal of attaining the promotion. She belonged in the office, not here among people she'd never see again. She knew what she wanted: dealing with procedural issues rather than in the thick of an operation. She had to carry through, successfully, to move up in rank, even if it meant Dante didn't get the sergeant's position.

And that made her feel just as bad as lying to these women.

"I just think I want more for my life."

"You aren't happy being married?"

"No. Dan is great and we get along. It's just..."

"Just what, dear?"

"Living here these past few weeks has been a whole new world for me. I'll miss it."

"Why on earth would you miss it? Unless..." Martha's face fell. "Are you thinking of leaving?"

"No. I mean, maybe eventually." Eloise shook her head. "I've enjoyed our times together. You've treated me like family and I'll never forget it."

"You're starting to worry me."

Eloise swiped at her watery eyes. "I'm just being silly. Grateful you're all here and ready to get back to our crafting."

Martha grabbed a tissue from the box on the counter. "When you're ready to confide in me, I'm only a short walk away," Martha told her. "We'll straighten this out."

If only that were true. By the time this op

wrapped up, Eloise would be back home and these friends would wonder whatever happened to Ellie and Dan Smith. All her training hadn't equipped her for the reality of the emotions resulting from being undercover.

Taking the tissue, Eloise blotted her eyes. Isn't this what she'd always wanted? To feel included? Why did she have to discover it now?

"Where's the... Oh." Betsy stopped in the middle of the kitchen. "Sorry to interrupt."

Eloise placed a hand over her swirling stomach. So much for keeping her gloomy mood a secret. She dashed a quick glance at Martha, then said, "It's okay. We were just chatting."

Betsy tilted her head, looked down at the hand Eloise had placed over her stomach and back up again. "You do seem a little... emotional today."

Eloise waved the tissue and laughed. "Don't mind me. It's nothing."

"What's nothing?" Stella asked as she joined the group, followed by Marie, who carried the nearly empty muffin tray and set it on the table.

"Eloise is crying over nothing," Betsy answered.

The room went silent. As the women exchanged glances, Eloise realized the dynamic had changed and she had no idea what was going on.

"And how long have you been upset over nothing?" Stella asked.

"I don't know. Recently."

"Is your stomach upset?" Marie asked.

"A little. What's with all the questions?"

Marie's head began to bob up and down. A knowing smile spread over Stella's lips. Then Betsy burst out, "Oh, my gosh. You're pregnant!"

Eloise blinked. Pregnant. What on earth…?

"I recognize the look," Betsy went on to say. "You've been preoccupied all morning and you have that queasy tummy expression."

"No. I'm not pregnant."

"Have you taken a test?" Stella asked.

"No. Because I'm not pregnant."

"How can you be sure if you don't take the test?" Marie asked as if Eloise were dense.

"Oh, dear," Martha muttered. "I'm afraid I've opened a can of worms."

"It's okay," Betsy said. "We were bound to find out soon enough."

"I'm not pregnant," Eloise repeated, drowned out by the flurry of comments and advice.

"I have a wonderful doctor I can refer you to," Betsy said.

"Oh, and we must go shopping for baby clothes," Stella interjected.

Frustrated now, Eloise held up her hands

and said loudly, "I'm not pregnant," just as the door to the garage opened and Dante stepped into the kitchen.

PREGNANT? ELOISE? DANTE stopped in his tracks.

The women went silent when he appeared, then they started talking all at once. He only had eyes for Eloise, her cheeks a bright red and a beseeching expression in her eyes.

He pushed his way through the group and leaned against the counter beside her. "Ellie, do you have something to tell me?"

She rolled her eyes. "Help," she whispered.

Taking pity on her, he held up a hand. "Ladies. How about you give my wife and me a minute."

The ladies happily agreed, moving back to the living room talking about babies and child rearing.

He struggled not to laugh. "Pregnant?"

"Martha and I were talking and I was kind of crying and Betsy jumped to conclusions."

He raised a brow.

"It would make sense if you'd been here."

"I'm glad I wasn't," he replied, grabbing a muffin and taking a bite.

"I wish I wasn't."

Chuckling, he finished off the muffin.

"What're you doing home? Thought you had a special morning shift."

"Rico let us go."

"Anything new happen?"

"Nah. Same old."

Since the night Dante had been sure Ramsey was following them, he hadn't learned anything new, but had heard an interesting conversation today before heading home.

"I should probably go in there," Eloise said, dread evident in her voice.

"It's not a firing squad," he teased. "It can't be that bad."

"Really? No one thinks you're pregnant."

"Yeah, well…impossible."

She playfully punched him in the arm and left the room.

Grinning, he went to his room and gathered up a change of clothing. Discreetly carrying a T-shirt and jeans to the master bedroom, he went inside and closed the door to change. When he reemerged, he leaned against the doorjamb, watching Eloise. The needles in her hands clicked as she threaded yarn over her fingers, top teeth worrying her lower lip. Could she be any more beautiful? Once he took his eyes from her, he noticed all the women were smiling at him and he understood Eloise's predicament. So he did what every good husband who didn't want to be a part of the conversation did; he escaped to the garage to work on his muscle car.

With a yank, he raised the garage door to let in the spring breeze. Before hoisting the hood, he gazed around. On the walls and piled in corners were years of stuff suburban home-owners collected. A box marked Christmas Tree on an overhead rack next to boxes with the printed word Ornaments. Tools neatly lined the workbench. A washer and dryer sat in the far corner near the kitchen door. Dust and cement gave the space a musty scent. He moved to the bench and opened his tool chest, the metal cool under his fingers. The sense of contentment that came whenever he began to turn wrenches soothed him.

He was getting antsy; he could feel it. Things at the auto garage were moving too slowly, but he hoped that would change. He'd overheard Rico talking on the phone, making a big deal about Tuesday night. He was more than ready for something important to happen.

Shaking off his mood, since he still had the weekend to get through, he focused on the pristine car engine. He'd been playing around with it for a while, adding specific requests from the buyer he'd already had lined up. Even though he was on the job, he'd promised a

252 THE LAWMAN'S SECRET VOW

due date for the customer and needed to keep working.

You could do this full-time.

The voice that reminded him he could make a good living from his mechanic skills mocked him. It hadn't been the first time, and like all the times before, he brushed it away. Ignored it. *You're a cop, like your father and brothers.*

Grabbing a socket wrench, he blocked the words he didn't want to hear and went to work. Engrossed in the project, he didn't realize how much time had passed until the ladies were in the driveway saying their goodbyes. Minutes later, Eloise came into the garage, two glasses of iced tea in hand. She set his on the workbench.

From her pensive look, he concluded she had something on her mind. He waited while she unfolded a lawn chair, set it at the head of the car and took a seat.

Finally, she said, "How do you do this?"

He knew she was talking about the job. "Pretend?"

She nodded.

"I'd say it gets easier, but it doesn't. I guess over time you just learn to handle it better. When the perp goes to jail and you've done your job, the end justifies the means."

"What about the people who end up being collateral damage?"

"There will always be those people. But we have to remember why we do the job."

Taking a sip of her tea, she stared at the headlights. When she didn't speak again, he went back to work, enjoying the companionable silence.

"You really like working with tools, don't you? You seem less…" She looked at the ceiling as she came up with the word. "Fidgety."

He wasn't surprised Eloise noticed. She had a keen eye.

"Tinkering with cars either helps me work through a problem or gives me some downtime. Depends what's going on in my life."

"I'm like that at the department. I actually like writing reports. Documenting an arrest or procedure."

"Everyone knows."

A slight grin curved her lips. "My parents wanted me to be a college professor. Like them. They were shocked when I decided on law enforcement."

"I could see you in the ivory tower."

"I love to read and am happiest with a book in my hands, but I wanted to do something more productive. More tangible. There is nothing wrong with teaching the classics, but my folks never considered anything beyond that world. I wanted more and the idea of protecting people's safety latched onto my brain and wouldn't let go."

"Do you see your folks much?"

"Not often. They're busy and I don't always fit into their schedule."

"That's cold."

"No. It's my parents. I've learned to accept we'll never be a warm, loving family."

"But you'd like to be."

"Yes. I suppose that's why bonding with these new friends bothers me so much."

"I get it."

A car zoomed down the street, followed by an angry yell. Silence returned, broken only by the occasional chirp of a bird.

"What's it like?" Eloise asked. "Coming from a large family?"

He leaned over the side of the car to peer in, loosening a bolt. "Claustrophobic."

"Sounds wonderful."

He lifted a brow at her dreamy expression. "I could see, as an only child, why you'd feel that way."

"But you don't?"

They were going to have this conversation? With a sigh, he stood, rested his hip against the Challenger. Decided what he should tell her.

"It was great when we were kids. We did all the usual stuff—family vacations, holiday dinners, birthday parties. My mom fussed over all her boys." He paused. Swallowed hard. "She was devastated when Dad died."

"So all of you, being good sons, decided to become overly protective?"

"We do keep an eye out for her. She's never been interested in another man before, so you can understand our concern."

"Maybe she's ready to move on with her life."

"And maybe we reserve the right to check up on any guy she starts dating."

Eloise's brow wrinkled. "That is awfully intrusive."

"Fair play," he said, glimpsing Eloise's annoyed expression. "You've never met my mother. She's made the act of interference an art. If I'd even breathed the fact that I had a female partner and we were pretending to be married, she'd already have a date at the church, reception venue booked and the baby room all planned out, even though we're on the job, not dating."

Eloise blinked like a deer in the headlights. "Oh, my."

"Yeah." He grinned, pride in his voice when he said, "She's good."

"Okay, your mom is a bit intense. And you

and your brothers were competitive growing up. Sounds idyllic to me."

"It was. But once we got old enough to outdo each other, things changed. I was about thirteen when I noticed it."

"In what way?"

"We were always trying to surpass each other. If Derrick made the softball team, Dylan also tried out for the team, made it *and* played football. Then Derrick had to make the basketball team. If Deke aced all his science classes, Derrick scored higher in his classes." The old frustration he thought he'd outgrown tugged at him. "It wasn't mean-spirited or ugly competition, it was just…exhausting."

Eloise crossed one bare leg over the other. "I imagine as the youngest you tried to best your brothers, too?"

"Yeah. But I wasn't as interested in sports like they were. And school?" He shrugged. "I did okay but I was no academic genius."

She nodded to the car. "This was your outlet."

He chuckled. "I was fidgety even as a child. My father saw my interest in anything mechanical, and through a process of elimination, we started working on cars together."

"You got to work off all that excess stamina and spend time with your dad."

"Best times of my life."

Daryl Matthews had figured out a way to channel Dante's energy and make it fun at the same time. They'd had more conversations about how to be a man over a brake job than sitting around the kitchen table or throwing a ball back and forth in the yard. His father made sure to have one special activity reserved with each of his sons, and now, years later, Dante missed him keenly.

"Fixing a problem with my hands made me feel like I'd accomplished something. I didn't have to prove myself, not to my folks or my brothers. I'm good fixing mechanical problems so my little hobby made me the family fix-it-all."

"Why did you go into law enforcement instead of working as a mechanic?"

He froze. Answered the question the way he always did instead of admitting the truth—that when he was on the job he wasn't the younger brother trying to prove himself. He wasn't annoying others by trying to work off his nervous energy. Instead, he said, "Everyone in my family is in law enforcement. I had to."

She peered at him for a long moment. "Had to because of family pressure or because you wanted to fit in?"

Now she was getting downright personal. "Has anyone ever told you you ask too many questions?"

"Yes." She wagged a finger at him. "And you can't evade my question. It's just the two of us here."

He pushed from the car. Paced beside it. "I wanted to become a cop. My father was police commissioner, and from the time we were toddlers, he emphasized the greater good. It didn't take much for Derrick and Dylan to jump on the bandwagon. They idolized everything about my dad's job."

"Deke?"

"Not as much. He had childhood allergies so he spent a lot of time indoors with his head in a book." He grinned. "Kind of like you."

"You said he's in forensics now?"

"He found a way to take his love for science and marry it to criminal investigation. He's good at it, too."

"Let me guess. You chose undercover work because it keeps you under the radar. That way you don't have to connect with other people if you don't want to. You go in, get the job done and get out."

He frowned. Is that why he liked going undercover? He'd never really analyzed it, but it made sense. He was actually good at his job, even though most days he felt like a poser.

"My dad, my brothers…they all belong in law enforcement. Most of the time I feel like I simply have something to prove."

He'd never said those words out loud before. Oddly enough, with Eloise, it seemed like the right time to confide the truth. To the right person.

She stood and came to stand beside him. Her perfume transfixed his senses, and when her long hair brushed over his shoulder, he fisted his hands together to keep from bringing her into an embrace.

"You are good at your job, you know."

Dante sent her a sidelong glance. "Really? I don't think our superiors would agree with that assessment."

"You have a tendency to be the lone wolf too often. That's their main concern."

"I've always worked better alone." Their shoulders brushed. "Until now. We make a good team."

"We do. But we still have our work cut out for us."

"Are you finished grilling me about my family?"

Her small smile didn't quite dispel the sadness in her eyes. "For now."

Back to business. Good. He'd revealed too much of himself already. And from the way Eloise distanced herself from the conversation she'd initiated, so had she.

"I overheard Rico on the phone this morning. Something is planned for Tuesday."

She angled away from him, outrage plain on her face. "And you are just now telling me?"

"Well, between you entertaining guests and the pregnancy rumor, I didn't have a chance."

She coughed out a laugh. "I can't believe they misinterpreted hiding my guilt with being pregnant."

"You're the right age. We're married. It was an honest mistake."

"I guess." She settled back beside him. "Back to Tuesday. What's going on?"

"I'm not sure, but I hope it's a break in the case. We need some action."

"I've still been trying to find anything on Griffin Enterprises. No luck so far."

"Keep digging. You'll discover something."

Their gazes met and held. He wanted to lean closer.

You're straddling the line again, Matthews.

She blinked and the connection was gone. "Thanks. When we go back to the garage next week, we'll need to be especially vigilant. It feels like we're getting close."

True, but the closeness he was worried about was this domestic situation with Eloise. He liked being pretend married to her way too much for both their sakes.

CHAPTER TWELVE

BY FOUR O'CLOCK Tuesday afternoon, Eloise still waited for Rico to make some sort of move. Dante had seemed sure that whatever Rico had been discussing on the phone was a big deal. When a normal day passed, she wondered if what Dante overheard was incorrect. Still, there was an underlying tension in the shop that couldn't be missed.

Finally making headway in the data entry, Eloise hoped that Rico would allow her access to the second office. Her fingers itched to open files on his computer and find out just how deeply entrenched her boss was in this car theft ring. Just in case she had a shot, she'd been carrying a flash drive in her shorts pocket. There was no doubt Rico was involved in one way or another, at least moving stolen vehicles. The big man was dodgy and nervous, constantly looking over his shoulder. And with Ramsey now dogging Dante, the brittle tension in the garage rose daily.

After a more sweeping background check, it

turned out Ramsey had been a person of interest many years ago in a smuggling ring case, but no charges were filed. The man appeared clean, at least on paper. But now?

The blinking cursor on the computer screen snagged her attention and Eloise went back to her task, her mind mulling over events so far. Dante was sure this garage was changing VINs. They'd followed a carrier with assumed stolen vehicles to a warehouse, which they'd checked to discover were still parked inside. Eventually, the cars had to be moved to the final destination, but when and where? Ramsey was suddenly interested in them, his mood changing from easygoing to dark and suspicious. All in all, the scenario raised more questions than answers. With a sigh, she continued typing.

A knock on the door startled her. She looked up to find Dante, hands braced on either side of the doorjamb, a frown marring his brow. He glanced over his shoulder and back, then lowered his voice. "Anything?"

She shook her head.

He rubbed a hand over his chin. "Maybe I misunderstood."

"It's possible, but Rico's been jumpy all day."

"I noticed that, too."

She closed the program and powered down the computer. "I've been putting it off, but Rico mentioned he wants me to run out for parts. It's getting late. I don't have an excuse not to go."

"You should get moving. We need to act as normal as possible."

She grabbed her wallet, keys and cell phone. "I have to get the list from the boss. I'll see you later."

He nodded and squeezed her hand as she passed by. Shivers cascaded over her, but she ignored them. She met his intent gaze for a moment, imagined that the uneasiness she glimpsed in his eyes matched her own. The longer the op went on, the more antsy they both became.

The boss was nowhere to be found in the hectic garage. Mac was singing, off-tune and loud, over the rattling generator. Dante returned to the oil change he'd started, tossing an empty bottle in the nearby trash can. A customer paced the sidewalk out front, talking on his cell phone, while waiting for his car. The prevailing scent of gasoline turned her stomach, already churning with the anxiety of waiting for something to happen.

Ramsey was also missing, unusual when they were this busy.

If Rico wasn't in the garage, he was sure to be found in his other office. She headed there, stopping short when she spied Rico and Ramsey standing in the grass outside the building out back and having an intense conversation. Anticipation spiking, she eased back into the garage, peeking around the open bay door to spy. Rico's face had turned a bright red, his hands flying as he rapidly spoke. Ramsey gave him a slit-eyed look, cutting into Rico's tirade to make his point. Clearly, there was a major debate going on. One that might help their investigation?

"I don't care what you're doing," Ramsey said, his voice louder as he spoke over his boss. "We need to go now."

"I can't leave. You know that."

"Quit with the excuses. This is important."

Rico ran a shaky hand through his dark hair, his expression torn.

"You agreed to this."

Rico clapped Ramsey on the shoulder. "Fine. Let's go."

Seeing her chance, Eloise strolled out of the garage, purposefully running into the men.

"Hi, Rico." She nodded to the other man. "Ramsey."

Ramsey merely nodded, moving fast.

Angling into his path, she cut off Rico's passage. "Boss, do you have the parts list ready? I'm running out to the repair shop and want to make all my stops in one trip. Mac said we're nearly out of timing belts."

A flash of frustration crossed his face. "It's in my office out back. I'll have to get it later."

Eloise stood her ground. "But you told me we need the carburetor back by end of work today."

Rico faltered. "You're right, I did." He glanced at Ramsey, who had stopped when he realized Rico wasn't following.

"The repair shop called and said it's ready," she reminded him, pushing the issue since Rico looked to be operating on his very last nerve. "They close in thirty minutes."

"C'mon," Ramsey shouted, irritation deepening his voice.

Eloise made sure to keep a confused expression on her face, while secretly hoping they might slip up and reveal their mission. "Should I wait until tomorrow?"

"No," Rico snapped, digging in his front pocket. "We need the parts now." He tossed her a ring of keys. "The list is on my desk. Get it so you can pick up everything today."

She caught the ring. "Thanks."

"Hurry. I need the key back before I leave." She'd taken two steps when he yelled, "And no messing around in there. Get in and out, got it?"

"On it," she called, holding back the urge to cheer as she jogged to the building. Behind her, Rico and Ramsey renewed their argument. Before unlocking the door, she heard a phone ring. With a quick glance over her shoulder, she saw Rico take a call while Ramsey threw his hands up in the air.

Deftly unlocking the door, a haze of cigarette smoke assailed her as she entered. When had Rico started smoking? The other office was smoke-free. Could the stress be getting to him? Sure looked like it, especially with Ramsey goading him.

Once inside, she pulled the flash drive from her pocket and inserted it in the port on the hard drive. Her fingers ran over the keyboard as she pulled up the command to copy the system drive.

"Hurry, hurry," she muttered under her breath, not sure how much time she'd safely need to get the information. The screen showed the computer directories being copied. While waiting, she searched for the parts list, buried—surprise, surprise—under a stack of papers. As she moved things around, she bumped the ashtray, spilling stubs on the desktop. Her movements jerky, she scooped them back into the glass tray. The man really needed to learn how to keep his work spaces tidy.

Finally, a beep and the drive flashed at her. Extracting it, she shoved it in her pocket, made sure the screen looked the same, took the list and grabbed the door handle, just as Rico opened it and pushed in.

"What's taking so long?" he barked.

"Sorry," Eloise said, haltingly, heart racing. "I had to search your desk."

Rico stomped to the desk, investigating the area. He turned to her and held out his hand. She dropped the key ring in his palm.

"Let's go." His voice brooked no disobedience.

Eloise stepped outside, her mouth dry as she controlled her pumping heart. She hustled down the path, Rico muttering as he locked the door and fell into step behind her.

Her chest squeezed tight. What if she'd taken a few seconds longer? She would have been discovered and the entire op would have gone down the drain.

"When you finish the run, you can call it a day," Rico said as he caught up to her. He jumped into the front seat of Ramsey's old beater car, which seemed odd since Rico normally drove his flashy, brand-new and ironically immaculately clean red truck. Driving around in Ramsey's car was equivalent to driving around in his messy office.

"I will," she answered, truck keys in hand. Once inside, she blew out a gush of air and started the ignition, her hands trembling. She pulled into the street, unintentionally tailing the men in the car in front of her. Suddenly, an idea struck her. Why not deliberately follow them? No way was she going to miss this opportunity to find out what Ramsey was all stirred up about.

Ramsey turned right, but Eloise had to wait for cars to pass before pulling onto the main thoroughfare. It was already late afternoon; folks were starting their trek home, making traffic heavy. Her stomach sank when she immediately lost sight of the old car. Craning her neck, she kept driving, on the lookout for her quarry.

At the next light she caught a glimpse of the car, stopped in the left lane at the red light. Her blood pulsed. She still had a chance to discover their destination. When the light changed, she switched lanes, staying far enough behind as not to draw suspicion. The old car moved into a left-turn lane. Eloise, with a buffer of four cars ahead of her, also moved into the lane. She just made the turn before the light changed, again holding back so she wouldn't be noticed. Finally, Ramsey pulled into the parking lot of a strip mall. Eloise passed, turning in at a different section of the same center.

Parking at the far end, she gathered her bearings to get a lay of the land before observing the men. They stood on the sidewalk outside a cell phone store. Rico checked his watch while Ramsey kept up a conversation. Rummaging around behind the seat, she pulled out the binoculars so she could better see what transpired. The glasses zeroed in on Rico as he nervously tugged on a cigarette, smoke lifting over him in ragged puffs.

They must be waiting for someone. Grabbing the digital camera from the glove box, she readied it to take pictures.

Moments later three boys showed up. Well, more like young men, by the looks of it. Her pulse leaped again.

The boys wore hoodies, even in the heat of the day. Ramsey did most of the talking. One of the boys, his aggressive manner identifying him as the leader, held out his hand. Ramsey dropped an object into it and the boys nodded and started walking away. Ramsey grabbed one of the boys by the shoulder, yelled close to his face, then pushed him off. Eloise noticed a white lightning bolt on the back of the jacket. The leader shouted and gestured rudely at Ramsey, then they rounded the building and were out of sight. All the while, Eloise kept snapping pictures.

Not taking a chance at being discovered, Eloise backed out of the space, turned away from the men and pulled out into the street. A few blocks later she doubled back and went to the carburetor shop, thankfully making it before closing time. From there she finished her errands, securing everything on the boss's list.

On the way back to the garage, she puzzled over a niggling image from the scene she'd just witnessed. Finally, revelation slammed her. When she'd gone on the call to the Parson's Auto Mall the day after the car thefts, she remembered the perps in the surveillance video also wore black hoodies. They'd managed to keep their sides to the camera, but the video had picked up a white blur on the back of their jackets. She realized now it was a lightning bolt, just like the jackets of the boys she'd just seen walk away. She couldn't be 100 percent sure they were the same suspects, but her clenched gut shouted otherwise. When she got home, she'd pull up the crime scene video to compare.

Finally, a break. One they hadn't actually been searching for, but found just the same. Was Ramsey running the gang of kids who stole cars from dealerships? And if so, was it connected to the elusive head of whatever was going on? Were the cars she and Dante had seen loaded onto the carrier the other night the work of these boys? She couldn't wait to compare notes with Dante and see what he thought.

Arriving back at the garage, she handed the carburetor off to Mac before placing the parts in the supply room. She returned to the office to collect her belongings, then locked up the office for the day. Trying to contain her excitement, she forced herself to keep a measured walk as she made her way to Dante. He lowered a raised hood and turned, a genuine smile crossing his lips when he saw her. His warm gaze sent mind-of-their-own tingles over her skin.

"Heading home?" she asked, her tone nonchalant. She wanted to share her news.

"Yeah. No overtime tonight."

"Great. I have *news* I'm dying to share with you."

He cocked his head, brow crinkled until he grasped the code word. His eyes lit up, twinkling just the way she liked. "News, huh?"

"Yes. You're going to love it."

ON THE DRIVE HOME, Dante listened carefully as Eloise filled him in on her unexpected surveillance. As soon as they walked in the front door, she rushed to the home office, pulling up the Parson video.

"See," she said, pointing to the blurry image of what they now knew to be a lightning bolt on the back of the hoodies. "It has to be the same crew."

"Why risk getting noticed with a big old sign on your back?"

"These are kids, Dante. They want to make a statement, never considering the risk of getting caught."

"That is true," he muttered, pacing the room as restless energy zinged through his blood. "Okay, let's suppose these two enterprises are connected. Surely the person in charge wouldn't want these kids announcing who they are to the world."

"Ramsey did grab one of the boys before they left and yelled something at him. I couldn't make out the words. A warning, maybe?"

"If it were me, I'd be telling these kids to keep a low profile."

"If only it were that easy." Eloise sighed. "Remember the boy I arrested six months ago? His sister had stolen a car, crashed after a high-speed pursuit and died, yet he still continued to boost cars in the neighborhood."

He recalled the case. Eloise had been shaken

up afterward, but remained professional in spite of the circumstances. It was never easy when dealing with kids.

He stopped. "Then we agree Ramsey is probably the guy really in charge of illegal activities at the garage?"

"Yes. Despite his bluster, Rico crumbled under Ramsey's commands." She turned in her seat. "If we catch the boys in the act, we might be able to get them to turn on Ramsey."

He started pacing again. "Still, it doesn't get us to the top. There's no way these guys are operating alone."

"Dante, you have pictures of Mac changing VIN plates. Once I retrieve the data from the flash drive, I'm hoping there's more incriminating evidence. That alone will get Rico and Mac arrested. Then we make sure to connect the boys, and the stolen cars, to Ramsey. It will be a good bust."

"But it doesn't complete the investigation."

"Maybe, but we will have put a dent in the operation. Get these guys off the streets while we keep searching for the ringleader. If we press hard enough, dangle some incentives before them, maybe they'll give up the boss's identity."

Dante sent her a wry look. "You really think they're going to give in that easily?"

"No, but Rico has a family. The despair on his face today… It seemed like he finally realized he's in too deep. If giving us information can get charges reduced or at least give him a shot at a deal, he might be willing to offer up the names."

"I'm not disagreeing with you, but what else do we have to go on?" He pointed to the computer. "What about Griffin Enterprises? Have you figured out if it's the name of someone involved in this scheme?"

"No. All I know is that it seems to be a dummy corporation. It's registered offshore, has a very professional logo and a very vague website, but I can't find any legitimate business dealings. Every time I try to get into the internal workings, a firewall pops up. That alone rings bells. I finally sent the information to the department. Hopefully one of the techs can get to the bottom of it."

"Still a dead end."

"Unfortunately, for now."

While his mind worked overtime, Eloise placed the flash drive in the port. "Give me time to upload the files and study the data. Maybe we'll have more to go on." She waved him away. "Why don't you make dinner while I work?"

"Who can eat dinner at a time like this?"

"I can. I'm getting hungry. And to be honest, pacing behind me isn't going to make me analyze any faster."

"Right." He rubbed the back of his neck. "Any requests?"

Her fingers were already tapping over the keyboard. "Anything," she muttered, focused on the screen.

After changing out of his work clothes into a comfortable T-shirt and shorts, Dante got to work in the kitchen. He needed to give Eloise space, no matter how much he wanted to add his two cents. Preparing dinner would keep him busy until his partner finished up. Since he actually enjoyed cooking, he scoured the refrigerator, finding chicken and vegetables to toss together in a skillet.

Twenty minutes later the bold scent of garlic and spices permeated the kitchen. He'd just finished slicing fresh tomatoes for a salad when Eloise materialized.

"Mmm. Smells good in here."

"I found chicken in the fridge." He nodded to a pot on the stove. "Mind checking the rice?"

She placed the paper she was holding on the counter and removed the lid. "Finished."

"What did you find?" he asked, carrying the salad bowl to the table.

"Rico kept a file on the VINs. Since they are being cloned, he has the make and model of each car along with the new number recorded. I noticed a bar code label printer in his second office. That must be where he's creating the counterfeit VIN labels. I even discovered that he's creating vehicle title documents to match the new numbers."

"The mother lode." Dante whooped, grabbing Eloise and lifting her off her feet to twirl in a circle. She grabbed hold of his shoulders, her lilting laugher encasing his heart, and he found himself in deep water yet again.

The line, a voice whispered.

Setting her feet on the floor, he barely pulled away before she leaned in, her lips curved, her eyelids at half-mast. The air grew heavy around them. Between her welcome proximity and just plain being happy in her presence, he let her take the lead. Soon, her lips brushed and captured his. Her arms circled his neck and he tugged her close, neither in any hurry to disengage from the heated embrace.

The stove timer shrilled, a stark reminder that as much as Dante wanted Eloise in his life, it would have to wait. They wrenched apart, a telltale flush creeping across Eloise's face. There was no denying she enjoyed his attention, just as much as he enjoyed doling out kisses. The invisible line continued to be a barrier between them, but he couldn't dismiss the longing that had taken up residence in his heart the longer they were together.

Slowly releasing her, he moved to the stove and silenced the noisemaker, then removed the skillet from the burner and turned it off. Meanwhile, Eloise gathered plates and utensils, and before long, they were digging into their meal.

"Sorry about that," Dante started.

"No, I shouldn't have…"

He cleared his throat. "So, ah, how's the rice?"

"Fluffy."

At the choice of her one-word description, a smile tugged his lips. Yeah, Eloise was always surprising him.

After the awkwardness of their spontaneous embrace passed, Eloise said, "I can do a search. Find out where the original VINs were registered."

"Let's hope it eventually leads us directly to the head honcho."

Eloise placed her fork beside her plate. "I called Chambers. He's pleased with what we've uncovered."

At her expression. Dante pushed his food

around on his plate. "Why do I hear a 'but' coming?"

"Chambers agrees with me. We can arrest Rico now on the VIN tampering charges."

"But?"

"He also agrees we should keep at it until we can connect Ramsey to the gang. There was another dealership break-in last night. Four cars were stolen. It looked like they used the keyless entry devices again. I wonder if that's what Ramsey handed off to the boys?"

"I haven't seen anything like them at the garage."

"Me, neither. Chambers has a team pohring over surveillance video to find any similarities to the Parson's Auto Mall theft."

"Let me guess. Once we can prove Ramsey is working with the gang, the entire auto garage goes down."

"Yes," she said. "I know you think we should keep searching—"

He jumped up. "We're close, Eloise. I can feel it."

"But at the risk of losing what we can prove for sure?"

"I know you want the promotion, but we have to consider the big picture here."

She jerked back at his words. "You believe I want to stop now just to get the promotion?"

He ran a hand over his head. "It sure seems like it."

"I'm doing smart police work."

"We'd be doing better police work if we figured out who's heading this entire operation."

"Then I could throw your insinuation right back at you. You want to find the leader to secure your place in running for the promotion."

Did he? He wanted the job, but not enough to risk blowing the capture of the entire ring.

"I want the truth."

"So do I."

At the verbal standoff, Dante swooped up his plate and carried it to the sink. "How much time is he giving us?"

"Not much. As it is, I'm afraid Rico is spooked enough to take off. Chambers wants us to monitor Ramsey and eventually bring him in."

Pacing again, Dante tried to channel the frustration coursing through him.

"What about going back to the warehouse tonight?" Eloise suggested, "Maybe we missed something the first time we were there."

"It's a long shot, but what do we have to lose? With new cars recently stolen, maybe we'll finally get lucky." He checked the clock. "It'll be dark in an hour or so. We can take another look."

Eloise stood, catching his arm as he passed by. The soft touch of her hand, the jasmine perfume flitting around him, made this entire situation more emotionally charged than it needed to be. Now was not the time to think about Eloise as an alluring woman, about how her mere presence in the house kept him awake at night. How each day he pictured what a future with her might look like, when in reality, once the competition for the promotion was over and the new sergeant was named, they'd likely end up miles apart.

He agreed, in principle, to what Eloise and Chambers wanted them to do, but he sensed if they hung in just a bit longer, their search would take them to the leader.

"Thank you," she said. "I know you want to wait it out."

"I don't agree with either of you, but what choice do I have?"

"We have orders."

Right. Orders. The bane of his existence. If it weren't for the fact that Eloise was directly involved with any off-operation decision he made, he'd be handling things differently. At this point, he'd gladly throw the promotion aside to catch the real leader behind the thefts and close the case for good.

Shaking off her hand, he said brusquely, "I'm going for a run."

He had to hand it to her, she barely winced at his brush-off, because let's face it, that's exactly what it was. He needed space and he needed it now.

"You cooked, so I'll clean the kitchen."

He took off for his room, changed and was soon pounding the pavement. Heavy metal roared through his earbuds. He tore up the asphalt, pushing himself beyond endurance so he didn't have to think about Eloise, the case or the possibility of never discovering who was behind the ring. He wanted it all, but experience had taught him no one ever really got everything they wanted in life. It came down to choices. Between right and wrong. What he would decide now would be the most important move in this time and place. Once he acted on it, there was no going back.

By the time he returned to the house, slowing his pace to even his breathing, he'd decided one thing. He was going to find the leader, with or without Eloise's help.

An hour later they were back at the warehouse. Taking position across the street, Dante peered through the binoculars.

"It's pretty deserted." Eloise spoke up from her shotgun position in the passenger seat.

She'd been subdued since he returned to the house. Not that he could blame her.

"Nothing's moving," he confirmed.

They waited fifteen more minutes. He cracked the window, letting the fresh air wash over him. There was no traffic tonight. A deserted vibe hung over the industrial park. A perfect time to carry out another clandestine search of the place.

"I think we can safely approach the building," he announced.

He and Eloise slid out of the truck cab. Together, they crept along the shadows, cautiously making their way to the warehouse. This visit they carried their firearms, just in case the situation went south. Once they reached the concrete driveway, he held out his hand to stop her, holding their position to scan the area one last time.

"Ready?" he asked, barely above a whisper.

"When you are."

"Go."

Heart pumping, he swiftly moved to the glass door of the office, Eloise by his side. Dante crossed his fingers they found another clue to keep the op running.

Once at the door, he cupped his hands beside his face to peer inside. The office was completely dark, but one light burned in the vast space beyond, revealing the worst-case scenario.

"The cars are gone. All of them."

CHAPTER THIRTEEN

"WE MISSED THE TRANSFER," Eloise said as they jumped back into the truck. They hadn't been able to enter the building, not that it would have mattered. Instead, they'd walked the property but didn't find any evidence left behind. It was as if the cars stored here never existed.

Dante started the truck and peeled out of the parking lot. "You said Chambers had a detail watching the warehouse."

"Hold on." She yanked her phone from her pocket and tapped the number for the department. Asked for Officer Syms, one of the men on the warehouse detail. When she was told he wasn't in, she identified herself and asked about the status of the detail. Frowned when she heard the answer.

"Chambers had to pull them," she said after hanging up. "He needed them for more important calls."

"Thanks for letting us know," Dante muttered under his breath.

"I should have asked for an update when I had the lieutenant on the phone, but we were discussing the dynamics of the case and then Chambers got another call."

When Dante didn't respond, Eloise tried to keep from squirming in her seat. The missing cars put a big knot in their investigation. They needed to follow the trail to uncover the next layer of the organization. Without them? Proving anything just became more difficult.

If they'd had a heads-up… It didn't matter. The cars were gone and they were back to square one. "We can still focus on the garage and Ramsey's gang."

"If that's even real."

"It is. If you'd seen how intense Ramsey was with those kids, you'd agree."

Dante's thumb tapped the steering wheel in a steady rhythm. His terse tones communicated he was still miffed over their dinner conversation. She knew he wanted to keep digging until they got to the root of the car ring, but she was more practical. And, ultimately, not as daring in his eyes? It wasn't that she didn't think they could find the source—she did—but given the circumstances in just the last few days, they had to strike now.

"I've documented everything we've discovered so far. Until Chambers says otherwise, we keep following leads."

He still didn't answer.

"What are your thoughts?"

He shot her a black look. "You don't want to know my thoughts right now."

She swallowed a sigh. "Which means you've come up with something."

"Not all the way. I need more time."

"So share what you've got so far."

"We have Rico. It's Ramsey, the kids and the cars we need to focus on. You said a dealership got hit again?"

"Yes."

He was quiet for a moment. "Check with Chambers to see if any other dealerships have been hit since we started the investigation. Most specifically, last Tuesday night when the cars showed up at the garage."

"You're thinking that if everyone is connected like we think, another carrier with the newly stolen cars might show up?"

"It's a long shot, but all we've got. Too many players are overlapping now."

She stared out the window in deep thought. What was out of place? After a few minutes, she turned to Dante. "The only guy not entirely in the loop is Greg. Maybe he's the link between the activities at the garage and the ringleader."

"My thoughts exactly."

"We need to find him."

"I'll come up with something before I go back to work tomorrow."

As Dante pulled into the driveway and parked, Eloise placed her hand on the door handle ready to exit. The tension in the truck cab grated on her nerves. Dante's mood was getting to her. She needed to be alone to steady herself.

The kiss in the kitchen, the kiss she'd initiated, weighed heavily on her. All she'd wanted was a chance to prove herself to her superiors. Move up rank. Show her parents that she'd chosen the correct career path. Yet every time she was within touching distance of Dante, all her good intentions fell by the wayside. How on earth had he become so important to her?

If she were honest with herself, she'd admit it was more than the kisses. Sure, she wouldn't deny the attraction they'd played around with before the op, a fun flirtation that wasn't going anywhere. She liked the real Dante. There was a depth to him he hid from the rest of the world and she felt privileged that he'd let her in enough to get a glimpse of that man.

More so, though, he was a good partner and

had a big heart. Trusted her decisions, even if he didn't always agree with her. And his sense of humor? The way he pushed her out of her comfort zone? A bright light in the structured life she'd created. So yeah, her heart was in real trouble of falling dangerously close to love. Which was crazy. He might kiss her a little more often than was appropriate considering their undercover status, but she didn't stop him. Did that make her a hypocrite?

Rules were important to her. She didn't need grand plans and gestures to get the job done. That might work for Dante, but not her. She needed the facts laid out before her, and right now, the facts were telling her they had a reasonable case, even without the leader. But if waiting to discover the identity of the ringleader made the case stronger, was she wrong to put Dante off?

This is all about the promotion, a tiny voice nagged. *You're playing it safe.*

Yes, she wanted the job, but on the merits of good police work. At this point did good work mean they should throw caution to the wind and delve deeper *in case* they found the ringleader? Accusing Dante of going after the ringleader just to get a promotion, well, that wasn't fair. He wanted to solve the case as much as she did. Was in just as deep. Could they come to the same conclusion using different methods?

Her emotions were running away from her like a high-speed roller coaster, and if she didn't get her act together, she might derail.

Dante turned off the ignition. Stayed in his seat. Curious, Eloise waited.

"You know I respect you," he finally said.

Okay, not how she'd like a conversation with Dante to start, because respect meant distance and despite everything, despite all her arguments not to push this attraction, she still wanted to get closer to the man sitting mere inches from her.

Cautiously, she asked, "Do I want to hear the rest?"

The garage lights illuminated the inside of the truck cab. She could see his features as clear as day, closed off and serious.

His voice was steady when he said, "I'm going to get this guy."

The intense focus on his face made her wary. "Of course we are. Together."

He shot her an enigmatic look.

A shiver ran over her skin. "Dante…"

"Just remember that."

He exited the cab. A million thoughts raced through her head. One stood out from them all. *He's going to do something impetuous.*

For the sake of everyone, it was up to her to stop him.

She finally opened the door and stepped into the temperate night, perfumed with traces of night jasmine. Stars studded the sky. Crickets hummed. All normal, yet chills pebbled her skin. She was about to go inside when she noticed the front porch light on at Martha's house. Odd. The woman usually retired early.

She walked over to investigate, surprised when she glimpsed the silhouette of someone sitting on a rocker.

"Martha?"

"Ellie, dear. I didn't expect you to come by so late."

"I saw your light on. Are you okay?"

"Having trouble sleeping."

Eloise knew the malady. "Can I get you anything?"

"No. Sitting in the silence is good for the soul. When I have an off night, I like to come out here and think about my life. All the wonderful memories with my husband, children and grandchildren." Her gaze glistened as she met Eloise's. "A lifetime's worth, like you're making with Dan."

Since she couldn't answer, Eloise sank onto the top step of the porch, angled to face her friend. "What would you say were the most treasured moments of your marriage?"

Martha chuckled. "Do you have an hour?"

"Actually, I do." Eloise spoke honestly. She had no desire to go into the house just yet. Not with her revelations about Dante so raw.

The wooden porch creaked as Martha rocked. Eloise found it comforting. Steady and strong, much like she imagined Martha's marriage to George.

"I almost didn't marry George," Martha said.

Eloise's mouth fell open. "What?"

"It's true. I had this notion that I wanted to become a nurse. Help sick people, maybe work in a hospital." She shrugged. "Wasn't sure it would ever happen."

"Why not? It's a wonderful dream."

"It would have been, until I turned fourteen. My father had recently died and my mother had to work to keep the family above water financially. To help out, I worked odd jobs to supplement the family income. It was pretty clear we would never have enough money to put me through nursing school, but I kept my hopes up. A pipe dream, really."

"When did George come into the picture?"

"Four years later, he walked into the store where I was shelving merchandise, shopping for a present for a woman he'd corresponded with when he was in the military. He said he took one look at me and lost his heart forever."

"And the other woman?"

"She'd moved on, George found out." Martha went quiet, staring out over the night shadows. A car drove by, breaking the silence. When she spoke again, a profound sadness laced her tone. "The years after my father died were difficult, almost like a bad dream. My mother changed, for the worse, then quickly remarried a man I didn't like. My older brother got into trouble with the law. We had once been a close-knit family and, suddenly, we were strangers. Nothing was what it seemed."

Eloise might not be remembering painful memories, but she understood the concept of nothing being what it seemed. Right now her life was entirely out of whack.

"Did you return George's feelings?"

Martha shook off the melancholy. "Not right away. It wasn't until my stepfather told me they weren't behind my dream to go to school. I fell apart. It was like my heart was wrenched from my chest."

Eloise recalled her parents' disappointment when she announced she wouldn't follow in their footsteps. "I always craved my parents' approval. Never got it, so I can relate."

Martha dabbed her eyes. "I walked around in a fog for days. Back then, it was difficult to go against your parents, especially a female, but my stepfather was especially hard. All I wanted to do was help people and they denied me."

Blinking the moisture in her eyes, Eloise confided, "I had a different type of argument with my folks. They wanted me to attend college, on their terms. With the major they picked. Even though I bucked their demands and chose an entirely different path, I think, in a small way, they were proud I carried through with my decision."

"I'd like to believe so."

A long moment passed as Eloise pondered the journey of her life. A journey that led her to Dante.

"Tell me, Martha, how did George finally capture your heart? You mentioned something about a grand gesture?"

A smile curved her lips. "We had been seeing each other for a few months by the time I learned I wouldn't be going to school. George came upon me as I was leaving work one day. I was trying desperately to keep myself together, but apparently not succeeding. He could see beyond the fake smile I presented to the world. When he asked why I was upset,

I just broke down and cried. I'd never told him of my desire to become a nurse. I finally pulled myself together, explaining how my parents were not supportive and that my dream would never become a reality."

Eloise straightened. "And?"

"He told me he would put me through school."

Placing her hand over her heart, Eloise blinked back fresh tears. "How sweet."

"He believed in me."

I respect you, Dante had said. Was that the same as believing in her?

"It took many years. We married, then had children. I finally graduated when I turned thirty-five. Fulfilled my wish of working in a hospital."

"George clearly loved you." Eloise brushed her tears away. "You made me cry with your lovely story."

"Well, my dear, you started it by asking about my marriage."

"I did indeed."

A faraway look reflected in Martha's gaze. "George always supported me. Laughed with me. Cried with me. We had a wonderful life together."

"And to think, you didn't even want to get married."

"Sometimes the things we want are right before us and we can't even see them."

Dante's face materialized in Eloise's mind. One didn't have to be a therapist to know what Eloise wanted.

Martha started to cough, startling Eloise from her thoughts. She jumped up. "Can I get you some water?"

Tapping her chest, Martha nodded.

Eloise ran inside to the kitchen, familiar with the floor plan by now after having spent many hours with Martha, and hurried back with a cool glass of water.

Martha drank, clearing her throat before she was able to speak again. "Thank you."

"Are you sure you're feeling all right?"

"Not as spry as usual, I will admit. I'll call my doctor in the morning." She placed the small glass on a table beside the rocker. "Maybe I'm coming down with a cold."

Eloise hovered over Martha, shaken by the sudden coughing spell. "You did get the flu shot, didn't you?"

Martha grinned. "Yes. My granddaughter asked me the same question when I spoke to her this morning."

"We're just looking out for you."

"And I love you for it."

Eloise's heart seized. She realized she also

loved Martha, a woman who had drawn Eloise into her life and cared about her, even if they weren't blood relatives.

A grin curved Martha's lips. "I just knew from the first day I met you we'd be grand friends."

Eloise took Martha's hand, her paper-thin, cool skin the most precious object Eloise had ever held between her fingers.

With a sigh, Martha reached out with her other hand for her cane. "I'll go inside now. I'm finally feeling tired."

"Do you want me to stay for a while? I don't mind at all."

Martha waved her off. "All I needed was some fresh air and heartfelt conversation."

Eloise helped her friend rise. Gave her a quick peck on her soft cheek.

"You promise to call if you need anything."

"I promise. Go home to your husband."

"Thank you, Martha."

"For what?"

Eloise swallowed hard, the depth of her emotions rising. Her voice caught when she said, "I don't have many friends, but you're one of the best."

Martha patted her arm. "Back at you, my dear."

Eloise helped her through the door, then

waited until she heard the lock click. Minutes later, the lights went out inside. Swallowing the lump still taking up residence in her throat, she made her way across the damp grass. She quietly entered her house, hoping Dante had turned in. With her emotions so close to the surface, she didn't think she could handle a conversation with him right now.

"C'MON, MAN. I asked for your advice about the op, not Eloise."

"Aren't they the same thing?" Dante's brother Derrick asked from the computer screen.

"You know I could just shut the laptop and tune you out until Dylan logs on."

Derrick smirked. "You could, but then you'd miss all my older-brother advice. It's priceless, you know."

"So you tell me every time we talk."

"And I'm right, aren't I?"

Dante's lips twitched. Derrick was nothing if not self-evolved.

"Thanks, but right now, I only want your take on the op."

Coming home after the disappointing rendezvous, Dante had bits of ideas forming in his head. He'd intended to hole up in his room to think, until a text from Derrick popped up on his private cell phone screen, informing Dante that there was new information on their mother and he should log on for a video chat. As usual Dylan was delayed, so Dante had brought his brother up to speed.

"Sounds like you need to go back to the beginning," Derrick said. "Go over every event and person you've come across so far. The answer could be staring you right in the face."

"Good advice. Eloise has detailed notes. We'll go over them from front to back."

Derrick's amused expression turned to concern. "Sounds like she's turned into a valuable partner."

"She's smart. Has great instincts."

"And that line we talked about? Have you stayed on your side?"

Dante fought to hide any telltale emotion from his brother. "Why would you ask me that?"

"Because whenever you mention her name, you get that twitchy guilty look I remember from when you were a kid."

Dante scoffed. "Like you paid that much attention."

"You'd be surprised what I noticed."

"Like what?"

"How handy you were around the house fixing things." A genuine smile curved Derrick's mouth. "Mom couldn't believe she had a child who could take care of broken appliances. It was like she had her own private handyman. And then the cars you and Dad worked on? We were all proud."

"Wow. I didn't think you'd paid any attention."

"You probably also never paid attention when I took the Mustang you and Dad were tinkering with out for a ride."

It took a moment for Dante to speak. "Wait. You took the car on the road?"

Derrick shrugged, like revealing this piece of information was no big deal. "Not before I checked with Dad to make sure it was safe, but yeah, I took it."

Dante gaped at his brother. "Unbelievable."

"Would you have let me take it if I'd asked?"

"Of course not!"

Derrick grinned.

"There were times I thought the car had been moved, but I figured Dad had been working on it. Never thought my sneaky brother took it for a joyride."

"Best car I ever drove," Derrick reminisced with a great deal of awe.

Dante shook his head. "Well, I can't be all that mad at you."

The teasing expression on Derrick's face vanished. "Why?"

"Remember that bike you saved up all your allowance and birthday money to buy?"

"The ten-speed with the navy blue color scheme."

"The same."

Derrick aimed him a dirty look.

"I kinda borrowed it when you went to base-ball camp one summer."

"Kinda?"

"Did. And I crashed it. Dad helped me bang out the dents before you got back."

"I… You… Wow. You are way more than a pretty boy."

"Been trying to prove it."

"I guess we're even, then," Derrick conceded.

"A car verses a bike? Hardly. But it's all water under the bridge now."

"What bridge?" Dylan asked, finally logging on.

"Nothing," Dante said. "Just some child-hood memories."

Dylan nodded, then jumped right into busi-ness. "You guys ready for an update?"

"What about Deke?" Derrick asked.

"He must be out of cell range. Couldn't get ahold of him."

"What's up?"

"The man Mom is dating is James Tate."

"You finally met him?" Dante asked, noticing a shadow in his peripheral vision. Eloise materialized, then when she saw he was busy, backed up. He waved her over.

"Are you sure?" she mouthed.

"You're welcome," he said.

"Why are you thanking me?" Dylan asked. "I haven't told you everything yet."

"No. It's…" He reached out and grabbed Eloise's hand, tugging her beside him. He angled the laptop to capture both their images.

"Guys, this is Eloise."

"Hi," she said, waving at the screen.

"Finally, we get to meet the brains of the operation. I'm Derrick."

Eloise nodded. "And you must be Dylan," she said to the other image.

"That's right. I was just giving my brothers the lowdown about our mother."

"Oh, then I'll leave you be."

"Don't rush off," Derrick said.

Dante smiled. "It's okay. I want you to stay."

She shot him a surprised glance, then moved behind him to get a better view of the screen. This close, her jasmine scent stirred his senses, made him acutely aware of her presence in the room. Looked like his awareness of Eloise wasn't going away anytime soon.

It was official. Eloise was definitely under his skin.

"Like I was saying," Dylan went on. "James Tate. I met him yesterday."

"And," Derrick prompted.

"Mom mentioned he was doing a little handiwork at her condo. He told me the name of the company he worked for and I looked it up. Public record."

"Let me guess," Dante said, controlling a laugh. "He's a fine upstanding citizen and Mom is furious with you for interfering in her life."

"The exact opposite. I called and the company said they have no record of him. Concerned he might be ripping Mom off, I did a basic background check. Prior to ten years ago, James Tate didn't exist. At least not a man of his age and description."

Dante leaned back, stunned. Eloise laid a hand on his shoulder and he reached up to take hold. "Did you tell Mom?"

"I mentioned it, but she said she's a good judge of character, there are things we don't know and to butt out of her business."

"Are we backing off?"

Dylan's cynical expression conveyed *Not in this lifetime.*

"What do you want us to do?" Derrick asked.

"I've got a friend I can get to do a deeper background check. He's on a job and will be out of town for a few more weeks, but he said he'd help then," Dylan answered.

"In the meantime, aren't you concerned about this guy taking advantage of Mom?" Derrick pressed.

"Now that we've met, he knows not to pull anything. I'll keep an eye on this end."

"I start a new assignment tomorrow," Derrick said. "Keep me in the loop."

"And we're still undercover," Dante added.

"I've got it handled for now," Dylan assured them both.

A ring sounded from the other room. "Oh, that's me," Eloise said. She leaned close to Dante, her hair brushing his shoulder. "Nice to meet you both."

Derrick winked. "Same here."

"Keep an eye on my brother," Dylan warned. "He has a tendency to do his own thing."

Dante rolled his eyes. "Thanks for nothing."

Eloise waved again and left the room.

"So, to wrap up," Dylan said. "I'll hold down the fort here."

"But you'll call if you need us," Dante re-affirmed.

"Absolutely."

The brothers signed off. Dante raised his arms, linked his fingers and rested them behind his head. What was their mother thinking? Jasmine had a mind of her own, but surely—

"Dante, come quick."

Hearing the panic in Eloise's voice, he jumped up and charged into the living room, only to find her running out the front door.

CHAPTER FOURTEEN

ELOISE SPRINTED ACROSS the damp grass, nearly losing her footing as she raced up the steps to Martha's porch.

"Slow down," Dante called from behind, rapidly gaining on her.

"It's Martha," she called needlessly over her shoulder. Once at the porch, Eloise crouched down to hunt for the plastic rock placed beside a planter that held a spare key to the house. "Her number showed on my caller ID, but when I answered, all I heard was a loud noise, like she dropped the phone."

Having found the key, she stood, trying without success to unlock the door. Dante snatched the key from her shaking fingers and stuck it in the slot. Why was this process taking forever?

Soon enough, Dante was turning the knob. Not waiting for him to fully open the door, Eloise barreled inside. The dim bathroom light illuminated the path to Martha's bedroom. Charging in, Eloise gasped when she found her friend lying on the floor beside the bed. "Martha," she cried, kneeling next to the woman. Even in the dismal lighting, Martha's face was deathly pale. Eloise called out her name, but the woman didn't answer. She finally had the presence of mind to check for a pulse. "Thin," she sputtered, her voice barely working.

"I'm calling 911," Dante said, phone in hand.

"Please, Martha," Eloise whispered. "Be okay."

"This is Detective Matthews, Palm Cove PD. I need an ambulance at 1025 Orchard Street. Possible cardiac event." He spoke to the person on the other end, giving all the pertinent information.

Clasping Martha's cold hand in hers, Eloise's heart pounded. Nothing could happen to this wonderful woman. She'd become a friend. A mentor. Eloise refused to think the worst, even with the reality of the situation staring her square in the face.

Seconds later, Martha's lids fluttered. "El—"

"Don't speak," Eloise instructed, forcing a calm and professional tone she didn't feel at the moment. "Save your energy."

"What…?"

"We've called for an ambulance."

Martha's lids wavered. "My medicine…" Then her eyes closed.

Eloise glanced up to meet Dante's worried gaze as he hovered over them. "Do you see any medicine on the nightstand?"

Switching on the bedside lamp, Dante searched. "Nothing."

"Try the bathroom."

Dante moved with purpose and speed, gone mere seconds before returning with a small medicine container. "Looks like a prescription for nitroglycerin."

Martha's lids fluttered again.

"Should we give her a pill?" Eloise asked, not sure what to do. Panic gripped her. Why didn't she know what to do?

"Ellie, I'm not sure we should take a chance. She may have already swallowed some—" A siren sounded in the distance, growing closer. "Let's wait for the paramedics."

Eloise nodded. "Help is here," she said to her friend, tightening her grip. "Hang on, Martha."

"I'll meet them at the door." Dante squeezed her shoulder, then bolted from the room.

Voices soon filtered into the bedroom from somewhere, but Eloise couldn't drag her gaze away from Martha's pale face. Eloise wanted to gather her close instead of leaving her on the hard floor, but realized she shouldn't move her friend. The night turned into a complicated twist, surreal and intense at the same time, leaving Eloise helpless.

She imagined the scent of coffee mingling with Martha's floral perfume, the comforting aroma she smelled every morning when they met on the patio to start the day. Tried to make this situation seem less serious than it was.

"Please hold on," Eloise pleaded, her voice thick and cracking with the emotion overwhelming her. "I know it's selfish, but I need you to get better. You've come to mean so much to me… I don't think…" She brushed the hot tears blurring her eyes. "I really want more time with you," she started blabbering. "I haven't gotten this whole knitting thing down. And then there's our morning coffee. Who else gets excited about trying different creamer flavors with each cup? I look forward to starting my day with your pearls of wisdom." She choked over her words, but forced her thoughts out, anyway. "I still have things to tell you."

Before she could utter another sentence, two men carrying medical equipment pushed into the room. She refused to budge, until strong hands gripped her arms and moved her out of the way to give the medics plenty of space to do their job.

Dante, she realized as he pulled her against

his warm, solid form. She reached up, her hands covering his, needing the lifeline as her friend's life hung in the balance. Her shoulders shook and her knees nearly buckled, but the tears were gone. She'd said her piece. Martha heard her, right?

"I'm sure she heard you," Dante whispered into her ear.

Had she said her thoughts out loud? What was wrong with her? She was a detective, trained to be calm in adverse situations. Yet here she stood, a bundle of nerves as the paramedics revived Martha. After what seemed an eternity, one of them said, "She's stable. Let's move her now."

"Move her where?"

The dark-haired paramedic glanced at her. "Coastal Hospital."

Someone new came in with a gurney and they gently lifted Martha from the floor. Her face was still a ghastly shade of white; her eyes remained closed. Eloise reached out as they passed by.

"Is she…?"

"We're doing everything we can to help her," one of the EMTs said as they exited the house, Eloise right behind them, dogging their footsteps. Before she could climb into the ambulance, Dante stopped her by taking hold of her hand.

"Ellie." When she didn't respond, he said her name again, louder.

She turned to face him. "What?"

"Take a couple breaths. We'll follow the ambulance in the truck."

"I should be with her."

"You can't. They need to be ready to treat her if necessary and you'll be in the way."

Yes. That made sense. She ran a trembling hand over her brow. "Then let's go."

Dante stopped her again. Placed a hand on her arm to turn her. "We need to go back to the house. For a minute."

She blinked at him.

"You need to pull yourself together."

Together. Right. She needed her cop face right now because she didn't know how else to cover the riot of emotions battling inside her. Taking a deep breath, she met Dante's shuttered gaze. "I'm good."

"No, you're not," he muttered as he took her hand and practically dragged her across the lawn, his bossiness almost bringing a smile to her face.

Once inside the house, Dante said, "Let me get my wallet and keys."

She nodded, on autopilot as she went to the

master bathroom to splash water on her face. Her heart still raced and her head pounded. She glanced in the mirror. Cringed. Her mascara had smeared around her eyes, her skin was just as ghostly as Martha's had been and her hair, sticking out all over the place, looked like she'd run her hand through it a hundred times. Grabbing a brush, she worked through the tangles, then wiped a washcloth over her face. Her contacts were gritty, irritating her eyes. She removed them and felt around for the spare set of glasses she kept in the bathroom.

"Ready?" Dante asked, his voice calm, yet commanding, from the doorway.

She turned, anxious to leave. Her eyes met his through the glass lenses and suddenly her feet were as heavy as cement blocks. The concern etched on his face—for her, for their friend—nearly brought her to her knees. She'd never experienced the depth of anyone caring about her during a life-altering event like this. Never. And suddenly it became all too real.

"I can't do this," she whispered, removing the glasses to rub her eyes.

Dante moved into the room with one step and tugged her into his arms. He held her tight as the tears she'd thought were gone returned with a vengeance. She couldn't control the sobbing or trembling, and while Dante's actions should have comforted her, she found herself embarrassed.

She pulled back, swiping at her wet cheeks. "What is wrong with me? I'm always calm under pressure. I know how to handle an emergency situation. I'm a police detective, for Pete's sake."

Dante propped a shoulder against the door frame. "You haven't had a person close to you experience this kind of distress?"

"No. My folks are healthy. I… You know I don't have a lot of friends. This is…"

"Out of your realm of expertise?"

She nodded, the lump in her throat making it impossible to answer.

A look she couldn't decipher in her current distress passed Dante's face. "Martha would want you to be strong, Ellie." He reached out to thumb the tears from her face. "And since I know there's steel in your bones, you can do this."

"And if the worst happens?" She sniffed.

"We'll get through that. Together."

Seeing the confidence on his face, Eloise took another breath. Replaced her glasses. Squared her shoulders and tried for a modicum of calm. "You'll stay with me at the hospital?"

"For as long as it takes."

She stepped forward, intending to exit the

bathroom, but instead wrapped her arms around his neck. When his strong arms circled her waist, she whispered, "Steel?"

"Hey, I'm trying," he muttered.

She drew back and sent him a teary smile. "Thank you."

He grinned. "Anytime."

Finally under control, Eloise hunted for her purse and soon they were on the road to the hospital.

DANTE HID HIS surprise at the depth of Eloise's reaction to Martha's apparent heart attack. He knew she wasn't close to her family, was a bit of a loner. But had she been lonely? Is that why she'd found solace in Martha's friendship? Why the woman's attack hit her so hard? The two had grown close in the short time they'd been neighbors, but for Eloise to break down as she had? It shook him. She was always in such control, always steady in an extreme situation. But tonight? She'd lost her cool. Bigtime. Yet her show of emotion only made him love her more.

Whoa. Love? Had he really gone there?

He took a sidelong glance at his partner seated on the passenger side as she worried her lower lip. Yep. Love. Because all he knew was that he wanted to stop the pain and make the events of tonight go away so she'd smile—any kind of smile—at him again. He'd take humor or frustration, as long as she went back to the woman who had it all together.

He shouldn't be surprised at this "aha" moment. He'd kept trying to cross the line, hadn't he? Had he been in love all along? Why else would he risk it?

But what about Eloise? Would she return his feelings? He really didn't want to ponder the idea, not when this was neither the time nor place to have a discussion about love and all the ramifications. Deep in his bones, he knew a relationship wasn't going to be easy, but he wanted her, anyway.

Eloise blew out a loud puff of air, distracting him from his thoughts. He eyed her again. Her face was still pale; lines of worry creased her skin, and he imagined it was all she could do not to place her foot over his on the gas pedal so they'd arrive at the hospital faster. He wished he had the right words to say, but sensed silence was better.

He stuck to Eloise's side once they arrived at the hospital. After an official inquiry—since they were the first responders at the scene—they learned Martha was still in the ER. They couldn't say more, which meant Eloise paced the length of the waiting room and back, multiple times. He tried once to get her to sit, but that had lasted a whopping two seconds before she was up and at it again.

He wasn't a fan of hospitals, having spent time in another room very similar to this one on the day his father died. The stark lighting, the staff running to and fro, the prevailing scent of antiseptic covering sickness—it reminded him of heartrending days he'd rather forget.

Stifling a yawn that crept up on him, he checked his watch. After 2:00 a.m. It was going to be a long night.

"I'm going to the vending machine for some coffee. Want a cup?"

Eloise's brown eyes looked huge behind her glasses. "No. I'm too jittery."

He nodded. "Be right back."

He started down a hallway, coming to an alcove with tall machines side by side. He pulled a few coins from his pocket and slipped them in the slot, then waited for what he was sure to be the worst cup of coffee ever.

As the dark liquid slowly filled the cup, his cell phone sounded. Who would be calling at this time of the morning? He checked the caller ID and frowned. His contact Ben, the colleague who'd gotten him the job at Rico's garage.

"Ben. What's up?"

"Passing along some intel you might find helpful."

"At this time of the morning?"

"I thought I'd get your voice mail, but this is better."

"What have you learned?"

"Those cars that were stashed at the warehouse?"

"Yeah?"

"They showed up at a new dealership thirty miles south of here."

"How do you know they're the same cars?"

"Chambers sent me the list you and your partner compiled. All accounted for."

"How did you stumble upon this?"

"My contact. The case I'm working is more closely connected to yours than we originally thought. The garage cover isn't limited to just Rico's. Turns out there's a network of garages changing VINs and moving cars. The guy I'm working for is just as involved as Rico."

There it was, the lead they'd been waiting for. "The stolen cars are all going to new dealerships?"

"Looks like it. New VINs translate into moving the stolen merchandise to a whole new location. Someone is about to get a lot richer."

"But who?"

"Still a tightly held secret."

Dante ran a hand through his hair. "We're nowhere closer?"

"Oh, we're closer, thanks to the list you provided," Ben said. Dante could hear the smile in his voice. "I heard chatter about another shipment scheduled for Rico's garage. Two nights from now. Because of you and your partner, we should be able to tie this case up."

"Thanks, Ben."

"You got it. We're gonna get this guy—I can feel it."

Dante signed off, hoping this was indeed the truth. He wanted this op to close on a positive note, which meant key players behind bars. Then maybe he could figure out what to do with his emotions for his partner.

The coffee finished filling the cup with a sputter. He removed the beverage from the machine and went back to the waiting room, where Eloise was still pacing.

"Wearing a path in the floor isn't going to make time move faster."

She shot him an annoyed frown. "It makes me feel like I'm doing something positive."

He took a sip of the coffee and grimaced. Yeah, worse than he thought.

Setting the cup on an end table, he walked to the bank of windows overlooking a small enclosed lanai. A sanctuary garden, he guessed. As he'd hoped, Eloise stopped pacing and joined him. They stood there for a few minutes, taking in the scene: a slim tree with lots of branches, several bushes dotted with small white flowers, lush tropical plants and a bench.

"I remember when my dad died," he said, his tone quiet. Was he hoping to distract her by relating his story? "It was a total surprise. He got up like he did every morning, dressed in his uniform and went to work. Only that day was different." He paused. Swallowed. "He didn't come home."

Eloise took his hand and squeezed. "You don't have to do this."

He turned his head to her. "I think I do."

She nodded.

"We all ended up in a waiting room very similar to this. After a while, they let my mom go back with him. I remember saying, 'Dad will be fine. He's too tough to die.'" He shook his head. "Derrick punched me in the arm. Dylan stayed seated, staring into space, and Deke? I think he might have been reading a magazine. It seemed like hours before my mother came back, her face streaked with tears. She didn't have to say a word. We knew."

Her shoulder brushed his. "I'm sorry, Dante."

"I'm not telling you this to prepare you for

the worst. Really, I don't know why I said anything at all. I've never talked about that day. To anyone."

"I'm honored," she whispered, her voice shaky.

They stood together, staring at the garden. How odd that he seemed to be sharing his strength *with* her. He'd always been the one to lead the way, take the castle by storm, make sure he rounded up the bad guys. When had he decided he needed to be strong for Eloise? Did it come from the helplessness he'd experienced the day his dad died? Realizing the depth of his feelings for her had put her first in his mind? He was no counselor, but it wasn't too hard to put the puzzle pieces together.

"My grandmother died when I was young," he heard Eloise say. A small smile curved her lips. "Grammy Beth and I were pretty tight. I spent hours at her house when I was a kid, playing and having a good time. When she died, so did my childhood. My folks expected me to grieve in silence. Act all grown up and cover my feelings. When I couldn't, that's when I started staying in my room, out of their way so they couldn't see what a disappointment I was."

"C'mon. They were that detached?"

Her chest rose and fell as she took a breath. "It felt like it at the time. Now I'm not so sure."

He shook his head, his heart going out to her and her unhappy memories. "As much as my brothers make me crazy, at least we had each other."

"And no matter what happens to Martha," she said quietly, "I have you?"

He leaned over and kissed her on the cheek. "Yeah, you have me."

Once their little heart-to-heart ended, Dante got Eloise to sit. His coffee had gone cold, so he abandoned it. After a while, he felt Eloise move against him, then her head landed on his shoulder, her jasmine scent invigorating him. It shouldn't feel right, but it did. Like she was meant to fit into the curve of his side. Instead of pushing his feelings away like he normally did, he wound his arm around her shoulders and she nestled in beside him. It felt good to be needed and to comfort her in return.

She'd just dozed off when a doctor appeared. "Detective Matthews?"

Eloise jumped up as Dante answered, "That's me."

"I'm Dr. Hayes. I wanted to tell you that Mrs. Jamison is finally stable. Apparently her chest grew tight after she went to bed. When she rose to get her medicine, she got dizzy and fell. We're moving her to a room." His eyes grew somber. "Thanks for alerting the rescue team. Your quick timing made all the difference."

"It was Detective Archer's fast reflexes, really."

The doctor glanced at Eloise.

"Can we see her?" she asked.

"She's just being settled and I'm not sure if she'll feel up to visiting." The doctor must have seen the disappointment on Eloise's face because he said, "It's much too early for visiting hours, but for the detectives who saved her life, I can make an exception. Give her some time to rest, though."

Eloise lit up. "Thank you, Doctor."

"She's in Room 223. Keep it quick."

"We will."

The doctor walked away. Dante felt Eloise tug on his sleeve, moving toward the elevator. Once on the designated floor, Eloise resumed her pacing.

"Do you think enough time has gone by?"

He wasn't sure, but considering Eloise's restlessness, she'd waited long enough. "Why don't you look in on her."

Eloise grabbed his hand. He didn't put up a fight as she pulled him down the hallway, but once they were outside of Martha's room, he held back.

"You go," he told her.

"Are you sure?"

He nodded. "I'll wait in the lounge by the elevators."

"Okay." She gave him a tight hug and then, taking a breath, disappeared into the dark room.

ELOISE TREADED ON light feet. A steady beep, beep, beep filled the silence. She wrinkled her nose at the disinfectant smell, then at the tubes attached to her friend. Lying on the white sheets, hooked up to machines, Martha seemed smaller than Eloise remembered. Pulling a chair to the bedside, Eloise gently took one of Martha's hands in hers. After a few moments, she began to speak.

"It looks like you're going to be okay, but I have to say, you scared the life out of me."

She was rewarded with a trembling smile. Relief washed over her.

"I really hope this is a onetime thing. I couldn't handle another call like the one I received from you tonight. Or rather, this morning."

"I knew you'd come," Martha whispered.

"Don't wear yourself out," Eloise chided.

Her lids fluttered, then Martha's gaze met hers. "Thank you."

"Are you kidding? How could I not make sure to get help?"

"The doctor said…bad attack. Up on my feet…soon."

As Martha spoke, her voice grew a little stronger. Eloise said a silent prayer of thanks.

"You'll have to take it easy for a while."

Martha shrugged. "A day… Or two."

Eloise chuckled. "I'll make sure you have whatever you need once you get back home."

Martha frowned. "No."

"It will be my pleasure."

Martha's lips wobbled again and her lids closed. In the dim room, Eloise took comfort in knowing her dear friend would see another sunrise. That she'd have more time to spend with this woman who had filled an empty spot in her heart. She hadn't realized how important this was, how much she'd needed Martha to fill Grammy Beth's place. Except Martha hadn't really taken her grandmother's place; instead, she'd added new memories, a new voice for Eloise to cherish.

Thirty minutes passed and Martha stirred again.

"I'm going to rally the neighbors to pitch in and help so you don't have to worry about a thing," Eloise said after having time to think. "I'll take time off from work."

Martha's lids opened. "Can you do that?"

"Of course. Just a day here and there until we get this sorted out."

Martha stared at her, alert, despite the night's events. Her voice gained strength the longer Martha was awake. "Ellie, I heard Dan call for help."

Oh, boy.

"I know he's a detective. I'm guessing you are, too?"

Shocked, Eloise leaned back in the chair.

"It makes sense actually. Ted and Janice taking off suddenly. It didn't seem right."

Eloise wasn't sure what to say, so she kept quiet.

"Then newlyweds moving in next door, asking all kinds of questions about the neighborhood."

Had they been that obvious? And did she admit the truth now that her friend had discovered their real identities?

"Wait. You are Ellie, aren't you?"

"My name is Eloise, but I like being called Ellie."

"Then Ellie, it is." Martha shifted her hand to cover Eloise's. "Don't worry, my dear. Mum's the word."

Eloise's heart squeezed. She had no doubt Martha would keep the truth to herself. "Thanks."

Martha closed her eyes again, drifting to sleep. Eloise rose, tiptoeing from the room to find Dante. He was sound asleep on the couch in the lounge.

"Hey," she said, tapping his arm to wake him.

He jerked, eyes wide. "What? I'm awake."

She chuckled and sank onto the couch beside him.

When he realized it was her, he relaxed. "How's the patient?"

"Sleeping."

"So we're heading home?"

"Actually, I'd like to stay if you don't mind."

He searched her eyes. Cupped her face with both his hands. "Sounds like a good idea."

She beamed at him.

"I'm sure her family will be here as soon as they've been notified, then we can get back to the job."

Her smile slipped. She hadn't thought about family coming to the hospital. Being involved in Martha's recovery.

"I have some news on the case," he went on to say, "but it can wait until later."

"Are you sure?"

"For now."

"Thanks. For everything. For bringing me here. For talking me down."

"The out-of-control Ellie was kinda scary."

She playfully slapped his arm. "Despite your attempt at humor, it meant a lot for you to stay with me."

"Who said it was humor?"

She rolled her eyes.

"Besides, where else would I be?"

Where else indeed? she wondered. Took him at his word.

Their gazes caught and held. He leaned in, hesitated. She blinked, waiting, then he kissed her. Gently, at first. Then with a little more passion. It took her breath away, leaving her wanting more when he pulled away.

"I'll go home, keep things running smoothly. Call me when you want me to pick you up."

She nodded, unable to speak. This kiss was different. It was…right. Honest. True.

Home.

When they stood, she walked him to the elevator. He pressed the button. Flashed her a grin. "Miss me, okay?"

She laughed instead of answering. The door opened and he stepped inside, giving her a snappy salute as the doors slid closed.

Shaking off her powerful reaction to his kiss, she moved quietly to Martha's room.

Would they find a way to work out a relationship once the case was over? No matter who got the promotion? She touched her lips, still feeling the warmth of his kiss. She hoped so.

CHAPTER FIFTEEN

TRUE TO HER WORD, Eloise had taken the next day off from the garage, hovering over Martha, but couldn't risk the operation by missing a second day of work. Dante had filled her in on their part in Ben's latest intel and she knew it was now or never to wrap up the case.

A half dozen cars had been delivered to the garage yesterday for the crew to work on and Dante expected more would arrive today. Eloise needed to be there to keep an eye on everyone's movements, but she dropped Dante off at the garage and hurried to the hospital to check on Martha before the day began.

Coffee in hand, she swerved around busy nurses and other hospital personnel en route to Martha's room. Just before she reached the door, a woman with blond hair, looking close to her age, stood in the doorway. "Yes, Grandmother, I know you'd like a different breakfast but the doctor is limiting your sodium intake."

A disgruntled voice sounded from inside

the room and the woman laughed. "I love you, too."

The woman turned and barreled straight into Eloise. "Oh, clumsy me."

Fast on her feet, Eloise sidestepped and balanced her coffee to keep it from spilling. "It's okay."

The woman smiled. "Good. I'd hate to make you waste your coffee. It is the most important way to start your day."

Eloise laughed.

"Do you know my grandmother?"

"We're neighbors. My, um, husband and I brought her here two nights ago when she had the heart attack." She stuck out her hand. "I'm Ellie."

"Oh, my gosh! Grandmother has told me about you. I'm Kristin."

Martha had talked about her? Her heart swelled just thinking about it. "Your grandmother has mentioned you, too. Nice to meet you," Eloise said after the shake. "Is Martha doing okay this morning?"

Kristin's expression took on an amused air. "Ready to get out of here."

"I can imagine."

"I have some arrangements to make, so I'm glad you're here. I don't like the idea of leaving her alone."

"I planned on sitting with her for a little while."

"Perfect. We got in late last night and I have tons to do."

"I thought I saw a car in her driveway."

"We came as soon as we got the call." Kristin's expression turned serious. "Thanks for looking out for my grandmother. I hate to think what might have happened if you hadn't called 911."

"Thankfully she'll be okay."

"Yes, and now I get a chance to pamper her, even though the stubborn woman will fight me tooth and nail."

Eloise chuckled. Kristin had described Martha to a T. "She is independent."

"To a fault. That's why I'm glad she finally agreed to come home with us."

A flutter of surprise swirled in Eloise's stomach. "Home? Where is that?"

"Ohio."

Eloise coughed. Ohio. At least a day or two drive from Florida.

Kristin dug around in her purse and extracted her cell phone. "I'll be back in an hour."

"Right. An hour."

The perky woman hustled along the hallway, greeting the staff like they were long-lost friends. Eloise helplessly watched her progress. Martha would be leaving? The thought never occurred to Eloise. She expected her friend to always be there when Eloise needed her.

Standing outside the door, her thoughts tumbled over each other. Did Martha want to leave? Was her granddaughter forcing her? She needed to hear it from her friend. Determined to get to the bottom of this newsflash, Eloise marched into the room, thrilled to see Martha sitting up in the bed. Color had returned to her face and her eyes were bright. After worrying over her friend for the last forty-eight hours, she couldn't have asked for anything better than Martha resembling her old self.

"Ellie. I'm glad you're here." She shifted as if looking around Eloise and said in a stage whisper, "Can you get me a cup of coffee?"

"I understand the doctor has you on a special diet."

"A boring diet," Martha groused.

"You better stick to his orders until you get home."

Martha crossed her arms over her chest. "Which can't come soon enough."

Eloise set her purse and cup on a rolling stand. Martha was in rare form this morning.

"Speaking of leaving, I ran into your grand-daughter in the hallway," she said, lowering herself into the chair beside the bed and deliberately moderating her tone. "She mentioned you're going home with her?"

Martha unfolded her arms, picking at the white blanket with nervous fingers. "Yes. I know it's a long trip, but it's been an ongoing discussion. After this latest…episode, Kristin and the family want me settled someplace where I'll have constant care."

"What about the rest of the family?"

"My children have downsized. It would be difficult for me to move in. Kristin has a big house and her husband does quite well for himself, and since she doesn't work, she's offered to take care of me. The other grandkids are farther away. She's my best option."

"You'd actually move that far away?"

Regret flickered in Martha's eyes. "I'm afraid so, my dear. As much as I love my home, I can't take care of it like I used to. The yard work is too much. Housekeeping wears me down."

Eloise understood. Didn't like the idea of her friend leaving, but realized Martha needed to live in a place with less responsibilities.

"What about our morning coffee together?" she asked in a teasing voice, covering the quickly mounting sorrow at the loss.

"How much longer would you be living next door to me, anyway? Once your job is finished you'll move on."

Martha nodded to Eloise's work clothes. She'd dressed like she did every day, in one of Rico's garage polo shirts and khaki shorts.

True…but… "I had this crazy idea we'd be friends even after I returned to regular duty."

"Which I would love, but it will have to be long distance. Kristin is helping put the house up for sale."

Sadness washed over her. Eloise suspected they might not see each other every day after she returned to her normal schedule, so why did the idea of Martha moving hundreds of miles away make her heart ache even worse?

"About the job," Eloise said, quickly pulling herself together to cover the pain spreading across her chest. "I'm sorry I lied to you. We're working undercover."

"Which requires secrets, I would imagine."

"In order for it to work, yes." She turned to stare blankly out the window, then met Martha's patient gaze. "Dan and I aren't really married."

Martha tilted her head. "I could see you have feelings for Dan, but there was something missing whenever you two were together. Not a tangible thing, really. More like a heart connection."

"You mean like real marriage vows?"

"That would do it." Martha chuckled. "But what about a future with Dan after the job? What's standing in your way?"

"Let's see, the case we're working, the fact that we're at the same police station and—the bigger and most complicated hurdle—we're both up for the same promotion."

"You don't make life easy, do you, Ellie?"

Actually, before this op, her life had been pretty simple. She went to work and took care of her apartment. But after sitting vigil with Martha all these hours, she realized she'd fallen in love—a revelation she'd mull over in detail later—and made friends she really liked.

Martha interrupted her thoughts. "What do you want, dear?"

What did she want? *Everything.* But hoping for it all was counterproductive. She did, however, want to discover what could be with Dante, along with earning the promotion.

"Well?" Martha prodded.

Eloise met Martha's perceptive gaze. "I was just thinking, could I have both?"

"I suppose that depends on Dan."

Yes, there was that small obstacle of Dante wanting the sergeant's position, too.

"I told you how much I wanted to go to nursing school, the story of how I got there. I still managed to find love and fulfill my dream."

Eloise leaned forward. "You're telling me to go for the promotion?"

"If you are very sure it's the job you want."

She was sure. "And a relationship?"

"I'm a firm believer in if it's meant to be, you'll be together."

If only she had that much faith. "I guess we'll have to sit down and figure out our relationship once we finish the investigation."

Martha patted her hand. "I have no doubt you will."

Fighting against the hot tears welling in her eyes, Eloise blinked them away before Martha could notice. Bidding farewell was going to be like saying goodbye to Grammy Beth. A sense of loss and helplessness engulfed her and she wished for more time.

An hour passed quickly and Kristin returned. "I need to get to work," Eloise said as she rose, hooking her purse strap over her shoulder to evade Martha's gaze. If Martha saw her telltale tears and commented on it, Eloise was sure she'd break down on the spot.

"It is going to take some time before I move. You will come see me, right?"

Bending down, Eloise hugged Martha's thin frame. Drank in the comforting scent of her floral perfume. Took consolation in knowing Martha would be taken care of by a loving family. A family she was not a part of. Was that what she'd miss the most? Feeling like she'd almost had the real thing with Martha and Dante? It was bad enough her friend would be leaving, what if Dante steered clear of her once this case was over? She'd never be happy going back to her old life. The alternative was too depressing to contemplate.

As she pulled away, Martha patted her cheek. "I will miss you, Ellie. Promise me we'll talk over the phone on a regular basis."

Eloise tried to smile, a wobbly curve the best she could muster. "So much so you'll get tired of me."

"Never."

Emotion clogged her throat.

"You know you're going to be just fine, no matter what happens."

Eloise didn't know any such thing, so she hung on to the promise of those words.

"Make sure you tell me the outcome of your job," Martha said with a wink.

"I will."

Taking her coffee cup, Eloise nodded to Kristin and swiftly made her way through the hospital corridor to the truck, then drove to work, ignoring the heavy sense of loneliness settling over her. It was silly, really, to feel such a loss at the idea of Martha moving away. It wasn't like she was a relative. Or that they'd have stayed close after Eloise moved out of the house next door. If she got the promotion, maybe she'd become too busy to visit her friend. Or worse, by not living next door, they might drift apart. Yes, this made sense. The change was best for Martha's health and well-being. Eloise would just move on. She was used to not having close friends. Martha's departure from her life wouldn't affect her at all.

She'd convinced herself that everything had worked out the way it should when she pulled up to the garage. Rolling her neck and getting back into character, she exited the car, more than ready to close this case. No sooner had she stepped into the garage than loud voices greeted her. Mac and Ramsey were having an argument over some kind of air hose hanging from the ceiling. She glanced at Dante, arching a brow. He nodded to the office. Moments later he joined her.

"What's up with the guys?" she asked as she took a seat behind the desk.

"Tempers are running high this morning."

"I can tell."

"How's Martha?"

"Good." She kept her voice controlled. "I met her granddaughter."

He searched her face. "And?"

Her eyes narrowed. "Why do you assume there's more?"

He crossed his arms over his black, button-down work shirt and leaned against the door frame, his posture portraying, *Really?*

"Okay, there's more." She tidied the already neat desk. "Apparently Martha is moving to Ohio."

"What's in Ohio?"

"Her granddaughter, whom she'll be living with."

Dante pushed from the frame and moved closer to the desk, his eyes never leaving her face as he placed both palms on the surface and leaned in. "I'm sorry. I know you two have grown close."

She shrugged. "Things happen." She picked up a stack of invoices and tapped the sides until the edges were straight. "Life moves on."

"C'mon, this has to be a shock."

"I'll get over it." She met his gaze. "Right now we have more important things to worry about."

"More important than—"

She held up her hand. "End of discussion. Tell me what's been going on here."

He studied her for a long-drawn-out moment. Opened his mouth to speak, then seemed to think better of it. When he finally spoke, he gave her the rundown for the day.

"More cars are arriving later today. Rico is antsy, smoking like a maniac. Told me to expect a late night. Whatever is going down is happening soon."

"Okay." She reached for another stack of invoices to straighten. "We should get back to work. Act as if this is just another business day."

Dante nodded as one of the guys called his name.

"I'll check back later."

"Fine."

Once she was by herself, she slumped in her seat. Allowed herself one final pity party. Her chest ached, and as much as she wanted to cry, she tamped down her emotions to stay alert. If this job had taught her anything, it was to be ready for things to change without a moment's notice. She didn't have time to mourn a friendship. Not with criminals to catch and emotions to bury.

By seven in the evening, Dante's nerves were on edge. Eloise had gone home hours ago. Just like Ben had reported, cars arrived. Mac was busy changing the VIN plates. Ramsey had taken off at one point, leaving Rico to inspect the incoming cars alongside Dante.

"Make sure you check the battery terminals," Rico ground out as he passed by.

"Boss. Chill. I got this."

Rico muttered something Dante couldn't decipher.

"What's up with you today?"

Rico ran a hand over his chest. "I'll be glad when we hand off these cars."

Dante shrugged. "Only makes room for the next batch."

At his response, Rico turned pale and headed out the open bay door, fishing a cigarette out of the pack.

"Something I said?" His cell rang. Grabbing a towel, he wiped his hands and swiped the screen. "Dan here."

"It's your wife, *Dan.*"

Dante grinned. Eloise had been subdued all day after her visit to Martha. She'd probably never admit it, but clearly the idea of her friend moving had her tied up in knots.

"What's up, wife?"

"Just wondering what time I should pick you up tonight."

"Hold on."

Rico was nowhere to be found, so Dante yelled to Mac, "What time are we finishing up tonight?"

"Boss said midnight."

Dante relayed the time. "We'll camp out down the road and wait for the carrier."

"I'll see you then."

"What, no small talk for your hubby?"

He could imagine her rolling her eyes. "Right. I have to get back to the roast in the oven."

With a chuckle, he ended the call.

Even with cars to service, time dragged on. By midnight it was all Dante could do not to run up and down the street to burn off his excess energy. When Eloise pulled up in the truck and honked, he nearly sagged with relief.

He jumped in beside her. She'd changed into a navy shirt and jeans, her hair pulled back into a high ponytail. "Circle the block and park down the street like last time."

She did as he asked, although he was disappointed she had no snappy comeback.

"You okay?"

"Sure. Just preparing myself for what lies ahead."

This time, the stakeout wasn't as drawn out as the first time. The car carrier arrived thirty minutes later. Like before, they followed the loaded truck to the warehouse parking lot, only this time the cars stayed loaded.

"Why the change in operations?" Eloise wondered out loud.

"If Ben is right, they're going to the dealership in the morning."

A car rattled down the street. Through his binoculars, he watched Ramsey's beater making tracks to the warehouse. "Looks like we have action."

Eloise straightened in her seat and peered through the lens of the camera to document the night's events. Once the car drew up to the carrier and parked, Ramsey climbed out of the driver seat. The passenger door opened and three teens piled out.

"Those are the kids I saw Ramsey meet the afternoon I followed him."

The young men took up position around the carrier while Ramsey spoke on his phone.

"Lookouts?" she asked as she snapped pictures of the crew.

"Most likely. Hope they aren't carrying."

Eloise lowered the camera. "Most of the kids we've arrested for stealing cars haven't graduated to guns."

"Something tells me this time is different."

Once the young men settled in, Dante leaned back. "Now we wait."

Hours passed with no activity. He ate a sandwich and changed into the dark clothes Eloise had brought for him. Dawn was beginning to light the sky when Eloise spoke up. "Is this it?"

Facing her, Dante shrugged. "I hope not."

Just after 6:00 a.m., the engine of the semi-truck fired up. During the night, Dante and Eloise had switched positions. She wanted to be able to capture the action and Dante was too jacked to sit still while she drove.

Waiting until the carrier and Ramsey's car departed, Dante tailed at a safe distance. The lead vehicles pulled out onto the interstate, driving south for thirty miles. Once off the highway, the carrier pulled into the parking lot of a car dealership.

Eloise leaned forward in her seat to peer through the windshield. "The place is brand-new."

"Agreed." He scanned the location. "I don't see a name anywhere."

"Maybe it's not open for business yet."

Dante passed the lot, circled around and found a place to park across the street. Binoculars in hand, he watched the progress. Ramsey gave instructions to the boys and before long the teens were off-loading the cars.

Eloise, readying the camera, asked, "See any new faces?"

"Not yet. Only see the driver, Ramsey and the boys."

"Someone has to be calling the shots."

Minutes later, a sporty car zoomed into the parking lot. "Bingo," Dante said.

Eloise raised the camera and peered through the lens. "Greg?"

"We haven't seen him in a while."

"Last time he was checking on the cars," she said, taking pictures of the entire operation. "His job must be to make sure the merchandise gets to the designated location."

He watched Greg speak to the carrier driver, then Ramsey. After a short conversation, Ramsey went back to oversee the activity of the young men. Greg walked across the blacktop, pulling something from the pocket of his dark suit as he approached the building. Keys. Unlocking the showroom door, he let himself in.

Dante lowered the binoculars. "Think he's getting a dealership of his own?"

Eloise snapped shots. "I guess that would make sense. If he's earned his way up the ladder—" A luxury sedan pulled into the lot, parking near the main door. "Looks like another player."

Dante peered into the glasses again. A woman dressed in a black sheath dress and high heels emerged from the sleek sedan. She tossed her hair over her shoulder as she retrieved a large tote bag. "I don't recognize her," Dante said.

"I do." Eloise took a few more pictures until the woman disappeared inside. She turned to Dante. "Her name is Stacy Monroe. Remember the Parson's Auto Mall theft?"

He nodded.

"She was the office manager."

"Convenient."

"I had one of the guys at the station do a background check on her, but then we were assigned to this job. I never read the finished report."

"You suspected her?"

"Not at the time. She was jumpy, but I attributed that to the theft. At the time, I asked for the backgrounds of all the employees. Detective Gates took over that case."

The door to the showroom opened and Greg walked out, talking on his phone. Seconds later Stacy followed, speaking to him. Greg waved her off and she grabbed his arm to claim his attention. He took the phone from his ear, turned and engaged in what looked like a heated conversation. After going back and forth, Stacy turned on her spiky heel to head inside. Greg resumed his call.

"I'd love to know what that was all about," Dante muttered.

While the exchange was taking place in front of them, Eloise pulled out her phone to call the station. "Hey, Brandy, is Gates available? Off? No, it's okay. Listen, can you pick me up? I need to do some digging at the station." She rattled off the location. "Thanks."

"What are you thinking?" The corners of Dante's eyes crinkled in curiosity.

"That I need to look at the file. Do a detailed computer search. Check Stacy's background and find out what she's doing here. You?"

"I'll stay put until one of them makes a move."

Twenty minutes later, Brandy pulled up beside Dante's truck. Eloise angled herself toward him. "I'm hoping it won't take too long to gather the information. Don't do anything until I get back to you."

He shot her a grin. "We're in this together."

Her frown said she didn't quite believe him. Turning the handle, she opened the door. "I'll call you as soon as I go over the file."

"I'll be here waiting."

ON THE WAY to the station, Brandy made small talk while Eloise's mind raced. Stacy? How was she involved? Logically, the case could be made that the evolution of the players was now clear, except for the boss. Rico and the guys at the garage, the boys stealing cars, Greg and Stacy. Who were they missing?

"...and I know you said you didn't want to work with Dante, but it looks like you two were on the same page."

Eloise shook her head. "What?"

"You. And Dante."

A topic she wasn't ready to discuss with anyone, even Brandy.

"Sorry. My mind is on this newest development."

"Sure. I just thought—"

"How about I give you the lowdown after we tie this up?"

Excitement lit Brandy's eyes as she glanced at Eloise. "It's a deal."

As soon as they arrived at the station, Eloise jogged inside. She made her way to Gates's desk and stared riffling through the folders piled in the corner.

"Archer," Lieutenant Chambers said as he crossed the room toward her. "What's the latest?"

Finding the file she was searching for, she

tucked a loose strand of hair behind her ear as she faced her superior. "Could you give me a few minutes, sir? Then I'll fill you in."

His brow rose. "By all means."

Eloise weaved through the empty desks to her own and fired up her computer. While waiting, she pulled out Stacy Monroe's sheet. Chambers sat on the corner of her desk, arms folded over his chest. When she'd read it through completely, she explained what had transpired in the last twelve hours.

"How does this woman fit in?" Chambers asked.

"According to her employment history, she's worked at three different dealerships in three years. Gates made a notation that each lot had been hit by car thieves while she worked there. Sometime after the cars were stolen, she quit."

"Sounds like a pattern."

"I agree. The interesting thing is, she quit Parson's Auto Mall two days after the robbery. Gates went back for a follow-up interview but she was gone. Mr. Parson didn't know where she went and there's no current address available."

Chambers rubbed his chin. "Part of the ring, but how?"

Eloise started tapping on her keyboard. "I'll

check her social media. See if she's posted anything recent that will give us a clue."

For the next fifteen minutes, Eloise scrolled through Stacy's favorite social sites. Finally, she went back far enough on Stacy's Facebook page to find a picture of the woman at a party, smiling. Eloise's finger froze on the key. Standing beside her stood Marcus King, the Car King of the South. And by the cozy way they were leaning into each other, Eloise decided they were more than friends.

She grabbed her phone, hitting Dante's number.

THIRTY MINUTES LATER, Greg pushed through the door of the dealership and strode to his sports car. On the way, Ramsey stomped over. Focusing the binoculars on the men, Dante was able to make out Ramsey saying something about "my money."

Whatever Greg's reply was, it didn't pacify Ramsey. He pushed the younger man and said, "Now."

Greg held his hands up and backed away, then turned to climb into his car. Dante started the truck, ready to follow. Was Greg headed to the leader? He had to find out.

Yeah, he'd promised Eloise he'd stay put, but his gut propelled him to follow this guy.

Cautiously leaving his spot, Dante eased out into traffic to follow. Greg headed north. A short while later, he pulled into the lot of an office building, parked and headed inside. Dante parked on the far side, waited a few minutes, then after readying his firearm, grabbed and donned a ball cap from the storage area behind the seat and followed Greg inside. Once in the lobby, he read the building directory to get a sense of where Greg was headed. His heart accelerated at the name of the company occupying the entire third floor. Griffin Enterprises. He reached for his phone, only to realize that in his haste he'd left it in on the seat of the truck. The elevator dinged and he quickly ducked into the nearby office for cover.

"HE'S NOT ANSWERING," Eloise told Chambers. By this time, Brandy had wandered over to the desk, inserting herself in the conversation.

"Just because she had her picture taken with Marcus King doesn't mean they're involved," Brandy pointed out.

Eloise held up her hand. "There's something…" She racked her brain to figure out what was nagging at her. When it wouldn't come, she scanned the picture again, but it revealed nothing. Finally, she tapped through the timeline again until she came upon a shot of Stacy standing beside a car, keys in hand. Then it hit her. "Griffin."

"Come again?" Chambers said.

"In the course of the investigation we've been trying to uncover who owns Griffin Enterprises. The day I talked to Stacy at Parson's Auto Mall, she had a square key ring with an animal printed on it. I didn't really focus on it at the time, but something's been bugging me all along the investigation. Could the animal have been a mythical griffin?" She began to type into the search engine, hunting for any overlap between Griffin Enterprises and Marcus King. Finally, she located an address for the enterprise in an office building owned by King. "This has to be it." She jumped up. "I need to get there now."

Chamber nodded at Brandy. "Go with Archer. I'll call for a warrant and send another team, as well," he said as he hurried back to his office.

As they ran out of the station, Eloise tried calling Dante again. "No answer," she muttered, hoping—but knowing otherwise deep in her gut—that he hadn't taken matters into his own hands. "We need to notify Dante."

Taking precious time they couldn't really afford, Eloise drove back to the parking lot

across from the dealership where they'd seen
Greg and Stacy. Dante's truck was gone. Be-
trayal, swift and hard, curled in her belly.

CHAPTER SIXTEEN

CLUTCHING A CLIPBOARD he'd commandeered from a desk in the office to use as a prop, Dante climbed the stairwell to the third floor. He opened the heavy door just a crack, peering down a dim hallway. Empty. Easing forward, he pressed against the wall as he cautiously moved from one glass office door to another.

At the fourth door, he managed a quick look inside. A few desks were scattered about the open, mostly empty room. Crossing the hallway, he ran past the door, backtracked and peered in from a different angle. There he saw Greg lingering in the doorway of another office. Who was he talking to?

He couldn't risk moving inside, so he waited. He probably should have gone to the truck to retrieve his phone, but there was no way he'd risk losing sight of Greg. Not now, when they were close to learning important information. Greg ending up here at Griffin Enterprises, the company they'd been trying to find information on, was no coincidence.

He couldn't walk away. Yeah, Eloise would be rightfully angry if she tried calling him, but she'd understand why he had to make this move.

Doubt niggled the back of his neck. She had to understand, right?

Greg turned and walked into the large office space, another man behind him. Dante's stomach lurched. Marcus King? Was he the ringleader?

It made sense. The guy had dealerships all over south Florida. Had he built his empire on stolen vehicles? Now that Dante put it together, it made an odd sort of sense. But where was the proof?

He didn't have any.

But he wouldn't pass up an opportunity to size up the current situation.

King disappeared, then rejoined Greg, handing him what looked like a stack of cash.

Tipping the bill of the ball cap down, Dante lowered his head as if reading a paper on the clipboard just as they looked his way.

"Can I help you?" came the cultured voice of King.

"I'm looking for…" Dante lifted the paper, lowered it, lifted it again. "Ah…there seems to be a mix-up."

Greg walked forward, his face etched with suspicion. "Do I know you?"

Dante scrunched his forehead together. They hadn't crossed paths directly, except for the one time he'd stopped by the garage at night. Shoot. Even though Dante had made himself scarce, Greg must have recognized him. "I don't think so."

He snapped his fingers. "Yeah. You work for Rico."

"No, man—"

"Be quiet," Greg all but spat at him. Dante dropped the board and held out his hands.

"Hey, guys, there's been a mistake."

"What do you really want?" King asked, his suave tone replaced by malice.

"See, here's the thing. A friend of mine has been searching for Griffin Enterprises and, well…" He shrugged. "Here you are."

"And, I'm afraid, there you go." King nodded to Greg, who attempted to pull out his weapon. Taking advantage, Dante leaped forward, knocking Greg over. They fell and, as they tussled, Greg lost his grip on his gun. Dante knocked it out of the way, then wrangled Greg to his stomach to subdue him. He quickly glanced around the room.

Great. During the process of stopping Greg, he'd lost track of King. Quickly cuffing one of Greg's hands, he dragged him into King's office and locked the other cuff to a filing cabinet handle. It may not hold him long, but Dante hoped for enough time to intercept King. Adrenaline fueling him, he hightailed it out of there.

Racing to the ground floor, Dante ran outside. King had already jumped into a car, squealing as he raced to the parking lot exit. Dante bolted for his truck when suddenly King slammed the brakes. Dante stopped in his tracks as two cars angled before the exit, keeping King from tearing down the main road. He caught a brief glimpse of Eloise exiting one of the cars, weapon drawn, before King reversed, flooring the engine. Dante dove out of the way of the rapidly moving car, pulling his weapon as he rolled on the gritty asphalt. King crashed into a parked car and his dramatic escape ended before it had a chance to start.

Before long, chaos ensued. Amid shouts and multiple commands, Dante shouted for a uniformed officer to retrieve Greg. Chambers, to Dante's surprise, had shown up, as well, on the phone barking orders for someone to hightail it to Rico's garage. Eloise was also on the phone, talking about picking up Stacy. Dante hoped the news of King's capture hadn't reached the grapevine so they had time to pick up all the players.

After King and Greg were hauled off, some of the officers returned to their squad cars, leaving behind the crime scene unit. Dante knew it was time to face the music with Eloise.

She stood with Brandy, her hair still in a loose ponytail, her cheeks flushed a rosy pink. She'd never looked more beautiful. Or more ticked off. When Brandy noticed him, her brows rose.

"I'll see you later," the crime scene tech said, then sprinted into the building to join the investigation.

Dante stopped Eloise before she could speak. "I can explain."

"Save it for your report."

"Eloise, I didn't ignore your request. I had an opportunity and took it."

"Without all the pertinent details. That's why you have a partner. And a phone."

He felt his face heat.

"We had this. If you'd have waited, we could have apprehended King and Greg together."

He tilted his head. "How…?"

"I found a connection between Stacy and King. Chambers called for a warrant in case we needed to seize any records. Because I wasted valuable time trying to find you, we almost missed our window of opportunity to pick up King. In your rush, he almost escaped."

"I…"

"You jumped the gun again, Dante. Nearly lost us King because you always have to do things your way."

"But in the end we got him. That's all that matters."

She stared at him, her eyes filled with pity. "You don't even see it, do you?"

"See what?"

She shook her head. "You and I don't stand a chance."

FOUR DAYS LATER, Dante sat at the round table in Jasmine Matthews's kitchen. He'd driven in last night, staying in the guest room of her condo as he tried to come up with a plan to fix the consequences he'd created by his impromptu actions.

"I messed up," he said as his mother joined him.

She sat and waited.

Dante ran a hand through his hair. "I nearly blew another case."

Thankfully, once all the players involved in the ring were rounded up, the connection to King was fully uncovered. Mostly because everyone was busy ratting each other out to get a deal. Officers had picked up Stacy before she learned they were onto her, the same with Rico, Mac and Ramsey. The teens stealing the cars were also brought in. The deeper they dug, the more King's reach astounded them. He had multiple teams of people working for him, stealing cars and changing VINs so he could sell them at his new lots.

Dante should have been happy to close the case.

Except the ending was not what he'd envisioned.

After explaining events to his mother, he said, "Chambers called me into his office the next day. Put me on desk duty indefinitely. I'm sure he's using me as an example and I don't blame him." He paused. "Worst of all, Eloise won't talk to me."

"And that bothers you the most?"

He rolled his shoulders. "Yeah." He'd called her cell phone numerous times but it had gone right to voice mail. He hadn't seen her at the station, or when he'd driven by her apartment. The depth of his mistake haunted him. Losing Eloise was a hundred times more painful. "We had a good partnership going. I blew it."

"Which partnership? The job? Or personal?"

Dante met his mother's perceptive gaze. "I'm in love with her, Mom, and I don't know if I can make things right."

"Well, it's about time you've met a woman you're serious about."

Dante nearly laughed out loud. No "I'm sorry, son" or "It'll be okay" speech. No, he only heard the "Fix it" tone in her voice.

"I knew we weren't supposed to cross any lines, but when we started working together, the lines got blurry. For both of us. But then I took off on my own in the case, and that was the deal breaker."

"Then come up with a deal she can live with."

"Live with what?" his brother Dylan asked as he strode into the kitchen through the back door, bringing a blast of warm air with him.

"I messed up. Big-time." Dante explained the events of the past few days again. "When Chambers suggested I take a few days off, I took it as a gift. If he had his way, I'd be suspended right now. Let's face it, if I strike out a third time, I'm done."

"So what're you doing here?" Dylan asked.

"Figuring out what to do with my life."

"He's in love," his mother couldn't resist adding with an annoying twinkle in her eye. He adored his mother, but admitting he was in love with Eloise was a tactical mistake on his end.

Dylan straddled the chair across from him. "Love, huh? Got a plan?"

"Actually, I do." The crazy idea had come to him before he drifted off to sleep the night before. He'd been considering it all morning. Was glad to have his mom and brother here to serve as a sounding board. "I'm thinking about quitting the force."

His mother's eyes went wide, her mouth forming an O.

Dylan reared back. "Come again?"

"Hear me out." He paused, getting his thoughts in line. "The Matthews boys have always been in law enforcement. I followed in Dad's footsteps, just like you and Deke and Derrick, but I realize now it's not my true calling. While there is great satisfaction in upholding the law, I can't say I wake up every morning excited to be on the job."

"But what about the promotion?" his mother asked.

"I'll admit, sometime during the operation I felt bad that we were even competing for the position. In the end, Eloise deserves it."

A contemplative silence blanketed the kitchen until his mother spoke. "Then what do you want for your life?"

"I've always enjoyed working on cars. I'd like to start out with a little business restoring old vehicles, then grow it and turn it into a full-time enterprise."

Dylan regarded him with those gray-blue eyes of his. It was all Dante could do not to squirm in his seat, reverting back to his younger-brother self who'd screwed up and had to pay the price.

"Like a specialized auto mechanic?" Dylan asked.

"In essence, yes. Restoring older cars is a hot market right now. I already have a few customers lined up and they have friends who have requested my services." He glanced at his mother. "Dad instilled and nurtured my love for older-model cars. I think I'd be better suited working with my hands instead of making my superiors' lives miserable."

His mother's eyes were blurry when she reached over to lay her hand on his. "Go with your heart, Dante. With your passion for restoring cars and for Eloise."

The blare from the cell phone sitting on the counter kept him from thanking his mother for her love and insight. His mother rose, blushing as she read the caller ID. "It's James. I'll be right back."

She tapped the screen and hurried from the

room, her voice growing softer as she moved to another part of the condo.

Dylan met his gaze head-on. "I agree with Mom. Go after your dream, Dante."

"You guys won't be disappointed?"

"Never." Dylan rested his elbows on the table. "You know as well as I do that if your head isn't in the game, people get hurt. You're a great undercover cop, but you don't play well with others. That can cost something very dear to you."

"Like my life."

"Or the woman you love."

Dylan had nearly lost a relationship with his girlfriend during an undercover operation taking place right under her nose. If anyone understood the cost of messing up, it was Dylan.

"I'd rather have Eloise in my life than bust criminals on a regular basis."

"Then you know what you have to do?"

"Win her back."

"It won't be easy."

He pictured Eloise's smiling face and his confidence grew. "She's worth it."

Dylan pulled a white square from his pocket and proceeded to unfold it. "Speaking of Eloise, we owe her one."

"What are you talking about?"

"She sent me information on James Tate.

My source has been out of town, but she got ahold of an investigator who sent us a lead."

Dante thought back to the night he'd included Eloise in the computer chat with his brothers. Even with Martha's medical scare and the case coming to an end, she'd still taken the time to get them background information on their mother's boyfriend. His chest squeezed so tight he could hardly breathe.

Dylan smoothed the creases and pushed the paper toward Dante.

"These are phone numbers," he said after scanning the page.

"From Tate's phone. See the yellow highlights?"

Dante looked closer. "I don't recognize the area code."

"North Georgia. He calls a number there regularly. The number belongs to a store called Blue Ridge Cottage located in the small town of Golden. The owner's name is Serena Stanhope."

"What's the connection? Is he seeing another woman at the same time he's dating Mom?"

"I don't know yet. I did a quick Google search. She's around our age."

Dante frowned. "He'd better have a good reason for these calls."

"I left a bunch of messages for Deke. He finally came off the Appalachian Trail and called me back. Since he's closer than all of us, he's going to check this woman out."

Dante pushed the paper back to his brother. "This guy better not hurt Mom."

"My sentiment exactly. We have to be careful. She's got radar when it comes to us digging behind her back."

"I'm not sure how she does it, but she's downright scary."

"And happy. I don't want—"

Their mother's voiced floated down the hallway. Dylan grabbed the paper to refold it and stick it in his pocket. When Jasmine entered the kitchen, her sons were making small talk.

She stopped short. Narrowed her eyes. "What did I miss?"

"Dante agreed to get on bended knee and ask for Eloise's forgiveness."

A small grin curved Dante's lips. At his brother's words, hope began to fill him.

A SMALL CROWD had gathered in the city council room located in Palm Cove City Hall. Half of the crowd was there for the meeting scheduled to take place to discuss city business. The others, mostly police officers in uniform and their families, mingled in the back. They'd gathered this afternoon to watch two rookies be sworn in, as well as to see Eloise move up in rank to sergeant. Yes, she'd gotten the promotion.

"Try not to act nervous," Brandy fussed. Even dressed in her uniform, Brandy was still able to pull off cute and fun. Eloise simply felt like her soul had been stomped on. Even the ceremony couldn't lift her spirits.

After the undercover stage of the Marcus King case had concluded, Eloise couldn't bring herself to talk to Dante. She was angry. Hurt, mostly, that he'd taken matters into his own hands without keeping her in the loop. She understood why he followed Greg; it was the manner in which he conducted himself that made her question everything between them.

Not that there was much to question. She was in love with him. Plain and simple.

But he knew how important it was to her that they complete the op together. If he'd easily gone off script on this case, what made her think he wouldn't do the same in real life? It boiled down to trust and although it tore her heart in two, she realized she wasn't sure she could trust him. And without trust, how did they build a relationship?

She blew out a sigh.

"I don't know why you stopped wearing your contacts," Brandy said, frowning at Eloise.

Today, Eloise had gone all official in her uniform, hair pulled back in a tight bun, glasses in place. What did it matter, really? Dante wouldn't be here to witness her rise in rank.

Which was the other fact that burned her. When she finally decided she could sit down and have a rational conversation with him, he'd up and left. Took a leave of absence, without telling her. No one knew where he was.

Guess those promises of a partnership were a lie. The kisses meant nothing. It was all part of the operation.

Even though she'd hoped otherwise.

The police chief walked into the room and voices lowered. Eloise took her seat, watching Captain Brewer greet the crowd, then lead the rookies in the police officer oath. Once finished, he called Eloise up to acknowledge her promotion and receive her new badge as she swore to discharge her duties as a Palm Cove police sergeant. She should have been elated, but instead, she felt hollow.

Besides her fellow officers, no one was here to cheer her on. Her parents, well, she knew that wouldn't happen so she hadn't bothered to call them. She would have loved to have

Martha here, but she'd already left for Ohio and her new life. As much as they promised to keep in touch, not seeing her friend every day would leave a big hole inside her. So here she was. Alone.

As she returned to her seat, she froze when she saw her parents a few rows back. Confusion overwhelmed her, but she quickly pulled herself together. Once the law enforcement presentations were completed, those not staying for the town council meeting left. Baffled by their presence, she approached her parents in the vast city hall lobby.

"What are you doing here?" she asked them.

"We could ask why you didn't tell us about the promotion," her mother said, the usual starch in her tone missing.

"We're proud of you," her father said, totally throwing her off balance.

"But…you've never liked my being a cop."

"It wasn't what we would have chosen for you…" her mother started to say.

"But you've done an excellent job and that's all we could ask for," her father finished. "We've missed you. We've missed having a daughter."

Okay, she hadn't drank anything strange before the ceremony. Why did she feel like she'd fallen down the rabbit hole?

"I've missed you, too. I'm just so shocked, but glad you're here," she finally said, deciding to embrace this change of attitude in her parents before they changed their minds.

"How about dinner sometime soon? We'll catch up."

Eloise blinked. Dinner? With her folks? "Sure. That sounds nice."

Lieutenant Chambers came over to shake her hand and speak to her parents. The lobby began to thin out as her parents said goodbye.

"Wait." Eloise stopped them. "How did you know? About today, I mean."

"One of your coworkers called us."

Odd. She hadn't said anything about her strained relationship with her parents to Brandy or any other colleague. Only… Dante.

Shock walloped her. Had he called them?

Her mother craned her neck and pointed over Eloise's shoulder. "That young man across the lobby."

Eloise turned on her heel. Dante leaned against the far wall, dressed in a button-down shirt, sleeves rolled to midarm, and jeans. He nodded when their gazes met.

"We'll talk soon," her mother said as they left.

As they walked away, she panicked. She wasn't ready to face Dante. Not yet. Noticing the new officers leaving by a side door, she ran to catch up with them before Dante could cross the lobby.

AN HOUR LATER, Eloise sat on a bench in Soldier Park, staring at a dazzling sunset. She'd managed to elude Dante, but once she got home and changed into a comfy sundress, restlessness made her stir-crazy and she needed to do something. She'd hopped into her car and driven aimlessly, finally pulling into the park where she'd wandered about before taking a seat to contemplate the beautiful vista before her.

The sky was brushed with streaks of orange and purple. The sun, perched on the horizon, burned brightly. The ocean waves hit the shore at a steady, soothing pace. Within minutes the stress of the day rolled from her shoulders and Eloise could breathe again.

How ironic that she sat before a gorgeous sunset, remembering Dante telling their neighbors at the block party that this was where Dan and Ellie had fallen in love.

Keeping her mind blank, she watched as the sun slowly disappeared before her eyes. Took solace knowing it would rise again tomorrow, even if she had no idea what would become of her. She might not have family to fall back on—the jury was still out on her parents—but she had police work and that would have to be enough.

Her thoughts were interrupted by the pounding of feet and the sound of heavy-metal rock music behind her. She whirled around, not daring to hope it might be Dante. She was disappointed to see a man she didn't recognize run by.

"Get a grip," she muttered as she resumed her seat on the bench.

True to her word, she contacted Tom Bailey once the excitement of the case was over and agreed to meet for coffee. It was awkward, on both their parts, and they decided to just be friends. Honestly, with Dante constantly front and center in her mind, no other guy would ever catch her attention at this point.

With a sigh, she continued watching the scene before her. A sailboat moved slowly in the distance. Wishing she were headed on an adventure, Eloise was startled when a person slid onto the bench beside her. She turned her head, swallowing her gasp. Dante rested one arm along the back of the bench, a satisfied smile on his lips.

"How'd you find me?"

"I went to the station and pinged your phone."

She went rigid with outrage. "You did what?"

He shrugged. "What's the worst that could happen? They give me permanent desk duty? Oh, wait, Chambers already did that."

"Dante—"

He held up his hand. "Hear me out. Please."

She pressed her lips together.

"I owe you an apology."

Her brow rose.

"Okay, probably more than one, but mostly for jumping the gun when we were undercover. I told you I'd stay put and I broke my word." He paused, then said in a quiet voice, "I don't want to be that man."

Her heart thawed a bit.

"I've done a lot of soul-searching since the hammer came down. Talked to my family. Came to a few decisions."

"Was one of them calling my parents?"

He squared his shoulders. "You're darn right. I called your dad. Spoke to him man-to-man and told him about your promotion. Suggested they make the ceremony."

"Guilted them, you mean?"

He grinned.

A breeze blew over the water, lifting a strand of her hair. She pushed her glasses up her nose, trying hard to remain angry with Dante and not succeeding.

"How did you know about the promotion? You'd left by the time word came down."

"Brandy texted me. Told me if I knew what was good for me, I'd get back here in time for the ceremony."

Eloise's heart squeezed a silent thanks to Brandy.

"Besides, I owe you."

She sent him a sideways glance.

"Dylan told me you were the one to find information on James Tate."

"I called in a favor."

"Why?"

"When I heard you and your brothers talking about your mom, and Dylan said he had to wait on his PI friend to get back to town before learning more about the man, I decided to move the process along."

"Thanks."

"And your mom?"

"Things are okay for now."

She nodded.

"But she can't wait to meet you."

Eloise's eyes went wide.

"Yep. And to make that happen, one of my decisions includes quitting the force."

She twisted in her seat. "What? No!"

Moving closer, he took her hand in his. Rubbed his thumb back and forth over her palm. "Yes. I'll admit, I've enjoyed the rush of working undercover, but the rest? It was never really my passion. I went into the profession because of my father and brothers."

"You're a good cop."

"But it doesn't inspire me. And it should. Like it inspires you."

She couldn't argue that point. "What will you do?"

"I've saved up some money. My mom is going to invest in a mechanic garage with me. I miss working on cars, and the time spent at Rico's made me realize I want to focus my energy on building a business."

She tilted her head. "You know, I can see that."

"I want to restore old cars. I've been doing it for a while, anyway. Have a knack for it."

"It will suit you."

"It will, but it won't be the same without you there."

She held her breath when she saw the desire and admiration in his eyes.

"I'd like us to be partners, Ellie. In real life. It's not a decision I can make on my own, so I'm asking you to think about it."

Her throat went dry and she had to clear it before speaking. "How do I know I can trust you?"

"By giving me a lifetime to prove myself to you."

At his declaration, her heart melted a bit more. "Oh, Dante."

He leaned in, his spicy cologne hijacking her senses. He brushed his lips over hers and she could swear she felt an eternity in that kiss. When he finally pulled away, she blinked, keenly missing his warmth.

Brushing a knuckle over her cheek, he said, "You keep fighting crime and I'll take old cars and make them new again. Win-win for both of us."

She bit her lip. She knew she loved him, but… Something Martha had said in their many talks came back to her. *Love can't be analyzed. It must be experienced.*

As much as Eloise was always following the rules, a little of Dante's instinctive way of looking at things had rubbed off on her. Life was too short to make a list of pros and cons when it came to a future with Dante. She was ready to jump in feetfirst right now. Besides, he'd had her heart since the day she met him.

"I love you, Ellie. Have ever since the day you took my challenge and raced through the mud right here in this very park. You hated every minute of it, but you showed me you had spirit, determination…honor."

She swallowed hard.

"What do you say?"

She stared into his beautiful eyes. Saw the love shining there. Knew this was her chance for love, a family, a place in the world. And she wanted it all.

Her heart turned to mush. "You make a very persuasive argument."

"And?"

"I love you, too."

He blew out a breath. "I need someone to keep me on the straight and narrow, Ellie. You're the only one capable of the task."

"Sounds like a full-time job."

He grinned and her heart melted for good. "I was hoping you'd see it that way."

With only one thing left to do, she kissed him, with a promise that would last a lifetime.

* * * * *

For more great romances from
USA TODAY *bestselling author*
Tara Randel,
visit www.Harlequin.com today!

HOME *on the* RANCH

Name _____ (PLEASE PRINT) _____

Address _____ Apt. # _____

City _____ State/Prov. _____ Zip/Postal Code _____

Signature (if under 18, a parent or guardian must sign)

Mail to the **Reader Service:**
IN U.S.A.: P.O. Box 1341, Buffalo, New York 14240-8531
IN CANADA: P.O. Box 603, Fort Erie, Ontario L2A 5X3

HRCBPA18R

Get 4 FREE REWARDS!

We'll send you 2 FREE Books plus 2 FREE Mystery Gifts.

FREE
Value Over
$20

Both the **Romance** and **Suspense** collections feature compelling novels written by many of today's best-selling authors.

YES! Please send me 2 FREE novels from the Essential Romance or Essential Suspense Collection and my 2 FREE gifts (gifts are worth about $10 retail). After receiving them, if I don't wish to receive any more books, I can return the shipping statement marked "cancel." If I don't cancel, I will receive 4 brand-new novels every month and be billed just $6.74 each in the U.S. or $7.24 each in Canada. That's a savings of at least 16% off the cover price. It's quite a bargain! Shipping and handling is just 50¢ per book in the U.S. and 75¢ per book in Canada*. I understand that accepting the 2 free books and gifts places me under no obligation to buy anything. I can always return a shipment and cancel at any time. The free books and gifts are mine to keep no matter what I decide.

Choose one: ☐ **Essential Romance**
(194/394 MDN GMY7)

☐ **Essential Suspense**
(191/391 MDN GMY7)

Name (please print)

Address   Apt. #

City   State/Province   Zip/Postal Code

Mail to the **Reader Service:**
IN U.S.A.: P.O. Box 1341, Buffalo, NY 14240-8531
IN CANADA: P.O. Box 603, Fort Erie, Ontario L2A 5X3

Want to try two free books from another series? Call 1-800-873-8635 or visit www.ReaderService.com.